THE BONE CLOCK

ANDREW JAMES GREIG

Storm

This is a work of fiction. Names, characters, businesses, places, events and incidents are either the products of the author's imagination or used in a fictitious manner. Any resemblance to actual persons, living or dead, or actual events is purely coincidental.

Copyright © Andrew James Greig, 2020, 2024, 2025

The moral right of the author has been asserted.

Previously published in 2020 as *Whirligig* by Fledgling Books and in 2024 by Holme Press.

All rights reserved. No part of this book may be reproduced or used in any manner without the prior written permission of the copyright owner. This prohibition includes, but is not limited to, any reproduction or use for the purpose of training artificial intelligence technologies or systems.

To request permissions, contact the publisher at rights@stormpublishing.co

Ebook ISBN: 978-1-80508-982-7
Paperback ISBN: 978-1-80508-983-4

Cover design: Blacksheep
Cover images: Depositphotos, Shutterstock

Published by Storm Publishing.
For further information, visit:
www.stormpublishing.co

ALSO BY ANDREW JAMES GREIG

Private Investigator Teàrlach Paterson
The Girl in the Loch
Silent Ritual
The Graveyard Bell

Detective Corstorphine
The Devil's Cut

Standalones
A Song of Winter

Dedicated to our children, for they carry the future in their hands

The whirligig of time brings in his revenges.
William Shakespeare – *Twelfth Night*

PROLOGUE
MAY 1997

'Please, you don't have to do this.' She tried to avoid the noose he slipped over her head, but he was too fast, too strong.

Rough rope fibres tightened around her neck. Her last breath formed a strangled plea for Abigail.

'I have a daughter. She's just a child.'

Her pleading was cut off as he pulled her higher into the tree, bracing himself until her feet stopped dancing on air.

'I was just a child too.' His voice was surprisingly gentle for a scene of such violence. He tied the rope to the old oak so that she remained suspended.

June Stevens' notebook lay on the ground. He picked it up, wiped off the layer of fine dust they'd raised during a short and unequal struggle, pocketed it and walked back along the track without a second glance.

Looking back only ever brought pain.

ONE

The front door slammed with such violence that the whole house shook, quivering timbers seeking comfort in the cold embrace of stone. Margo tensed in her bed, feeling the floor shake in sympathy. Nervously, she lay waiting for the angry wasp sound of his quad bike as it disappeared down the lonely track that led away from the isolated cottage. Only when the engine noise had faded did she allow herself to finally relax. He'd be gone all day, setting traps for the rabbits, laying poison for the birds of prey, shooting the mountain hares. Death. Death and violence were all she ever associated him with now.

Her hand tentatively reached out from under the covers and felt her face, flinching as her fingers encountered the bruise around her eye. It wasn't too bad. She had become a connoisseur of bruises, burns, broken bones. All of them her own. She could tell without looking that her eye would be swollen, the redness around the socket already turning to purple and black. She mentally ran through the foundation she'd apply, the beauty products she'd accumulated that artfully concealed the worst of the damage. Now that he was gone, the nervousness left her like a shed skin, a protective coat that was no longer needed. A butterfly flickered in her womb, and the nervousness returned – but this time it was visceral, this time the nervousness was for a life other than her own.

Margo had hoped, in the way that so many women do, that the announcement she was bringing his baby into the world would change him. Turn him from a sadistic bully into the man she'd always wanted him to be: tender, loyal, loving. Loving. The word hung in her mind like some impossible concept, a young girl's dream of how her life should have been before it had turned into a living nightmare. Instead, the announcement had only made him worse, and whatever demons drove him had been merciless in their response, leaving her concussed and broken on the cold stone kitchen floor. Margo's first thought had been for the new life she carried inside her, barely two months old. The second missed period had confirmed the truth of it to her, and then the doctor had made it official. She remembered the doctor's troubled eyes; they had shown concern, worry. 'Is there anything you'd like to ask me, anything worrying you?' Margo had attempted gaiety when she'd responded in the negative, and knew she'd failed when the doctor had lowered her voice to a conspiratorial tone. 'You know we're here to help. With anything, anything at all.' She'd almost run from the surgery, afraid that everyone could see through the makeup to the battered woman underneath.

It was their pity she desperately wanted to avoid. Their pity and judgement delivered with all-too-knowing eyes. The gamekeeper's cottage at least offered her the privacy to keep herself to herself, hide herself away, hide secrets that should never be allowed to escape. She swung her legs out over the side of the bed, with a sharp intake of breath as a healing rib complained, then walked to the bathroom to wash and repair what damage she could. Her face stared back at her, expressionless, beaten in spirit as well as in flesh. Margo waited in vain for the tears to flow. They never did these days. She told herself that she was out of tears, but she knew the truth of it. Tears were for those who still had hope, who still gave a fuck, if only about themselves. She glanced down at her belly, too early for any telltale bulge to show – but she felt different, her breasts felt different. She felt as if she was about to come into flower for the first time in her life, and that frightened her more than he did.

TWO

Mounted on his quad bike, Oscar seethed with anger, a litany of thoughts constantly revolving in his head and finding release in vocal outbursts as he accelerated down the glen. 'Stupid bitch. Fucking pregnant. Who wants a fucking kid?' The bike kicked under him as the tyres hit potholes and stray rocks, and he found some pleasure in forcing the quad back onto the track, wheels expertly placed within the ruts of previous journeys. The back of the quad was laden with snares, illegal snares designed to kill outright – or hold any unfortunate animal in agony until he had the pleasure of ending a life. A rifle was strapped into place beside him, although the local deer population would scatter out of the glen at the first sound of his coming. He glanced at the third item in his arsenal, a tin of strychnine masquerading as engine oil, wondering how much he would need to force an abortion, then turned his attention to the track ahead.

For some unaccountable reason, the memory of his parents came unbidden into his thoughts. Their holier than thou pronouncements were more often than not accompanied by the lash of the belt whilst he grew as feral as any wild animal. 'Fuck them!' he announced to the air. A fresh wave of anger broke over him as he faced the certain knowledge that he was in no way equipped to bring up a child himself. Anger had accompanied him all his life, a constant boiling of emotion under the skin. His peers understood it and knew when to back off. Like the deer, they valued self-preservation and took care wherever Oscar was concerned. As a result, he found from an early age that he was accepted as a leader, someone who acted as a beacon to those whose personal inadequacies and failings found a natural home in his company. His disciples only served to amplify his worst excesses, applaud his cruelty and encourage him to transgress those lines even they would not dare cross.

Oscar had left a trail in life as obvious as the one formed by his bike, crossing the glen day in, day out in all weathers. His employer knew enough about him, more than enough to hold him on a tight leash. But Oscar didn't care, he made a good gamekeeper – burning heather, feeding the pheasants and grouse, killing anything else with an enthusiasm his employer chose not to notice. He was cunning, though. Any tagged eagles he poisoned had their transmitter signals masked, tin foil wrapped around the leg until the bird resembled nothing more than a turkey ready for the oven. Oscar took great delight in transporting the corpse, sometimes for a hundred miles or more, until the signal was allowed to be detected far away from the estate he worked. Sometimes, he enjoyed targeting other estates, other gamekeepers who had looked at him in the wrong way. A rare smile touched his lips as he considered the latest victim of this ploy, due in court this week.

The smile swiftly turned downwards as he approached the oak tree. One day he'd burn the fucking thing down. It stood in mute judgement every day, since that silly bitch had been found hanging from its contorted branches. Perhaps the laird hadn't expected him to take the job, not when he had to face the tree every working day. But the job was the only one he'd ever been offered, and the cottage came with it – somewhere he could live without the pressure of eyes boring into his back. Plus, there was the bonus of work satisfaction, the killing. He'd almost inadvertently made the glen one of the top shooting ranges in Scotland, the number of birds that flapped inanely towards the guns increasing year on year.

It was, he decided, a mutually beneficial arrangement. One that also suited the inhabitants of the little Highland town where Oscar had been born, growing increasingly feral until he was ostracised to this lonely glen. Suited him, and suited the local police, tired of facing him after every violent episode. 'Fuck them!' He spat this last expletive out as he thought of the police, and the regular beatings he'd suffered in the holding cell after each arrest. Nothing stuck, no charges were ever brought to a satisfactory conclusion – he'd made sure of that.

The old oak whispered, fresh leaves rubbing against each other as a cool breeze caught the branches in a playful embrace. Concealed by the canopy, a rabbit gently swung from the wire wrapped around its neck, dropping so slowly that it appeared not to move at all. Minute increments, just one small step at a time. Measured.

The wire continued higher into the tree, where it joined with a peculiar mechanism constructed from bone and exquisitely carved wood. Each measured drop of the rabbit provided fresh impetus to bone gears, transmitting rotary movement via the main pulley, meshing with each interconnected neighbour in an intricate ballet of bone wheels, cogs and spindles, all held in place within a skeleton case of polished branches and carved twigs. In the heart of the caliber silently beat a balance wheel, a perfect disc of silver and gold. The mechanism had performed its purpose. Now the Hanging Tree waited. The tree loomed close, dominating the otherwise treeless landscape. A burn bubbled alongside the track, heather clung to sparse soil, the purple flowers scenting the chill morning air. Higher up the glen, bright yellow gorse and patches of broom signalled summer's approach and then a dark mass of cash crop conifers hugged the distant mountains until they, too, thinned out in the upper reaches. It was, in its own primitive way, quite beautiful. Oscar saw, but did not comprehend. He slowed down his approach. In places the tree roots lay exposed on the ground where the bike tyres had worn away the surrounding soil. He stood up in his seat to avoid having his bones rattled by the action of tyres over the uneven roots, and his head was at a perfect height to catch the near invisible wire noose that lay in wait.

The force of the impact caused the wire to bite deeply into his neck, almost severing his head from his body as his cervical vertebrae parted with an audible crack. The bike carried on without him, before a random stone tipped it into the burn, flooding the engine. The ensuing silence was broken only by the wet gurgling sounds Oscar made as he jerked uncontrollably on the wire, a percussive countermelody to the soft bubbling sound of the burn. His rough clothing was soiled as his bowels opened involuntarily, pooling under his twitching marionette body to mix with the blood pumping from a neck wound. The wire had opened his flesh to form a gaping red grin, a second mouth, mute and savage. The last thing he saw was the hanging rabbit's quizzical death face, looking more like a final valediction of justice before his world faded into nothingness.

The kinetic energy absorbed by the tree destroyed the mechanical construction in the branches above. Carefully carved and engineered bone cogs flew in all directions, the wooden infrastructure turned to matchwood. The parts landed silently in the surrounding heather or fell pattering like tiny hailstones where they impacted the track. Only two steel wires remained, suspending the rabbit and Oscar aloft where they performed an aerial pirouette, bloodied bodies coyly facing each other, then slowly turning away again. The sun shone through the branches and leaves, the dappled light lending a theatrical touch to the macabre scene. Before too long, the first flies scented the feast, and nature began the inevitable process to reclaim her own.

THREE

In the cottage, Margo was dressed, her long red hair tied back into the ponytail that Oscar preferred. She viewed her face critically in the mirror, the makeup and arnica barely disguising the darkening bruise despite layers of foundation. She pursed her lips, applying bright red lipstick as a distraction from her eyes. The sheets would need to be washed. There was a cut above her eye where she'd bled during the night. Margo stripped the bed, efficient in her movements even though she held herself awkwardly, body stiff on one side where the pain gnawed at her ribs. A new sheet pulled from the chest of drawers, fresh pillowcase all in white and scented with a hint of coconut from the gorse blossoms she'd collected, imprisoned in a muslin bag.

She held the bag in her hands, pulling it tight towards her face to drink in the perfume. She felt imprisoned too. Trapped in this loveless relationship, captive in this isolated cottage. 'You've made your bed and now must lie in it.' Her mother's voice, judgemental, strong with the certainty of religious fervour. Hateful. Margo's inability to blindly follow that same narrow path of righteousness her parents trod had driven her to this, unloved, discarded, unfit for the kingdom of heaven. Was it any wonder she ended up like this? Knocked up, knocked about – just another piece of human garbage nobody cared about.

The day stretched in front of her like a forbidden prize; hours without Oscar and his vicious quips, his punishing fists. This time would end too soon. The sound of the quad bike heralding his return would start her shivering with fear, painfully aware that any wrong move, any misstep, wrong comment or perceived inadequacy would be sufficient cause for him to lash out. She began with the kitchen, scrubbing the floor clean of her blood where she'd fallen last evening, rearranging the furniture, putting fallen chairs back upright. Her eyes fell on the knife rack, a housewarming present from one of the few women still willing to accept her as one of their own. In her darker moments, she'd imagined uses for those knives. A swift end to her own misery, a long deep cut up the arm. Or him. Taking a knife to him. She'd imagined it often enough, but it would have to be deep, and accurate – otherwise, he'd finish her in a moment.

The child inside her, though; what could she do? She couldn't stay with him, yet she had nowhere else to go. The only way out of the glen was along the track, and it would have to be by foot. He had the only transport. He'd see her for sure, watch her as she stumbled along the rough track, waiting to ambush her and deal with her as he wanted. He didn't want the child, and she knew he wouldn't hold back from punching her in the stomach to loosen the foetus's tenuous hold on life. Her hands instinctively cradled her womb, eyes wide with fright as she realised how trapped she was, how trapped they both were.

FOUR

'Good God!' Detective Constable Frankie McKenzie held her nose in mock horror, face gurning in disgust as she entered the back office. 'If that's your aftershave, Phil, then I have to tell you it's meant to attract a woman, not make her pass out.'

PC Philip Lamb stood adjusting his uniform, placing his cap at the regulation angle as he admired his reflection in the mirror he'd placed on his desk. It hadn't escaped Frankie's notice that this was the first item he'd used to personalise his space, an indicator as to his narcissistic tendencies. 'Some of us don't need any help to attract the opposite sex. It's not my aftershave – you're the detective, you work it out.' He turned away from his reflection to grin at her, the grin lessening as he caught sight of her expression, and he pointed a finger surreptitiously towards the DI's office by way of an explanation.

'Not another Tinder encounter?' The smell of aftershave pervaded the station. She'd caught the first telltale whiff at the sergeant's desk and the intensity had only increased as she approached the source. Frankie checked to see if the DI's office door was shut before venturing any further comment.

'No, this is Uniform Dating. She's a nurse.' The young constable was enjoying himself.

Sometimes, being the only female in the office carried a weight of responsibility over and above Frankie's job description, from acting as surrogate agony aunt to sole spokesperson for women's equality whilst at the same time being 'one of the boys'. It was, she felt, an impossible circle to square, especially when faced with a barely post-pubescent constable. She could see the desk sergeant's expression as he looked up from his screen at the front desk, a study in long suffering.

'Haven't you got a beat you're meant to be walking?' He spoke in a slow Highland drawl, leaving plenty of space between each word to allow them room to breathe.

'Sorry, sergeant; yes, sergeant.' PC Lamb marched smartly out of the room, new polished boots squeaking with eagerness. They both watched him go, fresh-faced youth facing the world with misplaced confidence, and exchanged a look. The desk sergeant gave a slight shake of his head before painstakingly adding data to his screen, one finger after another, as slow as his speech.

Frankie crossed over to her desk, catching the eye of DI James Corstorphine as he looked up from his screen, isolated from the general hubbub behind his office window. She smiled a welcome, but not too welcoming, preferring to keep a professional distance between them. She felt a twinge of sorrow for him, and his increasingly desperate attempts to find some sort of meaningful relationship since losing his wife five years previously. Corstorphine's forlorn love life was in danger of becoming the office soap with his membership of evening classes and rambling groups. At least he was able to laugh off those failed encounters that made it into the public domain – and with a town as small as this, that was almost all of them.

Frankie logged onto her computer and began entering the petty crimes she'd accumulated during the morning shift. Two shoplifters, both just girls really. They'd been cautioned previously, time and time again, almost ridiculously slapdash in their inability to steal clothes or cosmetics without drawing attention to themselves by giggling uncontrollably. She'd tried her best to talk the store out of pressing charges, but it was one time too many. Frankie paused, taking the opportunity to look at the welcome spring morning sunshine through the station window. She couldn't really blame the store; they were struggling to make ends meet as it was. Chances were it would never get to court anyway, too much pressure on the Procurator Fiscal's office to bother with two silly young girls. The threat of being taken to court and getting their names in the local press would be enough for the parents to come down hard, so it would be a result whichever way she looked at it. The window beckoned again, sunshine streaming in. Perhaps a tour of local farms, checking up on any rustling or fly tipping activity – that would seem a sensible use of her resources for the afternoon. Thank God for a small-town police station, she thought to herself. Nothing ever happened here. It was a sentiment shared by the entire staff, although they'd only ever be caught complaining about the lack of any proper policing work more becoming of their talents. The trick was to not complain too much, just in case they decided to transfer you somewhere busier – like Inverness.

Her attention was drawn back to the front desk as a distressed woman's voice increased in volume. The desk sergeant stood slowly, flapping both hands, palms facing down, in an effort to calm the woman down. The manoeuvre served only to agitate the woman to greater volume, the pitch of her voice sliding upwards towards hysteria. Frankie spun her seat around to see what the fuss was about and recognised Margo McDonald immediately.

'Bloody hell, what now!' She spoke the words under her breath, although the noise at the front desk was sufficient to drown out anything she said. Margo represented 'Trouble' around here, and her uninvited appearance at the police station front desk was worthy of investigation. Frankie joined the desk sergeant, his grateful glance offering fulsome thanks for the interruption.

'Margo, just take a breath. What's the matter?' The distraught face on the other side of the reception desk was covered in sweat, with mascara forming panda rings under her eyes – at least it looked like mascara. Frankie took an executive decision. 'Margo, come through here. You look like you need a seat.' She keyed the door release and led the way into the back office, Margo following her like an obedient child with a hand held tight onto an overnight bag, swollen to capacity. 'Hamish, could you get us both a cuppa?' The desk sergeant happily relinquished responsibility and moved with ponderous intent to the station kitchen, leaving the two women alone. The DI peered up from his screen, but Frankie shook her head. Whatever this was, it was easier with just the two of them.

FIVE

Margo collapsed in a chair, her eyes wild, darting from side to side like a trapped animal. One hand cradled her stomach, the other sought sanctuary on the desk between them, holding the wooden surface tight as if to steady the world. The bag lay on the floor. She tried to speak, but only primitive noises escaped in between desperate gasps for air. Frankie held up a hand. 'Take it easy. Just get your breath back and we can talk then. There's nothing that can't wait. We'll get you a nice cup of tea, things are always better with a cup of tea.'

Margo stared at Frankie, who seemed to have become the embodiment of her mother. Stock phrases coming hard on the heels of each other. Trite. Meaningless. She felt her breath coming back into more of a normal rhythm. She had left the cottage early that morning, gathering what few possessions she owned and bundling them into a bag in sheer panic in case Oscar came back and caught her in the act. He still hadn't returned home since he had left for work the previous morning, and her fear grew with every passing minute as she waited for the sound of his quad bike coming back up the glen. Oscar's normally foul mood had reached new depths since she'd given him the news, far worse than normal, and she envisioned him drinking the night away until he reached that point where he was capable of doing anything. No sleep had come to her. She'd lain in bed with the longest kitchen knife held tightly clasped in her hand, a cold sweat beading on her skin and every sense straining in the dark for any sign of his approach. As soon as the grey light of dawn touched the eastern horizon, she took the one chance she might ever have to escape him. She had to run away, far away from here, somewhere he could never find her. It was in that state of blind panic, as she hurried down the track towards the tree, that she saw the shape. She stopped suddenly, blood freezing in her veins, a cold pit forming where her womb lay. The shape rotated slowly, and as the face turned towards her, she saw dark shadows around the head resolve into crows. They flew off, cawing displeasure at being disturbed from feasting on his eyes, tempting morsels providing an aperitif to the main course. Her first instinct was to be sick, dry retching causing her to stagger away from the sight.

Margo made a detour around the tree, climbing some way up the rock-strewn slope to avoid seeing or smelling the scene, then once securely back on the rough track, half ran, half walked in a mindless fugue until she found herself at the police station. The reaction now came in waves: horror, shock, relief, all jumbled together in an incoherent mix of emotions. She sat facing the policewoman, her placid patience an antidote, as her feelings receded. Margo fixed Frankie with an empty look, and the policewoman made a show of picking up her notebook and pen and placing them on the table. An unnatural silence held the air between them, broken only by Margo's breaths becoming less ragged, more measured. Two mugs of tea arrived, held in Hamish's overlarge hands. He set them down on the table, swept a practised eye over Margo, and, apparently, decided she was safe to be left – for the moment.

Margo waited until the duty sergeant had returned to the

front desk, as if she wanted to share a secret that was just for the two women to hear. 'It's Oscar. He's killed himself.' Her voice was low, at complete odds to the banshee howl she'd issued at the front desk.

* * *

Frankie's pen stopped in mid stroke, and she engaged with Margo's eyes at last. They appeared as dark pools, hauntingly pretty in their own way, but unsettling in the depth of anguish they displayed. They say you can read a person's soul in their eyes. Frankie wondered, not for the first time, what horrors this woman sat opposite her had endured to give her eyes like this.

'Are you sure he's dead, Margo, could he just be unconscious or something? We ought to get an ambulance out to him just in case.' She adopted a sensible, businesslike tone. 'Now, where exactly is he? Can you tell me what happened?'

Margo's expression remained the same, but her voice now held a hard, sarcastic edge. 'He's hanging from the Hanging Tree, covered in shit, blood and flies. His head's half off. It will take more than a fleet of fucking ambulances to bring him back!' She laughed then, leaning back in her seat and baring her teeth to the overhead fluorescents. She smiled beatifically at Frankie as she composed herself once more.

Frankie felt a chill run down her spine. The woman was quite possibly insane, she might have even murdered Oscar. She tore her eyes away from Margo, risking a swift glance towards the front desk. Hamish was already making slow and steady progress towards them.

'Margo, we'll have to check, you understand that?' She spoke more calmly than she felt. 'Hamish here will take you to one of our rooms, where you can have a lie-down if you want. There's a toilet and washbasin if you need to freshen up.' She stood up, and Margo reached for her untouched mug of tea. 'It's

OK, I'll bring that for you.' Frankie carried the mug, the surface of the tea forming miniature waves as her hand betrayed her nervousness. Margo made to pick up her bag, but Frankie forestalled her. 'We'll keep that safe for you here.' Hamish led Margo into a holding cell, the euphemism 'one of our rooms' needing no translation.

'I'm sorry, but we don't have anywhere else to put you for the moment,' Frankie offered by way of an apology. The desk sergeant locked the door. Margo took the mug of tea through the hatch, and sat on the mattress, ignoring them both.

'I'll be back as soon as I can. Have a wee rest, and we can take your statement later.' Margo didn't respond, sitting with both hands clasped around the mug as if in prayer. They walked the short distance back to the office in silence, each concerned with their own thoughts.

'I'll get an ambulance sent out.' Hamish's measured tone helped Frankie calm down. Something about the manner in which Margo had delivered her message had unnerved her more than she liked to admit. 'And I'll keep an eye on her,' he added.

'Thanks, Hamish.' She flashed him a quick smile, grateful for his stolid presence. There were only the five of them working the station, two constables including the one fresh out of training, the two detectives – herself and DI Corstorphine, and Sergeant Hamish McKee. A small team more closely integrated than the larger stations, more like a family than colleagues. She tapped on the DI's door, and the pungent aroma of aftershave washed over her as she entered his office.

'I saw Margo McDonald. What's up?' Corstorphine leaned back in his seat, one eyebrow raised in his familiar interrogative stare. She stood in the doorway, working out her phrasing before speaking. It was a habit that led people to believe she was more slow-witted than she was, a perception she was in no hurry to correct.

'She said Oscar has killed himself. He's hanging from the old oak by the gamekeeper's cottage in Glen Mhor.' She refused to use the colloquial term for that particular tree, preferring to let the past remain dead and buried. She had been a young girl herself when the tree was christened, a lonely baptism of one young woman ending her life. 'I thought we should take a look before anything else.'

Corstorphine nodded, his expression unchanging. 'When was this meant to have happened?' His tone betrayed a detective's caution, treating every statement with a distrust learned from years of hard-won experience. He unwound his lanky frame from the comfort of the leather swivel chair he'd inherited from his predecessor, reaching for a mobile and a set of keys.

'She found his body this morning, so sometime in the last twenty-four hours presumably.'

'He's an unlikely candidate for a suicide.' Corstorphine voiced what Frankie had already considered. Some people are suicides-in-waiting. They give the impression of drowning on dry land, a futility of purpose, of having already given up the struggle. Oscar was the type who'd face down death, wrest the sickle from death's cold bone fingers and enjoy laying about him until stopped by a greater force.

'We'll take the Land Rover. That track's fairly unforgiving on the suspension.' He led the way to the station car park, the midday sun not managing to dispel the mood that was settling on them both.

SIX

The two detectives sat in the 4x4, staring at the figure swaying in front of them, blue strobe from the Land Rover's roof lights catching the body where it hung in the tree's shadow. It was apparent even from a distance that he was dead, the neck wound alone would have killed him in seconds. DI Corstorphine turned off the engine, and they dressed awkwardly in white forensics overclothes, pulling on blue latex gloves, incongruous in the rural setting, before reluctantly approaching the scene of the crime. The heather's perfume was insufficient to mask the earthly stench emanating from the body, a tang of iron from the blood discernible over more common odours. Tattered ribbons of flesh hung out of Oscar's eye sockets where sharp beaks had penetrated, and the steady hum of flies increased in volume as they approached the body.

Frankie raised the office SLR, taking shot after shot of Oscar's corpse, zooming to focus in on his neck. Corstorphine followed her gaze and spotted the rabbit dangling beside Oscar, strangely companion-like in death, and added a few shots of that unlikely pairing. The wires disappeared into the leafy canopy above, but Frankie took a few photos anyway. Corstorphine turned away from the macabre sight. He'd seen dead bodies before, it came with the job – but not like this. Oscar's body hung there like a medieval sacrifice, the gaping second mouth screaming silent obscenities at his back. He allowed himself time to process the image as he walked back towards the quad bike they had just passed down the track, spotting snares spilled on the ground as the bike had toppled into the burn. He retrieved the rifle from its side holster, sniffing the barrel to confirm it had been recently used, and took the keys out of the ignition. On second thoughts, he carefully fetched the engine oil tin, examining it suspiciously with a fair idea of what it contained. Looking back towards the tree, fresh tracks indicated where the quad bike had left the path, and no other tracks were obvious. The rifle and tin were placed in the back of the Land Rover, wrapped in a plastic sheet.

'Sir!' Frankie's voice carried a note of query. 'What do you make of this?'

He followed the line of her arm, a white stick lying beside the track immediately under the tree. It was a bone harpoon, more like the kind of thing he'd expect to see used by an Inuit fisherman than lying incongruously in some Highland glen.

'Could be one of Oscar's tools of the trade.' His response was neutral, unsure of the purpose of such a tool. 'Wouldn't put it past him to have something like that for getting at rabbits in burrows, perhaps setting snares from a distance.' He stooped to pick it up in a gloved hand, then noticed something, partially obscured by the heather overhanging the path. 'Now that's interesting!'

Frankie paused from photographing the harpoon to see the object he held up into the sunlight. It was a gearwheel, each tooth perfectly identical to the next as they wrapped a geometric pattern around the rim of a circular bone disk. He turned it, admiring the skill with which it had been manufactured. 'Was Oscar much of a creative artist?'

'Not to my knowledge, sir. He's...' She paused, then rearranged her words to account for the past tense: 'He was creative with his fists but more well known as a piss artist.'

Corstorphine nodded thoughtfully, placing the gearwheel into a plastic bag. He peered up into the tree, wondering whether he was still capable of emulating childhood feats of tree-climbing heroics to look more closely at the wire support. 'See if there's anything else unusual around here.'

They both undertook a fingertip search of the track, picking up tiny fragments of carved bone and wood and placing them into evidence bags as they went, with Frankie painstakingly photographing each item and location.

'You don't think it was a suicide, do you, sir?'

Corstorphine held her gaze for a long second before shaking his head deliberately side to side. 'No, Frankie. It doesn't feel right, not with all this paraphernalia under the tree.' He looked back at the quad bike, calculating the likely speed and force of impact. 'I'd say someone set a snare for him.'

Frankie nodded, moving upwind of the body.

She held her evidence bag aloft. 'What about these gears?'

He frowned. The gears were a complete mystery and would make their job that much harder to do. Then there was the dead rabbit, hanging next to Oscar's corpse in a manner that suggested someone was having fun at their expense.

'Would you say Margo could have set all this up?' He looked up into the tree again, searching for inspiration, something that would tell him what had happened here. He tried to envisage Margo climbing into the branches, setting a snare for her man.

'She had the motive, sir. It's public knowledge he knocked her about.' She sounded doubtful. Margo was a doormat. Whatever spirit she once may have possessed had been beaten out of her by Oscar.

'We can question her under caution when we get back.' He

lifted his head up from scrutinising the ground around the tree. An ambulance was making tortuous progress along the track. 'Here's the ambulance,' he said unnecessarily.

It took four of them to release Oscar's body from the tree and cut the wire with some difficulty from above his head. 'Try not to touch the wire, it may hold forensic evidence,' Corstorphine advised as the body was manhandled into a body bag. The ambulance crew zipped it up, noses wrinkling up against the smell, and laid it down on the gurney, securing the body into place with straps. The two detectives guided the ambulance as it executed a multi-point turn, stopping it as the wheels started to sink into the soft ground each side of the track, or threatened to drop into the burn at the end of each tortuous turn.

When the ambulance was safely away, Corstorphine manoeuvred the Land Rover under the tree and climbed onto the roof, releasing the captive rabbit into another evidence bag. From there he could reach the lower branches with ease and climbed gingerly into the upper reaches of the tree. The stronger of the wire snares was securely wrapped around one of the stout branches, where the force of Oscar's snaring had caused the wire to dig deeply into the bark. It was the rabbit's snare that caught Corstorphine's attention, though, looped around a large bone wheel that had jammed itself in between two smaller branches.

He called down to Frankie. 'Pass up the camera.' As he grabbed the strap, he caught her questioning gaze. 'The whole bloody tree will have to be a crime scene.' His mind was engaged with how to manage an oak tree and its surrounds as a forensics crime scene; they didn't teach this at police college!

They left the tree wrapped with police tape, instructing anyone unlikely enough to be in the vicinity of the deserted glen not to cross this line, then drove on to the cottage. The small sunlit stone building sat peacefully in the glen, making the nightmarish scene they'd recently left behind appear all the more unreal. Corstorphine pulled on another set of latex gloves and tried the door. It was unlocked, and with an unspoken agreement, they entered. The rooms were spotless, kitchen knives all in place in a wooden rack, bed made. They opened a few drawers, nothing out of the ordinary. The drive back to the station was interspersed with little in the way of conversation, both detectives too wrapped up in their own thoughts.

'Can it be a coincidence he chose that tree to set a snare?' Corstorphine queried Frankie. The knowledge of how the tree became known locally as the Hanging Tree was at the forefront of their minds.

'Who, sir? Oscar – or whoever laid the trap for him?'

'I think we can dispense with the idea of a suicide.' Corstorphine drove in silence for a while, concentrating on keeping the Land Rover's wheels inside the existing track ruts. 'I don't know what's going on with the gears lying around the tree, but nobody goes to that much trouble if they're killing themselves. The question we should be asking is who had the motive?'

Frankie sighed heavily. 'Who didn't have a reason to kill him? He's been making lifelong enemies ever since he reached nursery school!' She stared out of the Land Rover window, distant mountains wreathed in clouds threatening an end to the sunny spell they'd been enjoying. 'Do you think any motive may have a connection with the tree then, sir?'

'Probably just a coincidence.'

'But why leave a rabbit up there?' Frankie voiced just one of the questions that worried him too. Snared like a rabbit. Hung in the Hanging Tree. Bits of artfully constructed bone gears littering the ground. It made no sense, and Oscar wasn't likely to be offering them much assistance.

'We'll start with Margo; she must know something.'

'You think she's a suspect, sir?'

'At this stage, everyone's a bloody suspect.' He slowed as the vehicle reached the road, checked each way and then moved off at a faster speed towards the town. 'But do I think Margo killed him?' The silence that followed them back into town provided the only answer they had.

They sat in the interview room, Frankie and Corstorphine on one side of the table with Margo facing them. Three mugs of coffee sat untouched, thin tendrils of steam curling up into the stale air. Frankie switched on the voice recorder beside her, announced who was in the room and advised Margo that she was providing a witness statement of her own free will before Corstorphine spoke. He took the time to study her. She'd been beaten, and recently – the bruising was evident enough around her eyes despite the layers of makeup.

'Before we start, Margo, do you need to see a doctor? I can see someone has knocked you about.' Corstorphine had seen her wince as she lowered herself onto the hard chair. She'd clasped her hand to her side, before linking arms protectively across her chest.

'I'm fine.' The response was sharp with irritation.

'Alright.' He sighed, tired of always being seen as the enemy in these scenarios. 'I want you to go over everything that happened before you saw Oscar this morning. Try and remember every detail, even things that seem unimportant like changes in his routine. Did he appear unduly worried? Anything that you can tell us may help.'

Margo's breath came in short shallow breaths. She watched them through narrowed eyes before responding. 'We had a fight two days ago. I told him I was expecting.' Frankie's eyes widened and she focussed on Margo's stomach, clearly searching for a telltale bulge. Corstorphine just nodded encouragement for her to continue.

'Oscar wasn't impressed. He let me know he didn't want a child. Tried his damn best to get rid of it there and then!' She spat the last words out. 'He was never that good with words, preferred using his hands.' She laughed mirthlessly at her own joke, missing the quick glance that the detectives exchanged.

'And then?' Frankie prompted.

'He left the house yesterday morning just after six as usual. Oscar liked to be up early in case any animals were stupid enough to still be on the hills. I lay in bed for a while, then did a wash. The sheets were bloody.'

Corstorphine's pen scratched the details in his notebook.

'What did you do after that?' Corstorphine asked. 'Did anyone come to the house, or did you see any hikers on the path? Anyone that can substantiate your story?'

'Well, it's like a bloody motorway some days. I had thought about opening a café, maybe selling some home-made cakes. You know, make some money on the side to pay for foreign holidays.' The sarcasm met with a stony response. She breathed deeply, and then winced, before shifting position in the chair. 'No, nobody comes up the glen. There's fuck all reason to do so. It goes nowhere, there's no big hills to climb, no fish in the burn and no trees to cut down.' She paused for a second. 'Except the one.'

'So, what did you do the rest of the day?' Frankie asked. Details would help colour in the outline she'd given them.

'Made the fucking bed with clean sheets, cleaned the kitchen floor where I'd bled all over it and prepared Oscar's meal for him. The rest of the time I just looked out of the window and wished I could run away.' She blinked away the tears that were starting to form, before hurriedly continuing. 'When Oscar was late for his dinner, I thought he'd be down the pub.' Her eyes met theirs, the anguish in her gaze catching them both unawares. 'Then I was worried. I can just about manage him normal-like, but when he's drunk... You've no idea what he's like. He wanted the baby gone, I knew that.'

Corstorphine saw Margo's fist clench and wondered how

far she would go to protect her unborn child – even to the point of murder?

'When he hadn't come back this morning, I took my chance, packed my bag and left. I thought he'd see me on the track, and I couldn't run because of the pain in my ribs. Then I saw him, hanging from that tree. I couldn't work out what it was at first, then I saw it was Oscar.'

Her head tilted to one side as if she was reliving the moment, unconsciously mimicking Oscar's stance as he swung bloodily from the wire. 'I was happy,' she stated simply. 'He couldn't hurt me anymore. Then I thought whoever did it might still be around, and I had to run even though it hurt my ribs. You know the rest.'

Corstorphine regarded her steadily, the eyebrow refusing to lift. Insofar as anyone tells the truth, this was as close as it got. 'Who'd want to do this to him, Margo?'

She laughed, the sound short and sharp like a fox's cough. 'Who wouldn't!'

Frankie asked her again. 'Seriously, Margo, if you know anyone who may have done this, we need to know.'

Margo took time to consider as Corstorphine observed her, seeing the calculation in her eyes.

'There's a gamey Oscar set up some months ago, left a dead eagle on his beat. He's up before the court in Inverness sometime this week. Oscar said he'd know who did it, found it funny.'

'Do you have a name?' Corstorphine queried. Frankie's pen hovered over her notebook.

'John Ackerman. His patch isn't that far from Inverness. Everyone knows it's a setup. You don't shit in your own bed.'

Frankie closed her notebook. 'This interview is terminated at eighteen forty.' She switched off the recorder, whilst Margo looked at them quizzically.

'You're free to go, Margo. Get yourself checked out at the

hospital – do you want us to run you there?' Corstorphine's offer was met with a hostile stare.

'Think I want to be seen in a police car? No, thanks. I'll make my own way.'

'Where will you be staying, Margo, in case we need to get back in touch?' Frankie queried her as she held the door open.

Margo stared blankly into some middle distance as if she'd set out this morning without any destination in mind, save anywhere away from Oscar. 'Back home.'

'Before you go...'

Margo turned to see Corstorphine holding out a set of keys. 'From the quad bike,' he explained. She took them in silence and left the interview room. Corstorphine escorted her to the front desk where Hamish handed over her travel bag. They stood watching her as she retrieved a purse, making a show of counting her money out in front of them before abruptly leaving.

SEVEN

Corstorphine left Frankie at the station in the act of pinning a red thread between Oscar's photograph and a yellow Post-it inscribed with John Ackerman's name. As crazy walls go, this one was looking particularly sparse, and he had little confidence that their first suspect would prove to be the killer. Frankie had put Margo's name up on the board, but Corstorphine had a feeling that line of enquiry was a nonstarter. Whoever had set the snare for Oscar had planned his death carefully, more like a military operation than the desperate act of a newly pregnant woman. The forensics report would come later, once the SOC unit had made the round trip from Inverness and finished investigating the scene of the crime – a tree, that would be a first for them. Leaving Frankie to work the case on her own felt like a dereliction of duty, and it was in a conflicted state of mind that he crossed the car park, raising a hand in farewell to her outline in the office window. Still, there wasn't much more that he could do without the forensics report. The vision of Oscar's torn body hanging from the tree remained fresh in his memory, and it took a wilful effort to erase the image. He wanted to go home, sink into the settee with the TV on and a large single malt – but he had arranged to meet this woman. Corstorphine was too much the gentleman to stand her up, no matter how Oscar's death had affected him.

He checked the car dashboard: 19:15. Still in time to make his pre-arranged date at the village inn some way out of town. Raising himself slightly in the driver's seat, Corstorphine appraised his reflection in the rear-view mirror. Hair touched with grey, but no sign yet of the widow's peak that had adorned his father's head at this same age. Did he look forty-one? His hazel eyes engaged with their serious reflection, balancing the crooked ridge of a broken nose, the result of an overly enthusiastic arrest in his younger days. He had a face his wife used to describe variously as 'characterful' or 'rugged'. Towards the end, as she was anchored to the hospital bed with a morphine drip for the pain, her shaking hand had brushed his wet cheek and with a voice more air than sound, she'd told him it was 'lived-in'.

Corstorphine still felt guilty whenever he met another woman, concern that he was being unfaithful, disrespectful. His wife still sat next to him in his imagination, a comforting presence giving him 'that look' which told him he was being stupid, or stubborn, or frequently both. *'Go on and live life. That's the only gift you can give me. Live for both of us.'* It was, he felt, an admonishment to grief. They were among the last words she'd spoken, whispered with eyes momentarily unclouded before a replacement morphine drip took effect. Words that wounded him deeply. He turned to look at her, sitting beside him as he manoeuvred out of the station car park, and her smile was benediction enough. Corstorphine addressed the empty air. 'You're right. I know.'

The road followed the edge of a loch, grey waters cresting into white peaks as the wind intensified, miniature white horses riding each crest. Pine trees bent their tall heads, inclining away from the prevailing westerly fresh in from the Atlantic. A bird hung motionless in the agitated sky, an expert aviator bending nature's force to hold itself effortlessly suspended in space. Corstorphine gave up trying to identify it as he held the car to the curve of the road. Too small for an eagle, probably a buzzard searching for an easy meal – purveyor of the finest roadkill. He envied the bird its inherent ability to master the elements. For too long now, he'd felt his life was similarly suspended, hanging at some random point but exhibiting none of the graceful skill the bird presented. No, Corstorphine thought ruefully, his motion through life was more the stumbling random walk of the town drunk, greeting each new day with the dull surprise that he'd managed to get this far without falling flat on his face.

'Give it a rest, Corstorphine. Glass half-empty again?' His disembodied wife laughed beside him, poking fun at his moodiness, encouraging him as she often did to enjoy life whilst it lasted.

'Aye. I know, lass.' He spoke the words with the ease of someone long used to communicating with the dead. 'I always was a morose bastard.' She faded away as the village inn lights came into view, and by the time he'd turned into the car park, there was nothing left of her, just a touch of warmth around his heart. Corstorphine remained in the car for a few minutes, mentally filing the day's events away before he felt able to face the world.

There was a woman already sitting at the table the waitress pointed out to him, and her eyes flicked towards him as he approached. She looked no older than thirty, certainly a lot younger than her slightly out of focus online profile had suggested. All too often, people on the dating apps lied more than a politician, photographs taken before the last flush of youth had departed presented as 'recent'. The duplicity of those seeking a relationship was slightly offensive to his detective's mindset, but he knew enough about life to make allowances for the air of desperation that adhered to some of those serial daters he had encountered. This was a novelty for him, a woman appearing younger than her photograph. She raised her hand, her fingers performing a Mexican wave in his direction.

'James Corstorphine, sorry I'm late.' He proffered a hand to the woman, suddenly taken by the panicked thought that perhaps this wasn't his date and wondering how best to extricate himself, even as his hand was grasped by hers.

'Jenny Peck. No, you're quite on time. I'm early, so I started without you.' She tilted her head towards a glass of wine. 'Can I get you a drink?'

Corstorphine sat at the table, flustered by the role reversal that had taken place. 'No, let me.' His protestations went ignored. She had already raised her hand again, beckoning over the waitress with an imperial wave. 'I insist! What will you have?' They both stared at him, his date with an amused air as if he'd just said something witty, the waitress with professional indifference.

'Do you have a non-alcoholic beer?' Corstorphine suddenly felt ineffectual, off balance, wondering how the initiative had been so easily taken away.

'We've got non-alcoholic lager.' The waitress waited, stylus poised over some iPad arrangement that he supposed was electronically connected directly to the bar.

'Yes, that's fine. Thanks.' She placed the menus down on the table, and after a second's hesitation which wasn't lost on him, put the wine list down on Jenny's side of the table.

'Hard day?' His date asked the question whilst raising the wine to her lips, observing him over the upturned rim.

'Aye. Busy enough. How about you – you're a nurse, is that right?' Corstorphine felt instantly more at ease asking the questions and took the opportunity to search her face for any clues as to character. Apart from dark brown eyes that held his in an amused stare, he was none the wiser. Those detective skills, honed year after year from searching faces for guile or guilt, came back empty. She was attractive enough, a light touch with the makeup which was a relief, auburn hair falling naturally to her shoulders. A momentary panic hit him as it crossed his mind she might be younger than he first thought.

'Staff nurse,' she replied. 'I'm the battle-axe on the ward.'

It was Corstorphine's turn to smile, more out of a sense of relief that she couldn't be that young to be a staff nurse. 'I can't see you as any kind of murder weapon.'

She laughed, a light sound that he felt he'd like to hear more of. 'Well, I can see that you're a policeman. Murder weapon indeed!'

He took his time reading the dinner menu as a companionable silence engulfed their table, a small quiet island in the sea of conversation that murmured restlessly around them. Couples out for dinner, families celebrating a birthday or some other event, a few first dates like themselves – too old for nightclubs, too young to have resigned themselves to a lonely existence. The sound of a grandfather clock striking eight o'clock brought him out of his reverie. A sombre-looking instrument more than likely purchased from some house auction to provide much needed character to the otherwise anodyne restaurant interior. Now that his attention had been drawn to it, he could hear the metronome tick tock that accompanied the pendulum's swing.

'Can I take your order, or would you like some more time?' The waitress had materialised beside him, electronic notepad poised for their order. Corstorphine didn't need to check whether his table companion was ready; she reeled off her starter and main with decisive efficiency, ordering another glass of wine at the same time. He felt distracted – some vague coalescing thought was clamouring to be heard, but it had departed without leaving any memory of its passing. He ordered automatically, safe choices that wouldn't be challenging either to cook or to eat, listening with half his attention as Jenny asked him if this was a regular haunt of his.

'No, I don't come here that often. I quite like the food here, not too keen on that picture on a plate nonsense the trendier places dish up.'

'You're lucky if they serve it on a dish! These days they want to serve it on slates, or wooden boards – anything impractical that your dinner can just slide off. Totally unhygienic!' She paused as the waitress returned with the drinks, waiting for Corstorphine to touch glasses.

'Here's tae us!' He voiced the words, wondering if she, too, was running the rest of the reciprocal Scots toast in her mind – *Wha's like us? Gey few, and they're a' deid*. The thought suddenly occurred to him that she may be a widow, another soul cast adrift by the early death of a loved one. 'Do you do this sort of thing often?' The words came quickly, covering his momentary embarrassment.

'Date strange men?' Her eyes remained amused, focussing on the wineglass which she revolved slowly in long fingers. 'I could ask you the same question. Are you a serial dater, James?' She looked at him directly, the interest in whatever his response might be apparent in her quizzical expression.

Corstorphine struggled to answer. 'I've been on a few dates over the last year, none of them particularly successful.' He sipped his beer, wishing it was alcoholic now, something to erase the words he'd just blurted out before thinking them through. What was he even doing here, fresh from a murder scene? He sensed his wife giving him an encouraging look, willing him to keep at it. 'I'm sorry, I'm really not very good at this.'

She observed him keenly, giving Corstorphine the impression that she was making an analysis much as any good nurse would every day on the ward. 'How long have you been single?' Her amused expression now had an overlay of concern.

He saw the concern in her eyes – Corstorphine also read people for a living. *Christ, this is going well – now she's feeling sorry for me!* 'My wife died five years ago, cancer. I'm only just getting back into the dating game.' He grimaced. The words came out raw, exposed, like pulling off a plaster before a wound had healed. Nothing said romantic evening like dropping your dead wife into the conversation. 'Think I'm out of practice.'

The starters arrived, punctuating Corstorphine's statement with plate-sized full stops. They ate quietly, interspersing mouthfuls with satisfied comments about the food.

'You just have to be you, James.' The advice came as the plates had been cleared away, filling the hiatus between courses. 'My husband ran out on me, two years ago now. Had an affair with someone he met whilst out walking the dog.' She stared intently at the white linen tablecloth as if it held the answer to a question she'd asked many times before. She raised her head to lock eyes with him, no room for guile this close. 'She was just a lassie in her early twenties, almost half his age.' She shook her head in denial. 'Funny how you can't see something that's right under your nose. Do you get that, in the police business, clues so obvious that you wonder how on earth nobody could have spotted them at the outset?'

Corstorphine drank his beer, the cardboard taste that accompanied non-alcoholic beverages not so obvious after the first few sips. His palate must be getting used to it. 'The benefits of hindsight. Aye, we get it all the time, especially from the press – or anyone who doesn't have to join the dots as an investigation is underway. Sometimes, it's the smallest clue that brings it all together, or the modus operandi – habitual routines as easy to recognise as a fingerprint.'

The arrival of the main course interrupted his flow, and they leaned back in their seats as the waitress placed the plates on the table. Corstorphine exchanged a glance with Jenny, seeking a sign that they shared some interest apart from the food. The unvoiced response was non-committal, leaving him to wonder if he was ever going to find a way through the unmapped middle-aged courtship ritual he kept attempting. It was all so easy when the whole world was younger and less encumbered with emotional and physical baggage. They met in groups, they drank, danced and partied in groups. Eventually, they paired off, couple after couple as nature intended until only the oddballs, self-contained or unlucky remained. He was beginning to feel like an oddball himself, a misplaced sock in the drawer of life. He felt his wife's expression without the need to see it, lips pursed up to one side, head tilted inquisitively, requesting he just look at himself now. He took a knife to his steak, red meat exposed as the blade cut deep.

'What's the story with the garrotted guy they brought in today?' She asked the question before he'd had a chance to eat the first mouthful and the meal in front of him morphed into an atrocity, juice running red under his blade. Corstorphine drew a breath, his appetite completely gone.

'Sorry, I'm not able to talk about work.' He stared blankly at his plate, willing away the recent sight and smell of Oscar's body.

'No, of course. Silly of me to ask – it's just word gets around the hospital of anything like this. Left the ambulance crew a bit shaken, to be honest, and we talk these things over between us.' She looked apologetic. 'Helps to talk, makes it easier for us all to cope when something bad happens.'

'That's alright. Sometimes, the job throws up stuff that is hard to deal with.' He cut the steak into a mouth-sized portion. 'You just get used to it, I guess.' The steak tasted good as he dealt with the day's trauma in his own way, consigning it to that part of his memory marked Private.

'What made you want to be a nurse?' He steered the conversation onto safer ground.

'Oh, I don't know.'

Corstorphine imagined waking up to her smile.

'I feel we all need to help where we can. Do our bit.' She spoke in short sentences between bites. 'Not that much different to you, really. Taking damaged people and doing what we can with them.'

Her enigmatic expression gave nothing away.

'What about you, James? What made you join the police?'

He struggled for an answer appropriate for the setting, taking longer than necessary to finish his mouthful whilst her gaze remained uncomfortably fixed on him from across the table.

'Short answer. I don't think I'm suited to much else – and the bar's set fairly low.'

She responded to his attempt at self-deprecation with a raised eyebrow. 'I don't believe you.'

Corstorphine felt a blush starting under his collar. God, he was behaving like a teenager.

'Truth is I wanted to make a difference,' he blurted. 'Try and make society better by putting the bad guys away.'

'Don't they just come back again? Do a few years inside where they learn new tricks?'

'I have to believe I'm doing something worthwhile, otherwise what's the point?'

There was an awkward silence before Jenny changed the subject.

'Isn't it lovely now the evenings are longer?'

With work marked off-limits, the rest of the conversation dealt with inconsequential topics as they discovered a shared interest in nature.

'Would you like to meet again?' She asked the question over coffee, once he'd relented and agreed to share the bill.

'That would be nice. Aye – I'd like that.' Corstorphine felt the ground moving under his feet as if some giant continental plate had shifted. Every other date he'd been on had ended with the woman making hurried excuses, never to be seen again. They left the table, Corstorphine for once actually helping a woman on with her coat instead of proving an impediment to the process, and exited into the night.

'Good! Good night then, James.' She leaned forward, head demurely turned to one side to present a cheek.

'Good night, Jenny.' He waited until she'd entered the waiting taxi before walking in a daze to his car. His wife sat next to him on the journey home, a quiet smile sitting on her invisible lips.

EIGHT

The minister of St Cuthbert's made his daily pilgrimage from the manse, shuffling along a well-trodden path through an overgrown graveyard to the church. Each step brought with it a sharp stab of pain in his lower back muscles, and he silently invoked the Lord's Prayer until he reached the medieval church porch. A pair of ornate Gothic doors opened easily against his touch, and he tilted his head in obsequience towards the far altar before entering the cool, darkened interior. Half in hope, he glanced around the church in search of any parishioners but was unsurprised to find he was alone. Fresh flowers adorned the window recesses, a mix of wildflowers and roses adding a splash of colour to an interior that had otherwise been drained of joy over the centuries.

His flock was diminishing year in, year out as the grim reaper took a steady toll on the aged. Any new young faces that made an inquisitive appearance over the year were soon put off by the unwelcoming stares of his congregants, and instead often made their way to one of the evangelical churches that had sprung up in the most ungodly of places. The local cinema hosted one of these gatherings of bright-eyed born-again Christians, playing guitars and singing along to the bouncing ball as the words scrolled on the silver screen in the upstairs studio. On the ground floor, without anyone finding this at all unusual, bingo devotees sat in equal glassy-eyed reverence as balls dropped out of a machine and the numbers were intoned with meaning as powerful as the words spoken upstairs.

The minister knew all about evangelists. False prophets each and every one, most of them funded by shady American churches that monetised Christ. Slick organisations taking a tithe direct from wage packets to fund private jets and lavish lifestyles. How did the flocks not realise they were being fleeced? The similarities between sheep farming and religion were not lost on him, for God's sake it was even spelled out in the bible. He glanced at the figure of Christ on the cross, suspended for all eternity behind the altar and looking forlornly down on him. Was that an accusatory look? His eyes weren't what they used to be.

Pulling an oversized key from his pockets with some difficulty, he inserted it into the lock of an ancient oak door securing the entry to the bell tower. A turn of the key released the door, and it swung open to reveal the small stone ringing chamber at the base of the bell tower. With the habit of years, his eyes travelled up beyond the thick red and blue banded Sally until the rope disappeared into a hole in the ceiling some distance up the tower.

Many years ago, when he had first taken the ministry, bell-ringing was the job of the church warden. He remembered walking to church with a straight back, acknowledging the smiles and greetings of his parishioners as they heeded the clarion call of the single bell. Now there was nobody left with the strength to pull the rope, and soon the day would come when he, too, could no longer manage.

He locked the door back into place behind him to prevent it from swinging open, revealing the iron clasp set into stone that held the end of the rope. Ignoring the pain in his back, he unwound the rope and then wrapped it into three large loops, turn after turn held in his hand to form an intimate bond between himself and the bell high above.

He had instructed generations of bellringers in how to hold the rope, how to allow sufficient slack for the recoil as the bell traversed its arc above their heads, how never to wrap the rope around their arms. He pulled on the rope, feeling the weight of the bell resisting his initial attempts to overcome inertia. The strength in his arms alone was insufficient these days to pull the bell up successfully.

For the last decade, he had needed to add his body's weight, letting himself fall almost to the ground to bring the bell round into position. The corollary of this of course was that he was then lifted off his feet as the bell swung back, his arm attempting to pull the rest of his body heavenwards at each rotation. He imagined this must be what it would be like on the day of Rapture, when the godly were called to heaven. Bellringing had become a transcendent event for him. Every Sunday, his body fought against the increasingly reluctant rope, overcoming the adversity of gravity and friction before experiencing that brief dizzying moment when ascension appeared possible.

Gripping the rope hard, he threw himself towards the floor to start the heavy mechanism into motion. The rope lifted slightly, pulling him back to his feet and he threw himself down again, timing the force expertly to provide impetus at exactly the right moment. With increasing vigour, he repeated his solitary exercise before the bell started to ring in earnest and his body felt that miraculous moment of weightlessness. The pain in his back receded as his spine was stretched, nerves free for the moment from the punishing effects of gravity on ruined cartilage.

High up in the belfry, the force of his endeavours was transferred via a secondary mechanism, quite separate to the bell. A large circular bone cog connected to a reciprocating steel saw, a parasitic addition which had never been imagined by the original medieval craftsmen who had built this tower. The saw was cutting upwards through the oak beam that held the cast bronze bell aloft. The minister was correct; over the last few months the bell had been increasingly resistant to his efforts.

A younger bellringer might have been less likely to blame the inadequacies of an aging body and had the bell tower mechanism investigated, but the minister put the increasing stiffness down to age and infirmity. Then, without warning, the oak gave way, parting along the line of the saw as the weight of the bell and vibration proved too much. Old mortar crumbled as the oak beam twisted in stone sockets, the stone giving way almost as easily as the mortar and the bell began its fall from grace.

The minister felt something was awry as the vibration travelled down the rope, a sudden grip as the cord dug deeply into his flesh harder than a vengeful angel's clasp – then nothing. He stood looking upwards in confusion, the rope starting to gather in coils at his feet as the tower groaned like a wounded giant. In the few seconds it took for the bell to shake free, the minister realised his peril. There was nowhere for him to go, save through the locked belfry tower door which resisted his panicked attempts to pull open. A discordant peal alerted him to his fate, and his wide eyes stared heavenwards for the last time. The bell was in free fall; no longer held above the earth, it accelerated downwards, smashing through the fragile ringing chamber roof in a cloud of plaster dust and reducing the minister to bone, blood and offal in one final act. The bell lodged against the bell tower door, and dull metallic sounds still issued from its cracked surface as falling masonry hit the solid bronze before the church fell silent.

The small congregation had mostly taken their places in the pews. Faces turned to stone as the cacophony sounded, staring blankly at the white dust slowly filling the nave. Standing or sitting, frozen in shock, they remained mute until blood started trickling under the belfry door. The first scream cut the air like a knife, a release of tension that transferred to the other parishioners who reacted with a unity of purpose and vigour that would have put the young evangelists to shame. As one, they ran to push on the locked belfry door, but the oak remained resolute, jammed solid against the weight of the bell and fallen masonry.

A sizeable crowd began to gather outside the church, neighbouring houses alerted by the discordant clarion death call as the heavy bronze bell rang a final descent. It was an irony that would not have been wasted on the minister, had he still lived, the last sounding of the bell bringing the largest congregation for many years.

NINE

PC Lamb stared at the crimson puddle that was already congealing under the bell tower door. Bloodied footprints led the way to the church porch doors, held wide open to allow access to the compressed air hoses powering the saws, cutting through the hinges and lock holding the door in place. It seemed like sacrilege to him, destroying the medieval door; each attempt to force it open had caused greater damage. A floodlight cast an unforgiving illumination on the scene, catching the crucifixion in stark outlines where the figure of Christ appeared to be dancing in the firemen's shadows, bringing back visions from his first MDMA-fuelled rave. A loud crack from splintering wood brought him back to the present as the recalcitrant door timbers parted, and his stomach contents forced their way up his throat in response to the charnel house now revealed.

'Sarge?' He stood outside in the graveyard, after telling the firemen he was seeking a stronger radio signal but glad to be out in the fresh air.

'Sierra four-five, this is whisky tango. Did they not teach you radio technique at that police college, PC Lamb? Over!'

The sergeant's lugubrious tone helped to calm his nerves.

He took a couple of gulps of air, glad that he'd managed to keep his breakfast down. 'Sorry, sarge. I'm at St Cuthbert's. There's been an accident. Over.'

'Thank you, Sierra four-five. We've already been notified that there has been an incident, that's why you were sent there. Can you provide a level of detail above the obvious? Over.'

PC Lamb frowned at his radio transmitter. He could imagine the sarge doing a whisky tango. Feeling more upbeat, he continued. 'It's the minister. Looks like the bell came down on top of him. Over.'

'What's his status? Over.'

PC Lamb had seen his status, and it wasn't good. 'He's dead, sarge, he's a dead ringer.' Why had he said that? Something told him the sarge wouldn't appreciate his humour. 'Over,' he added quickly.

'Your career will be over if I hear you say that again. Secure the scene. We'll have to send in the DI. Just wait there and keep anyone not wearing a uniform out of the church. Over and out.'

PC Lamb clipped the transmitter back into place on his uniform and began herding the more inquisitive members of the public out of the graveyard. He spotted the young reporter from the local paper, waving her phone at him as she approached. His mood lifted; they'd shared a few drinks just the other evening and he thought he might be in with a chance. He straightened his back in case she took an impromptu snap and wondered if he could get the words bell and end into the newspaper report without incurring the sergeant's wrath.

TEN

Corstorphine stood in the shattered doorway of the bell tower, surveying the damage wrought by a 575kg cast bronze bell falling thirty metres. Parts of the minister were still recognisable, those arms and legs that protruded from beneath the bell. He went to scratch his head before remembering belatedly that he was wearing a safety helmet, and his arm fell back uselessly at his side.

'Jesus!' Frankie's offering had little to do with the sanctity of the scene. 'Have you seen the timber?' Her hand pointed at an upended oak beam, buried in the dust and rubble, the exposed end pointing back up the tower. It had been sawn almost completely through, just a ragged line of torn timber paid testament to the point at which the tensile strength failed.

Corstorphine nodded. 'That's not what bothers me.' She frowned at him in puzzlement, then followed his line of vision to see what he was focussed on. The rubble-strewn ground was covered in a fine layer of white dust, plaster that had turned into clouds when the ceiling immediately above their heads had been pulverised. It took her a while to spot what concerned him – a fragment of a gearwheel, too small to be part of the bellringing mechanism. The similarity to the gearwheels they'd collected at the Hanging Tree was clear.

'Jesus!'

'I really don't think he's going to help us, Frankie, no matter how many times you invoke his name.' Corstorphine shone a flashlight into the tower, the light catching quartz crystals in the stonework which shone briefly like stars, tiny pinpricks of diamond light in an otherwise dark square universe. He slipped the torch back into his pocket. 'There's nothing more we can do here until the tower's made safe. See if the church can be secured, I'll get hold of the forensics team again.' Corstorphine turned to leave. 'Put a rocket under the building surveyors when they get here, we need the body and bell removed and a fingertip search of all the rubble. I'll see you back at the station.'

As he left the scene, Corstorphine puzzled over what possible link could exist between the town bully and a minister. Was there even a connection to be made or was someone randomly killing for the sheer hell of it? Either way, two murders in a small Highland town would bring a level of scrutiny they were ill-equipped to handle. He keyed the number for the Inverness forensics team on the way to his car, this could be another first for them.

Once back at the station, Corstorphine added the minister's name, Reverend Simon McLean, to the crazy wall. His marker stood alone and unconnected, in death as well as in life. Sighing heavily, he drew a rough gearwheel in the middle of the whiteboard, linking it to Oscar and the minister. Somehow, they had to be connected. He keyed his computer into life, brought up Oscar's case notes and tried a cross link to the minister on the police VALCRI system. Quite why their inconsequential Highland station had been chosen to trial the new European software was a mystery, but at this stage Corstorphine was glad to use any tool at his disposal. Unsurprisingly, there was nothing. The minister had led a blameless existence as far as the police were concerned, not even so much as a parking ticket. He tried entering bone gears as key words, nothing. Corstorphine sighed again, staring at the computer screen as if by force of will he could entice it to impart some meaningful clue. The screen remained devoid of inspiration, and Corstorphine switched the computer off in disgust and pulled on his jacket. The forensics report from Oscar's death was due in tomorrow, and there was nothing he could realistically accomplish by staying here on a Sunday.

He took a well-used detour on the drive home, stopping off at the Indian takeaway to collect an early dinner. Once back at his house, Corstorphine switched on the TV, collapsed into a settee large enough for three and began forking mouthfuls of chicken tikka masala and pilau rice directly out of the tinfoil trays. The programme was something to do with antiques, the presenter a curious shade of orange like some overgrown oompa loompa. Delighted pensioners oohed and aahed over china ornaments and silver trays, trying to act as though they weren't on television. He let it all wash over him, the images and voices a substitute for company, a way for him to pretend that his loneliness was just an illusion. It wasn't meant to be like this – he never expected to be faced with nothing but his own company day in, day out. The two murders were a relief in one respect, something tangible to fill his time. If he concentrated on work, he had less opportunity to dwell on himself – a subject of diminishing interest and growing depression.

Monday morning brought the rain, sheets of water falling from grey leaden clouds and adding to the air of despondency that lay over the police station as they held the morning briefing. Corstorphine stood in front of the crazy wall, the two recent deaths of Oscar and the Reverend Simon McLean sharing pole position at the top. Margo and the gamekeeper John Ackerman held the centre of the display – subject to further enquiry. Both were tenuously linked in both Corstorphine and Frankie's view to the gearwheel he'd drawn yesterday; it was a modus operandi not suited to either of the two suspects' characters or abilities. The full team were in attendance, PC Philip Lamb accompanied by an older constable, PC Bill McAdam and Sergeant Hamish McKee. Frankie stood beside him, waiting to add what little she could to the briefing.

'As you all know, Oscar's body was found in the Hanging Tree on Saturday, on the track to the gamekeeper's cottage in Glen Mhor. We're awaiting the forensics report from the scene, but it seems most likely that someone, or some people, set a snare for him.' Corstorphine fiddled with a remote control, and a picture of Oscar's final moments appeared on the screen beside him. 'Death would have been instantaneous, he was on his quad bike when he hit the wire snare, so the force of the impact almost sliced his head off.'

'I've just had my bacon butty and tomato sauce.'

'Lamb!' The sergeant's disapproving voice cut across anything else the young constable was going to offer in terms of commentary.

'It's just as well you were present at the next death then, Lamb, otherwise this picture might have really spoilt your breakfast.' Corstorphine keyed the next slide, and the incongruous grouping of the shattered church bell and what was left of the minister filled the screen. The image was almost like a cartoon depiction, two legs and an outstretched arm visible under the massive bell. It was only the amount of blood that brought the picture out of the realms of humour back into grim reality. Corstorphine found he was pausing to allow Lamb time to interject another quip and hastily continued.

'The minister of St Cuthbert's died yesterday morning

when the church bell fell on him. We're at an early stage in the investigation, but I can tell you the timbers holding the bell in place had been sawn through deliberately.'

'What's this got to do with Oscar, sir?' PC McAdam voiced the question that they all wanted to ask.

'That's what we'd like to know, Bill. I can't give you any more detail at the moment, truth is we are as in the dark as the rest of you, but there are common elements to both deaths that make me believe there is a strong link. Do any of you know of any connection, however obscure, between Oscar and the minister?'

The small group looked at each other, puzzled expressions and shaking heads giving Corstorphine the answer he had been expecting.

'OK. Keep a lid on the rumour factory. I don't want word getting out that we think there's anything connecting these two for the time being. At the same time, see what you can find out about both of them, just in case there's something that can help us in the investigation. That's all. I don't want to hold you back from your work.' Corstorphine held out an arm to stop PC McAdam from leaving. 'Bill, we need to pick up this gamekeeper – John Ackerman. I want you to accompany Frankie and bring him in for questioning.'

'I understand, sir.' McAdam turned towards Frankie. 'Whenever you're ready?'

'No time like the present, Bill. We'll see you in a couple of hours, sir.'

Corstorphine watched them leave, and realised the sergeant was still in the briefing room. He stood awkwardly, as if some internal and unresolved conflict was occupying his mind.

'What is it, Hamish?' Corstorphine quizzed the desk sergeant.

Hamish indicated Corstorphine's office. 'Do you mind if we talk in there, sir?'

'No, of course not, come on in.' He shut the door behind the sergeant and motioned him to take one of the spare seats. Corstorphine sank into the old leather chair as the sergeant started speaking.

'There may be a link, sir, but I'm not sure if it's going to be of much use to you.'

'Anything you can give me at this stage is a bonus, Hamish. I've damn little to go on, and don't hold out much hope that this John Ackerman is going to fill in any of the blanks for us. What's on your mind?'

The sergeant shifted uncomfortably in his seat, the frown on his forehead deepening. 'When Oscar was five years old, he'd just started school. Well, he was the same as all the other kids as far as I could tell. I used to go around the local primary schools introducing myself as the local bobby, and I remember Oscar because he wanted to try on my helmet – almost lost him in there!' Corstorphine smiled in encouragement; he had no idea where this story was going but listened patiently.

The desk sergeant continued. 'It was several months after he'd started school when there was a bit of a stushie. He'd told one of the teachers that the minister had been "touching him". There weren't the same procedures to follow back then, and the whole thing was dismissed as a malicious prank. DI Brian Rankin, your predecessor, carried out an investigation and found nothing in it, nothing at all. The minister was quite upset for months afterwards, had a few meetings with Oscar's parents and the teachers. Oscar was given a fair larruping by his dad – they were members of the congregation, so Oscar's behaviour must have been mortifying for both his parents at the time. The thing is, I always had my doubts about it. No smoke without fire as they say. Not that there was ever any evidence,' he added quickly.

Corstorphine nodded in response. Child abuse was not something that anyone would believe of a minister back then –

how times had changed. 'What I'm trying to say, sir, is that nobody believed the wee five-year-old boy at the time.' He looked at Corstorphine in a way that reminded him of someone seeking contrition. 'With all the stories you hear today, I've sometimes wondered, what if he was telling the truth? The minister's dead now, so we'll never know, but Oscar was a fine wee lad when he started school and after that, he turned into what he was. I'd hate to think we had a part to play in that, sir, by never believing the wee lad.'

'As you say, Hamish, it's too late now. If you want my opinion, Oscar was a bad apple from the start – I wouldn't put it past him to try to get the minister into trouble just for the hell of it.' He stood up, signalling the end of the conversation.

'If you say so, sir.' The sergeant got to his feet, a frown of doubt still evident on his face. 'And it doesn't really help you, does it? Oscar would have been the one looking for revenge, but he's already dead.' He left the detective's office, heading back to his habitual position at the front desk. Corstorphine sat in silence, the sergeant's words repeating on a loop inside his mind. Hamish was a good judge of character – could there have been any truth in the allegation made by that five-year-old boy? Had something happened to turn Oscar into the man he became? It was a tenuous link at best.

Oscar could have sawn the beam in the bell tower, although he'd have had to get past the locked bell tower door. But then the gears, in both murders. If there was a connection, who would have wanted them both dead? More to the point, what if there were other people on the killer's list? Corstorphine was already facing an unprecedented crime wave; any more deaths and his team would be put under the microscope.

His email chimed, announcing the arrival of the Inverness forensics report – he scanned the document: no fingerprints, no DNA. There was a paragraph about the gears left in the tree, without any conclusion as to their use. One item leapt out at him. They'd performed a sweep with a metal detector around the bracken surrounding the tree and had found a single coin. The comment suggested it had only recently been left there as it was in near-mint condition, and no obvious signs of handling were visible apart from a fine metal spiral attached to the centre. He looked at the photograph more closely. This wasn't some loose change from Oscar's pockets, it was a thousand-lire coin minted by the Vatican. The profile of Pope Paul II adorned the obverse, bearing an uncanny resemblance to Marlon Brando in *The Godfather*. Corstorphine printed the forensics report and stared at the photograph they'd taken of the coin, spinning the page to read the date stamped into the gold surface – MCMXCVII.

Corstorphine wrestled unsuccessfully with the translation of Roman numerals to something that made sense, before finally giving up and entering it into Google – the result came back as 1997. The next page of the report showed a picture of the reverse of the coin: a coat of arms bearing crossed keys was visible as well as the date written in Arabic numerals confirming the Google translation. He leaned back in the leather seat, wondering if this was a deliberate message left for them to find. Did it signify a Mafia connection, or was there a link to the Catholic church? Corstorphine shook his head. That *Godfather* similarity must be clouding his judgement – even the Mafia's reach wouldn't extend to some rogue gamekeeper in a Highland glen. Oscar's autopsy offered no clues either. Cause of death was a broken neck and severed windpipe; no other significant injuries were reported.

Corstorphine leaned back in his seat, imagining Oscar's last few minutes. How had he not seen the snare? Had it been set overnight? That would explain why he hadn't noticed it during the day. Driving down the glen first thing in the morning, the sun would have been in his eyes, he could easily have missed seeing the snare in the tree's shadow. Then what was the point of all the bone gears? Was someone leaving a message or were they part of the snare apparatus? Whoever had left it for him must have known that Oscar would drive right into it; they weren't simply trying to frighten him. Same with the minister, dropping a bloody great bell on him from that height wasn't offering him much hope of survival. Two definite murders, almost certainly the same killer – yet the murderer was careful enough not to be present at either death or, so far at least, leave any forensic evidence that could be used in a prosecution case. Either the murderer was incredibly lucky, or was very, very careful.

Through the office window he saw Phil Lamb adjusting his tie in the mirror he kept on his desk, then flicking an errant lock of hair back into place. The PC caught Corstorphine observing him, some sixth sense alerting him. Lamb waved a hand at him, changing course mid-wave to turn the wave into a slack salute and marched out of the office to pound the streets.

Corstorphine sighed. How was he going to catch a murderer who left no trace when his only resource was a team of coppers eminently suited to a sleepy small-town patch. He had no delusions, the whole team were seen as second-rate coppers, including himself, left to police a backwater town and surrounding area. Hamish was the oldest, most experienced cop there, but the desk sergeant needed a new adjective to describe the ponderous speed at which he undertook any activity.

In effect, he was already retired, propping up the front desk where his only excitement was dealing with the two or three members of the public who strayed into his domain each day. Phil Lamb was barely out of school, and it showed in his puerile behaviour – one day he might make a good cop, but for the time being, everyone had to be patient and teach him the ropes. Bill McAdam was a solid presence, a diligent if unimaginative policeman, a good man to have around if a drunk decided to take a swing at you, but he'd never make detective. Frankie was the only one he could rely upon for help with these murders; she was perceptive, a damn sight more perceptive than she let on. It would have to be the two of them – but they needed a break, just a bit of luck. Corstorphine began methodically piecing together what they knew – no matter how clever this killer was, there had to be a pattern, a reason. His job was to find it before anyone else died.

ELEVEN

Margo straightened, pulling her shoulders back to relieve the ache that had been building as she tended to the small vegetable plot outside the cottage. The sound of a diesel engine had alerted her, the mechanical noise an alien note in the soundscape she inhabited. A Land Rover approached, bumping up the rough track and leaving a cloud of dust in its wake. Her eyes narrowed, recognising the laird's vehicle – this was going to prove difficult.

She'd returned to the cottage immediately after leaving the police station, squandering what little money she possessed on a taxi to avoid a wait for the last bus and the two-kilometre walk back along the single track down the glen. She also wanted to avoid walking under the tree, blue police tape lending a carnivalesque feeling to the scene of a particularly gruesome death. The taxi driver had quizzed her as they had approached, and she'd fobbed him off, *Oscar has had an accident, and yes, he's dead.* That had put an end to the conversation, the driver processing the information and impatient to disperse the news far and wide like a modern-day town crier. Margo was still in a state of shock, attempting to process the events of the last few days and coming to terms with what Oscar's death meant for her. His presence haunted the deserted cottage as if he lay in wait behind every closed door, and unable to settle, she had headed outside to work off her nervous energy in attending to the garden.

The Land Rover came to a halt on the stone track beside the cottage, and a florid-faced driver extricated himself with some difficulty from the seat of the Land Rover. He wore the tweed jacket and sensible trousers that were de rigueur for a country gentleman. In place of a deerstalker's hat his hair hung in listless strands from around a balding pate, the constant breeze funnelling down the glen unable to raise more than a flicker of movement from his greased mane. Two dogs started barking at her from the back of the vehicle, big brown animals with oversize jaws. Margo started at the sound, afraid he was going to let them out. What was it Oscar had said? Rhodesian ridgebacks or something, used for hunting lions.

'Shut up!' The dogs quietened at the sound of their master's voice, intelligent brown eyes watching him warily through the glass as if expecting violence. He turned away from them, smiling at Margo, wet lips stretching across dimpling cheeks as he approached, eyes wandering freely over her legs and chest. He stopped so close to her she could see the tributaries of burst blood vessels snaking across his fat cheeks, smell the whisky on his breath.

'Margo. I'm so sorry to hear about Oscar.' His voice was a poor actor's attempt at expressing concern, insincerity surrounded every word. 'Is there anything I can do?'

She had a reasonable idea of what he would like to do. His eyes held that same single-minded intensity that Oscar's eyes had exhibited when he wanted sex. Eyes the crows had eaten.

'That's very kind, sir, but I'm alright for the moment. It's come as a bit of a shock as you can imagine. I think I just need some time on my own to come to terms with everything.' Margo added the last bit as a hint for him to fuck off.

'Aren't you going to invite me in for a cup of tea?' His face adopted an overly eager expression, and she wondered what part of fuck off he didn't understand. Trouble was, he was Oscar's boss, and the cottage came with the job. Margo knew there would have to be some sort of negotiation to allow her to stay on, for a while at least.

'Of course, I'm sorry. Not up to my usual standards of hospitality. Come in.' She felt his eyes following the sway of her hips as she entered the cottage. The thought made her feel sick.

'Tell me everything that happened. I could only get the slightest information from the police.' He sat down at the table as if he owned it. 'Things ran a lot more smoothly when Brian Rankin was in charge!' Margo put the kettle on, realising he not only owned the table but used to own the police as well. She wondered if he imagined he owned her too.

'There's not much to tell.' Cups were retrieved from a kitchen cabinet, and she was relieved to see him looking around the kitchen rather than at her as she placed them side by side on the table. 'He'd not returned last Friday. I waited up all night for him.' She adopted the tone of the dutiful and concerned wife, omitting the fact that she had been holding a knife during the night in case he came home drunk. 'The next morning when he still wasn't here, I went into town in case he was locked up. You know, causing a disturbance or some shite. When I got as far as the tree, I saw him hanging there, his neck was sliced by the wire or whatever.' She paused, pouring dark tea into the two cups, seeing his face in her mind, twin bloodied dark holes where his eyes should have been. 'I could see he was dead,' she continued, pushing a mug towards the laird. 'So, I ran to the police station as fast as I could.'

The laird's small eyes squinted into her face, looking for what she wasn't telling him. 'Had he said anything to you, was anyone out to get him or was it suicide?' He slurped his tea, leaving thin lips wetter than they were before. Margo shivered in disgust. 'There, there, I realise this must be difficult for you.' He stood and made to put an arm around her shoulder, misunderstanding the reason for the shiver, and Margo moved quickly to the other side of the kitchen, pretending to look for sugar. He sat down again, looking displeased to have been rebuffed. 'I'm only trying to help, you know.' His voice carried a peevish tone that had been absent before, a little boy's selfish whine when every wish wasn't instantly gratified.

'I know, I'm sorry.' Margo dabbed at an imaginary tear. 'It's all been too much.' She made a show of regaining her composure, giving her time to think. 'The police don't think it was suicide, they had me in for questioning – as if I'm capable of anything like that!'

'Well, the police will find whoever was responsible, I'm sure.' He stood up, banging his half-full cup back down on the tabletop. Margo watched a wave of black tea wash across the surface of his cup and back again, back and forth. A mesmerising miniature tidal system enclosed in cheap china. Turning back from the door, he faced her as if issuing an ultimatum. 'You can't stay here, Margo. I'll need to find another gamekeeper, and when I do, you'll have to leave.' He attempted a kind smile, but it looked to Margo as if he was salivating over a fresh steak. 'I'll let you stay here as long as I can. We've always been good friends, haven't we, Margo?'

She nodded wordlessly, horrified at what might be the unsaid message in that exchange.

He looked satisfied, for the moment. 'Good. I'm glad we can help each other through this difficult time.' His smile remained as insincere as it was when he first arrived, and he turned away to leave, then paused in the doorway, blocking the only exit from the cottage. 'Does Oscar keep any papers here, any records?'

She looked at him in puzzlement. Oscar kept bullets, snares and knives – and poison. She'd never seen him with any paperwork. 'No, sir, none that I ever saw.'

The laird frowned briefly, then made light of it as if it didn't matter. 'Well, if you do find anything, be sure to let me know. They'll just be recordings of grouse numbers – boring things like that. Probably look more like meaningless squiggles that won't mean anything to you, but I need the records to pass onto the next gamekeeper. I'll come back tomorrow afternoon after court and have a rummage through the sheds in case he's left it all there. Will that be alright?'

She nodded again. 'Yes. Of course. No problem at all. I'll check through his things, see if there's a notebook in his pockets.'

The laird smacked his lips together in a sound of wet satisfaction. 'Good. That would be a help. See you tomorrow then.'

The Land Rover made its way back down the glen, and the sick feeling she'd felt earlier receded. Margo wasn't sure if her nausea was due to the laird or morning sickness. Either way, he was worried about something, something Oscar may have had on him. She shut the door firmly behind her and locked it for good measure. If Oscar had some paperwork the laird was desperate for, it sure as hell wasn't going to be about grouse numbers. With a sudden sense of purpose, Margo started searching the small cottage for anything that she might be able to use as leverage with the laird, or even exchange for hard cash.

An hour later and she admitted defeat. There was nothing to be found in Oscar's pockets, shirts or hidden in his socks. Nothing on top of the wardrobe or under the chest of drawers. She'd taken each drawer out, looking carefully underneath and behind each one. Every floorboard had been checked, none were loose. *Think, Margo, think*, she admonished herself. *Where does he spend time away from me when he's not in the glen?* Her eyes were drawn to the two stone sheds that hemmed in the courtyard, providing some shelter from the wind that incessantly blew up the glen.

Grabbing a searchlight, she crossed over to the first shed which served as the woodstore. The door wasn't even locked, just a bent nail served as a clasp to secure the door in place. The shed was already full of logs seasoning in preparation for the coming winter. If he'd buried anything under there, she'd never be able to find it. Clambering carefully over the stacked logs, she cast the flashlight beam over the rafters, looking in the corners and under eaves for any possible concealed documents. Nothing. She stood outside, wiping the dust from her nostrils and pulling old cobwebs from her hair. It had now gone eight, and she had just the one shed left. Margo looked at the dusk sky – she had just over an hour before she lost the light.

This one was locked. The padlock was fairly new and too substantial for the contents. 'Where does he keep the bloody key?' Margo spoke aloud in an urgent whisper, as if afraid that Oscar could hear her. She looked around her in fear; even when he was dead, he still frightened her. 'Get a bloody grip.' She thought furiously, all the house keys were kept in one of the kitchen drawers – there was nothing that would fit the padlock. She'd never even seen a key that might be the one. Where else could he keep any keys? The answer came to her as she imagined his body hanging in the tree. His pockets? No! He kept the only other set of keys on his quad bike. The same keys that copper had handed over at the station.

Margo ran back into the house, checking her coat pockets before pulling out Oscar's set of keys – that one looked like it might fit the padlock!

Hurrying back, she almost forgot the pain in her ribs that had slowed her down before, and ran to the locked shed, fumbling to present the newest key on the ring to the padlock. A turn, and the lock opened. She pushed open the door, and a smell of petrol and oil escaped. At first sight, she was disappointed. Just more gamekeeper paraphernalia – fuel cans, strimmers, place markers for the shooters, ropes and wire.

A set of steps leaned against one of the stone walls. She pulled them out, set them up and started exploring the roof. And there, inexpertly concealed behind a loose stone was a metal box, the flashlight revealing the gleam of metal in the shadows. The lid opened easily, and inside were rolls of fifty-pound notes held in tight cylinders with rubber bands. There must have been a few thousand pounds in there. Hands shaking with excitement, she tipped the contents onto the flagstone floor. At the bottom of the tin was a notebook and some old photographs of children she didn't recognise. Margo opened the notebook, only to read indecipherable scribbles that looked more like Egyptian heliographs than any writing she recognised.

She closed it in disappointment, then recoiled when she saw what was written on the back cover – *June Stevens, The Chronicle*. What was Oscar doing with the reporter's notebook? The woman who'd been found hanging in the tree back in 1997. The sick feeling returned, and she vomited against the wall. This time, she couldn't blame morning sickness, just a dawning realisation that Oscar knew more about that death than he had ever let on. She wiped her mouth, letting out a long shuddering breath.

The laird was looking for something – did he know about the money? A more sinister thought occurred to her – did he know about the notebook? If he did, then he was implicated as well. She had thought with Oscar gone, her life would improve, that there was nobody else who could threaten her. The laird could be a bigger problem than Oscar ever had been. He had money, he was a sheriff and he owned the land she lived on. There was always something funny going on between Oscar and the laird, she'd known it ever since he'd been given the job. Theirs wasn't the normal laird/gamekeeper relationship – they circled each other warily like dogs getting ready to fight. On the surface Oscar paid due deference to his boss, but it struck her now that Oscar held a royal flush and the laird didn't dare call him out. Was the notebook Oscar's hold over him?

Margo gathered the money, photos and notebook together, jamming them back into the tin and took it outside into the courtyard. She needed to find somewhere to hide it, somewhere the laird couldn't find it. The spade still stood upright in the vegetable patch, and Margo dug a hole deeper than was strictly necessary for seed potatoes. Before burying the box, she helped herself to one roll of fifty-pound notes with a rare smile – perhaps things were looking up for once in her life.

TWELVE

Margo called a taxi, handing the driver a handful of coins and her last tenner as he dropped her in the town. She'd left a note on the cottage door inviting the laird to let himself in and have a look around whilst she was out shopping in the town. A rare smile made an appearance as she imagined his fruitless search around the cottage and outbuildings. The notebook was safely buried in her vegetable plot where he'd never think to look. She congratulated herself on managing to avoid meeting him again, alone in the isolated cottage. A shiver went down her spine – he gave her the creeps.

She crossed over the road, heading for the cut-price supermarket. Entering the automatic door, her eyes were drawn towards the newspaper, headlines sharing the front page with an old picture of Oscar with *Gamekeeper Snared in Tree* printed above. Margo's breath caught in her throat as the shop tilted in her vision, causing her to clutch wildly in search of support.

'Watch where you're going!' A young mother took avoiding action with a pushchair, her pinched face changing from anger into concern as she caught sight of Margo's expression. 'You alright, love?'

Margo nodded, taking a few deep breaths to compose herself. 'Yeah, just feeling a bit faint for a moment. I'm OK now.'

The woman gave her an interrogative stare until her child shouted for a sweetie and she moved swiftly off down the aisle, scolding the child as she went. Margo watched her go, wondering if that would be her in a few years. Not if she could help it! There must be a way of making money out of that tin of Oscar's, something about that notebook she could use on the laird. She grabbed a trolley and started filling it with essentials, then added a few luxuries. Her life was going to change. *Every fucking cloud has a silver lining*, she told herself and grinned manically as she deliberately rephrased another of her mother's favourite sayings. *In for a penny, in for a fucking pound.* She added the newspaper at the checkout, offering a fifty-pound note which the cashier studied with suspicion before running it past the supervisor. She caught the telltale purple glow of an ultraviolet tester, checking the note wasn't a forgery. The cashier returned to the till, counting out three ten-pound notes and a handful of change as Margo filled a plastic bag with her purchases.

'Thanks,' Margo uttered without meaning it.

She stood outside, bag in hand and the first glimmer of an idea entered her head as she looked up at *The Courier*'s foot-high letters decorating the building above the supermarket. Papers pay for stories and Oscar was still in the news. 'Strike whilst the fucking iron's hot,' she told herself and rang the intercom at *The Courier*'s door. A rasping buzz invited her to push it open and she climbed stone stairs to the upper floor.

'Josephine Sables, senior reporter. Please take a seat, what can we do for you?' The woman must have been around the same age as she was, long, dark hair tied back into a ponytail and exposing her high cheekbones to their best advantage. Margo instantly disliked her, and her French accent. She felt the frown before it showed on her face, eyes closing to present angry slits to the world. 'I'm Margo McDonald. Your paper has my boyfriend's picture plastered all over the front page. How much will you pay me for my story?'

Josephine leaned back in her chair, openly appraising Margo. 'You're direct, I like that.' Her cool brown eyes took in Margo at a glance, saw the bruising, the victim. 'Let me be direct in return, we don't pay for stories – unless you've something that will help sell newspapers.'

Margo was taken aback, she'd thought the paper would offer her a few hundred pounds for her take on Oscar, provide her the opportunity to play the grieving widow.

'I lived with him for years in that cottage, we were like husband and wife.' She said this defensively, not liking the way the reporter stared directly into her eyes, understanding too much.

'Then maybe you can tell me who killed him, and why?'

'How do I know? Oscar had a knack for pissing people off – take your pick of anyone in this town.'

Josephine reached for her notepad and pen, laying her phone on the table to record the conversation. 'Tell you what, Margo. Why don't you tell me about you and Oscar, and how you discovered his body? Then we'll see if we can make an offer for your contribution to the paper.'

Margo stared back at her, feeling the bundle of notes pressing through her jeans pocket. 'Sod it. I'll tell you what I know, then you better pay me something.'

Josephine smiled in encouragement, and Margo began speaking.

'I knew Oscar all the way through school. He was always the coolest kid, not too bright but the other kids treated him with respect. I didn't really pay much attention to him until high school, then I noticed how good-looking he was. I knew he was trouble, even then, but you know how it is – there's something about a rebel.' Margo had trouble describing what she did like about Oscar, what had drawn her to him like a primeval force when hormones first started blazing through her body. Oscar represented all those film stars she fantasied over, the rock stars that sneered out of the TV when her parents let her watch what they supposed was an innocent music show. She would tame him, make him her own – and all the other girls would be jealous the day they got married. Of course, it hadn't worked out quite that way.

'We properly got together when I was fifteen, started walking out together.' Margo realised how old-fashioned that phrase sounded even as she spoke the words. What she should have said was when heavy petting turned into something that spoke to the animal in both of them. She'd felt it then, felt as if she'd conquered him even as he bragged openly about shagging her. She was made a woman, she knew things he didn't. She knew he was still a boy, and inside him was a need to be loved and held, warm and close to her skin.

'We were in love,' she said simply, unable to express something that felt so deep and true to her in mere words. 'My parents had a fit when they found out. I was locked in the house for a week, but Oscar climbed in through my bedroom window and helped me escape. It was pure *Romeo and Juliet*.' Margo smiled at the memory, the day she left her parents for the last time. They never spoke to her again. 'Although it did turn out more *Bonnie and Clyde* in the end.'

'How do you mean, *Bonnie and Clyde* – the bank robbers?'

Margo laughed at her pronunciation of robbers, the r rolling around her tongue in a parody of a French accent.

'Aye, ze bonk hrrobbers. We got involved in a few scrapes, nothing much but the polis started taking an interest. Oscar was beaten up more than a few times by the polis. Bastards!'

The reporter gave her a tired look before continuing.

'Are you saying Oscar was mistreated by the police?'

'Aye, they took him into the cells and took turns hitting him. Happens all the time, you just live with it.' She watched as the reporter's pencil raced across the notepad, then her eyes widened as she realised what the scribbles represented. 'Is that shorthand?' Her finger pointed at the notebook.

'Yes, any reporter should know how to use shorthand. You can't always rely on electronic equipment.' Josephine's eyes indicated the mobile phone lying innocuously in between them.

'No, guess not.' Margo filed away that information for later. 'Aye, well, it was just small-town stuff. You know, bit of drug dealing, stealing stuff people wouldn't even know was missing. Just making ends meet. Oscar was hardly a criminal, but he was a bit too quick to use his fists. I held him back a lot, stopped him before he did too much damage. People used to wind him up on purpose you see, especially when he'd had a drink. Thought that he'd be easier to take on if he was pissed, get themselves a reputation as the man who brought Oscar down. Trouble was, I couldn't control him when he was pissed – he really hurt some of those guys. It was their own fault, everyone knew not to wind him up when he was pissed!' She said this defiantly, still protecting Oscar even after he was dead.

'And when did he start hurting you?' Josephine's voice was quiet, the question unexpected.

When did it start? She cast her mind back to the early years, his playful hitting as he called it. She'd accepted the smacks as his way of showing he loved her – they weren't proper hits, just affectionate. 'We'd been together a couple of years, I'd caught him with another girl.' Her memory took her back to that day, the hurt she'd felt at being so easily replaced by another woman, the mix of anger and fear as she confronted him. He'd hit her properly then, she remembered her head exploding from the force of the blow before she learned how to move with his fist, reduce the force of the impact without avoiding it – that just made him want to hit her harder. Funny thing was she welcomed the pain, it hurt less than the feeling of rejection, of being used, of being disposable. In time, the physical violence became a natural part of their relationship, and like a whipped cur she crawled back to him every time.

'After a few years.' Margo's voice was a whisper. She'd never told anyone this before. Why now, sat before this French reporter, was she spilling out her soul as if she was sat in a confessional? 'It wasn't his fault.' She felt angry at letting down her guard. 'Oscar had a terrible childhood, no one ever believed him.'

'Believed what?'

Margo looked up from her lap, the calculating expression returning. 'I'll tell you what his demons were, but you'll have to pay me.'

Josephine toyed with her pencil, spinning it around her long fingers like a drum majorette on parade. 'I'm allowed to offer you a hundred pounds, cash. If the story is good, and we can lead with some insight into Oscar's murder, then I can go higher.'

They sat like poker players facing each other across the table, and Margo cashed in first.

'Where's the money? I'm not saying anything else until you give me a hundred quid.'

Josephine gave her a thin smile, then got up to leave Margo on her own in the office. She looked around her in disinterest, then turned the computer monitor around to see what the reporter was working on. A mock-up of the next *Courier* edition filled the screen, a photograph of the minister with a headline announcing his murder. She hastily turned the monitor back, thinking hard.

She sat motionless until Josephine returned and counted out five twenty-pound notes, placing them in front of Margo as if placing a bet. She pocketed the money and sneered at the reporter as if it was she who had won the round.

'Oscar was sexually molested as a young child. He told his teachers, his fucking useless parents and the polis. Nobody did anything about it. On top of that, Oscar was beaten, beaten hard by his dad and forced to spend hours alone with his fucking abuser. How do you think that affected him? Every week, he was forced to go to his abuser and face every fucking perversion the old sod felt like doing, safe in the knowledge that he was untouchable. It wasn't just the one old pervert either. Oscar told me he was taken to the orphanage and raped by people there, whilst the fucking nuns looked the other way. That's why he turned out like he did, that's why I stayed with him and tried to help him. I did my best.' Margo started crying, the tears leaving trails of black mascara in their wake. 'I did what I fucking could for him. I loved him, I just wasn't strong enough for him. No one was.'

Josephine handed over a box of tissues, and Margo grabbed it angrily, dabbing at her eyes too late to avoid smearing the makeup. 'The bastard had it coming to him. I'm glad he's dead!'

'Who, Oscar?'

Margo looked up at the reporter, contempt written across her tear-stained face. 'Not Oscar, I loved him.' She spun the screen around, finger jabbing with accusation at the minister's photograph. 'The fucking pervert minister of St Cuthbert's. He's the bastard that ruined Oscar.'

Josephine's pencil made indecipherable scribbles across the page. 'Tell me how you found him, the day he died.' Her voice was softer now, gentle.

'I'd waited all night for him, worried that he hadn't come home. First thing in the morning, I went looking for him, thought maybe the polis had him. I was only a little way down the glen when I saw him.' Her eyes widened as she relived the moment, saw the shape dangling from the tree. 'He was hanging from the Hanging Tree, dead. I saw crows picking at his eyes, his neck sliced open. That tree is fucking cursed, someone should chop the bloody thing down.'

'What then?' Josephine encouraged.

'I ran, I ran as fast as I could. I thought he'd killed himself but...'

'But what, Margo?'

'But Oscar wasn't ever going to kill himself, someone killed him. For all I knew they were still somewhere close. I ran all the way to the town and ended up at the polis station. I told them everything I know.'

'Did you tell them about the minister?'

Margo shook her head. 'No, but then they weren't offering me money.'

THIRTEEN

'Damn it!' The laird swore at the note pinned onto the gamekeeper's cottage door.

Gone to town food shopping, please let yourself in and look around. I couldn't find any notes. Margo.

He tried the door. It was unlocked, and he entered the small dark hall. Margo had left a faint scent on the air which he inhaled deeply, his imagination running riot as he pictured himself in closer proximity to Margo's body. Shutting the door behind him, he walked the few steps to the kitchen, eyes searching the shelves and cupboards. Selecting a drawer at random, his fingers rifled through the contents, then underneath them, before he lifted the entire drawer out of the unit. The procedure was repeated for each kitchen cupboard, the contents carefully examined and then replaced.

Pursing his lips in disappointment, he stepped through into the living room, turning the cheap cushions to look underneath, moving the heavy furniture that came with the cottage to investigate any potential hiding places – nothing. That left the upstairs bedroom and bathroom.

An hour later and he had to admit defeat. It didn't help that he had no real idea of what he was looking for, but Oscar had made it clear that he held written evidence which would look very bad for him were it ever to be found. A threat that had been left to hang over his head like Damocles' sword. He stood in the cottage bedroom, fingers absently stroking the fabric of Margo's underwear, which he had taken out of a bedside drawer with a reverence usually reserved for religious artefacts. Could Oscar have invented the whole thing? Maybe the only evidence that had ever existed had died with him. A smile flitted across the laird's face at the justice of the blackmailer's death, his satisfaction only tempered with a slight worry as to who was responsible for the murder on his land.

With regret, he laid the underwear down on the chest of drawers, but not before burying his face into the fabric and taking a long, deep breath. The sheds would have to wait for another day. He'd need them emptied first – which reminded him to retrieve a letter from his jacket pocket. He propped it on the kitchen table before leaving the house.

The dogs barked with excitement as he approached the Land Rover, expecting their confinement to be over. He ignored them, turning the vehicle around in the small area in between cottage and outbuildings before heading back down the glen. On an impulse he took the turn-off before the estate house, heading along a rough track that led into one of the conifer plantations he'd inherited from his father. The track split several times, and he unerringly took each choice without hesitation. One advantage of being raised as a child on an estate like this was to develop an encyclopaedic knowledge of the lay of the land, to know each track and path as well as an urban child learns the city streets around their home.

An abandoned stone building eventually came into view, trees growing almost up to the walls. The windows consisted of small slits, looking more like a Second World War bunker than a house. Iron bars covered the windows as if it were a prison, but the windows were too small for any human to climb through. He parked the Land Rover, then opened the back door to release the two big dogs which began running around in a frenzy, dropping noses to the ground in search of interesting scents to follow. 'Heel!' The word was spat out, the animals reluctantly running to shadow their master as he pushed open the solid wooden door that sealed the entrance. They filed in, the laird followed by the two large dogs, entered a square, stone room devoid of any furniture. Several rusting metal hooks hung from high ceiling beams awaiting the next slaughter. The room was cold, little sunlight reached the building through the oppressive fir trees and the sealed windows left the air stale, smelling of dust and that faint odour he associated with death and decay.

The building was once a cared-for home, a place to bring up a family and work the land, but whichever family had once lived here were long gone – forcibly removed with so many others once sheep grazing provided a better return for the laird's money.

It was now used as a cold store, a place to hang the pheasants, grouse and deer killed during the seasonal shooting sprees. He stopped in surprise, seeing a box of crisps left against the wall. Next to the box was an ornate hourglass, full of red sand. The laird picked it up, wondering who had been using his cold store as an impromptu hideout and wondering at their choice of accessories. The hourglass was heavy and rested on a base made of mahogany or some other valuable hard wood. It pivoted between two carved and polished leg bones, from a young red deer, he estimated, judging by the size. He thought it would make a handsome addition to the mantlepiece in his trophy room and inverted the hourglass to watch the red sand trickling through the pinched centre. What could it have been designed to time? The sand would take days to complete the journey from one side to the other. There was a coin embedded in the newly upturned base, Pope Paul II in profile. Holding it under one arm, he turned the handle and pulled on the door. The door wouldn't move. 'Blast! Must be the damp.'

The hourglass was placed on the floor, and he pulled at the door with more force – it still wouldn't budge. 'What the hell?' Bending down so his eyes were at the same level as the handle, he keyed the torch on his mobile and peered at the gap between door and frame. The mortice lock had engaged, he could see the over-engineered Victorian slab of metal bridging the gap and locking him inside. He stared stupidly at the empty keyhole – there had never been a key in the lock ever since his father had died, there was never a need this far out in the glen, especially for a building that remained empty most of the year. Nobody had locked it, he'd have heard the key being put in the lock, or the dogs would have barked at the first sign of anyone else being near. 'This is ridiculous!' He talked to himself, angry at being locked inside one of his own buildings. How could it have happened? He'd been in and out of the cold store for years, the door always swung shut on well-engineered gravity hinges and the latch held it shut. That was sufficient to keep any animals out of the cold store when he had game hanging, and a simple turn of the handle released the catch. He tried turning the handle again, watching through the narrow gap in the frame as the latch wound back into the door – but the mortice remained put.

The dogs panted up at him, wondering why he didn't open the door. There were interesting smells outside, new smells that needed investigating. One of the dogs whined impatiently only to receive a kick. 'Shut up, stupid animal, let me think.' The laird thought, and the more he thought, the more concerned he became. The cold store was well off any beaten track, the only person he could expect to visit it was Oscar – and he was dead. Nobody knew he was here. He checked his phone for a signal, knowing that the nearest phone mast was on the other side of the mountain. Nothing, no connections available. He checked the window – too small to climb through even if it didn't have solid steel bars. His father had insisted the cold store be made more secure after a deer carcass had gone missing one particularly bleak winter. With eyes growing ever more frantic, he searched the room for a way out; the walls were thick stone, the narrow windows barred, the ceiling too high to reach and made with solid wooden beams with lathe and horsehair plaster filling the gaps – and the door he already knew was impassable.

The next appointment in his diary was for the Sheriff Court in Inverness on Thursday, three days away. If he ate the crisps sparingly, he reckoned he could last until then – and surely someone would be sent out to look for him if he hadn't appeared or answered his phone? Then there was whoever had been using his store for their own purposes, perhaps they'd turn up any minute and help him out? Feeling suitably encouraged, he opened the first crisp packet and sat down on the floor, sharing a few packs with his dogs who wolfed the snack down as if it were their last meal. The box stated *twenty-four mixed flavour multipack, not for resale*. 'That's almost six packets a day, plenty to keep us going!' He grinned at the dogs, ruffling fur in a companionable way. They were all in this together so may as well make the best of a bad thing. The red sand still spilled in a minute waterfall through the hourglass, a gentle trickle from one glass container to the next. He made a bet with himself there and then, believing he'd be found and let out before the sand completely filled the lower glass.

As the hours passed, he tried to remember how long someone was meant to be able to survive without water – was it three days? That seemed an awfully short time, surely nomads crossing deserts managed longer than that. An uncomfortable thought occurred to him. Suppose whoever had left the hour-glass and the crisps had done so in the knowledge that he would be trapped here without water. The salt-laden crisps would hasten death, of that he had no doubt. He searched the room for anything that could be used to force the door, but there wasn't even a loose stone in the wall. The roof offered a possible way out, if only he could pull himself up using the metal hooks. After twenty minutes of launching himself into the air and cutting his hands on the rusty metal, he was out of breath, collapsing on the cold stone floor and coughing from the exertion. No way out, he'd have to wait until someone found him.

FOURTEEN

Margo had returned to the cottage only to find her knickers lying on top of the chest of drawers. She felt physically sick, violated in her own home. Without thinking, she threw them in with the rest of the dirty washing, shutting the lid as if that might help eradicate the vision of the laird fingering her underclothes. The nausea returned in waves, and she bent double over the toilet, dry retching wracking her body as she convulsed. As the sickness passed, she made her way back down the cottage stairs to the kitchen, putting on the kettle. 'Everything's alright with a cup of fucking tea,' Margo advised the empty room, murdering another of her mother's favourite adages.

With the mug of steaming liquid clasped to her body, Margo picked up the envelope left propped on the kitchen table. It was written in legalese, but the meaning was clear enough – she only had a month to find somewhere else to live. Margo sat looking out of the cottage window as the wind shook the frame in a sudden gust. She couldn't stay here; the laird was either going to stalk her like he did his deer or throw her out. Neither option held any particular attraction. She sipped at the tea, unconsciously cradling her womb with the other hand – still too early for any outward sign, but she felt decidedly pregnant. The foetus was already beginning to control her life. Margo wouldn't have welcomed the comparison but much in the same way as parasitic wasps turn their caterpillar hosts into zombies, whatever decision she took now had to be in her unborn child's best interests.

She sat nursing her tea. Everything felt unreal: her pregnancy, Oscar gone, the notice to quit the house that was her home. Even just sitting there quietly without the fear of him coming home unexpectedly and finding fault, that unbearable worry had gone. Why then did she feel the pain of losing him when he'd been so cruel? Margo felt more alone than at any time before in her life. In his own way Oscar had at least needed her, the two of them were together – perhaps not in a way commonly represented in romantic fiction, but they were together. Now she was truly apart, alone and adrift with nobody in the world who cared what happened to her. She felt the gravity of self-pity starting to pull her down into that relentless spiral she knew too well and fought back. Margo didn't need the world or its pity. The child she carried needed her and that was enough; for to be needed is to be loved and that was all she had ever desired.

Her first concern had to be money. There wasn't anything she could hope to accomplish without money. How much was there in that tin, was it even still there? A sudden panic attack hit her as she scrambled to the door, throwing it open to see whether the laird had dug up her vegetable patch whilst she'd been away. The spade remained where she'd left it, upright in the freshly turned soil where new plants held tight against the wind that threatened to lift them out of the ground.

She glanced down the track, then searched around the hills just in case he had someone keeping an eye on her. Clouds sped by overhead, urged on by the prevailing wind which regularly reached gale force up on the mountain tops. The hills around her weren't that high, but clouds covered the tops, wrapping the weathered rocks in moisture as water vapour coalesced in the colder air. The glen was empty, as far as she could tell. If the laird had already searched the cottage, then he was unlikely to want to search it again. She pulled on her wellingtons, grabbed a coat and collected the spade. With a final look around her, she dug with a single sense of purpose to retrieve the tin, hiding it under the folds of her coat as she took it back into the cottage. Door safely locked, and curtains drawn for good measure, she placed the tin on the kitchen table. Taking out the rolls of fifty-pound notes, Margo started counting them into piles, each one with five hundred pounds. In a few minutes, she'd opened the last roll. She sat back in her chair, her head reeling. £3250! Plus, the four hundred she'd hidden in her clothing and purse and the hundred pounds from the snotty reporter.

It was a good start, but not enough. She emptied the rest of the tin's contents on the table. The photographs she dismissed, nothing she could make out of them. Why did Oscar keep them? He was hardly the sentimental type. They looked like kids at school, were they his classmates? As she carelessly scattered them across the table, one flipped over and her heart chilled. Drawn on the back was a skull and crossbones, an image still found on some of the older gravestones she'd seen in the town. Picking up the photograph, she looked more closely at the picture. It was of a child, a tousle-headed boy of six or seven years old. Did this mean he was dead? Wordlessly she checked the other photographs. Out of the fifteen she counted, eight had the same inscription on the back, drawn carelessly in ballpoint.

The notebook caught her attention, black and red cover curled with age and damp. She checked the name again – definitely June Stevens. Why did she have to write in stupid bloody scribbles! Margo thought back to the French newspaper reporter. She knew how to write shorthand. She might even pay good money to get her hands on the reporter's notebook, who knows what secrets were inside?

She opened the biscuit tin and shoved in the notebook and photos. The money she slipped inside a pillowcase, that would have to do until she went back into town.

FIFTEEN

Corstorphine and Frankie sat in the interview room, running through the legal litany that informed John Ackerman of his rights. He'd been picked up from the Sheriff Court in Inverness that morning following a conviction for poisoning the golden eagle found on his estate, and his mood matched his ill-fitting dark suit.

Corstorphine started the interview. 'What can you tell us about your movements last week, between the dates of Monday 12th to Friday 16th May?'

'Is this to do with that bastard Oscar Anderson?' The gamekeeper almost spat the words out.

'I'll ask the questions, John.' Corstorphine could see the visceral animal hatred in his face, weasel features twisted into an ugly sneer. The sneer turned into a satisfied grin, exposing yellowed teeth that hadn't been near a dentist for many years. 'You think I killed him?'

'I don't recollect anyone saying he was dead, do you, Frankie?'

'Don't try that shit with me. It's common knowledge the

cunt was found hanging from that tree. Don't the polis read the papers like the rest of us?'

Corstorphine made a note to look at the day's press. He glanced towards Frankie who made a non-committal gesture with her shoulders, an imperceptible shrug expressing she was none the wiser either. 'Why don't you try answering the question. What were your movements last week?'

'I was on the estate all week. Didn't have much choice as your polis buddies at Inverness wanted to look in every bloody building. Looking for the poison, they said. Didn't make a fuck of difference they found none. Like I told them – it wisnae me did the poisoning! The guy they should have collared is that dead bastard.'

'Can anyone substantiate your story?' Frankie interrupted.

The gamekeeper looked at her with surprise, almost as if he was unused to a woman asking him questions. 'Aye. The Inverness bobbies of course, hen.' He shook his head as if she had just asked the most stupid question.

'And the Inverness police were with you every day last week?' She persevered, but Corstorphine could sense she was bottling her frustration for the moment.

'Pretty much. They were with me from first thing Monday all day. Then they came back on the Tuesday with some stuck-up RSPB types. Know what gets me about the RSPB? They get all hot and bothered about some bloody bird that kills other birds for a living, and then don't give a toss about the thousands of pheasants and grouse people like us make sure get shot every year. They're birds as well.'

'Just answer the question.' Corstorphine interrupted his soliloquy.

He received a sullen stare for his interruption. 'On the Wednesday I was on the estate all day, ask my boss. The Thursday I was showing some rich American the best places to stalk deer and had a few drinks at his expense in the Stag Hotel where he was staying. The Friday I had to go into Inverness to see the legal aid – total waste of bloody time, that was.' He looked at them both with open hostility. 'What's the bloody point of the law if the sheriff is as bent as his gamekeeper?'

'You're familiar with the concept of slander?' Corstorphine asked.

'Aye. And he's another one that has it coming.'

'How do you mean?' Frankie rejoined the questioning.

The gamekeeper adopted the same surprised expression at being questioned by a woman, quickly looking towards Corstorphine for confirmation that he was expected to answer. 'You don't know the half of it, do you?' He said this with apparent wonder. 'Those two have been hand in glove for bloody years. You ever wondered why Oscar never got prosecuted, not once?' He sniggered, a sound Corstorphine could picture him making all the way through school. 'You two should take up comedy, bloody class.'

'If you have any information that might lead us to whoever was responsible for this death, you'd be well advised to tell us now.' Corstorphine spoke quietly, making the full import of what he was saying percolate in the gamekeeper's consciousness.

John Ackerman sat back in his chair and regarded them with a pleased expression. 'Think I'm going to help you with your job when you've just lost me mine? Think again.'

They let him go after checking his story with the Inverness police who confirmed with Corstorphine that they'd spent the two days with the gamekeeper last week. The Procurator Fiscal had wanted more evidence to tie him to the poisoning, but it didn't matter in the end. The sheriff had come down hard on him, big fine and community service – would have been custodial for a second offence – and he lost his job, so good result as far as they were concerned. His employer, a financier from London, confirmed he was with him the previous Wednesday and that the American visitor had been walking the hills with him on the Thursday. Corstorphine couldn't see how the gamekeeper would have had the time to set such an elaborate trap for Oscar, much less have the IQ to do so. He did have the motive, however.

Frankie brought in the morning's *Courier* and placed it on his desk. The front page was a photo of the Hanging Tree still adorned with police tape, making it look like a festive maypole in the wilderness. Right month for it, Corstorphine voiced silently to himself. The headline shouted in large bold print *Gamekeeper Snared in Tree* with *Police investigate second death at cursed tree* as a strapline. An old photograph of Oscar stared sullenly from the page.

'So much for keeping it under wraps!' Corstorphine sighed heavily. There was no point in berating his staff, there were any number of ways the story could have got out. He belatedly remembered Jenny mentioning that the hospital staff were all talking about it. How long before the minister put in an appearance on the front page?

'Sir?' Frankie interrupted his thoughts. He looked up from the paper. Her forehead had developed several deep lines – her thinking face, he called it. 'What is it, Frankie?'

She hesitated, as Corstorphine willed her to start talking.

'What do you make of John Ackerman's comments about the sheriff and Oscar being in cahoots?'

Corstorphine wondered if Frankie had been watching too many westerns. 'In cahoots?' he offered.

'Yes, sir. John Ackerman suggested they were hand in glove. Do you think there's any truth in that? Oscar certainly seemed to lead a charmed life – not one prosecution ever stuck.'

Corstorphine shrugged. Not being born and brought up in the town meant that he was always going to be seen as the incomer. Local history and knowledge came to him drip by drip, and he often relied on Frankie and the others to fill him in on feuds and alliances that went back several generations in some instances.

'What do you think, Frankie? You've lived here all of your life, is there something we're missing, some other line of enquiry we should be following?'

'I don't know, sir. If John Ackerman says the sheriff has it coming, shouldn't we warn him he may be in danger?'

'I don't think that's necessary, Frankie. As a sheriff he's put any number of people behind bars, he knows to take precautions. I've been to his house on the estate, big wall around it, alarm system, CCTV – he'd not be such an easy target as Oscar was.'

'But if it's the same person that got to the minister...' She left the thought hanging.

Corstorphine remembered the coin that forensics had found under the tree and dug out the report from underneath the newspaper on his desk. 'When did that lassie kill herself, Frankie? What year?'

She adopted the same look of concentration, brows furrowed downwards as she retrieved a memory. 'I was seven at the time, so that would make it... 1997, sir.'

He passed over the photograph of the coin. She studied it in silence before they locked eyes. 'Looks like there may be a connection to her death after all!'

Corstorphine nodded. 'Let's not get ahead of ourselves. We'll see what they find in the bell tower first. Either way, we need to start looking for a connection between the dead reporter and Oscar.' It was Corstorphine's turn to frown. 'Who was the suicide anyway, do you remember her name?'

'Oh yes. She was the local reporter for the *Courier*. Her name was June Stevens.'

'Get down to the paper, try and find out who leaked the story to them, although it's too bloody late now. And have a look at what June Stevens was working on before her death just in case it's pertinent somehow.'

'Yes, sir.' Frankie turned smartly on her heel and left him alone with his thoughts. What if her death wasn't a suicide – was the same murderer repeating his crime twenty years later?

'Hamish!' Corstorphine called to the desk sergeant. 'Can you fetch me the case notes of that woman who committed suicide in 1997? June Stevens?'

'Certainly, sir. They'll be locked in the storeroom filing cabinet, files that old. May take a while.'

'I'll watch the front desk until one of the constables comes back. Then I want you to tell me everything you remember about the day she died.'

'Is there a connection to the present-day murders, sir?' Hamish appeared unnaturally ill at ease, uncomfortable in his own skin.

'I'm not sure, Hamish. Just something I need to explore.'

The sergeant returned after a while, a bulging file tied with blue ribbon under his arm. 'This is the lot,' he announced. 'The DI's notebook is here as well – I put it in here when he retired. It was the only important case we ever had whilst he was in charge.'

'Thanks, Hamish. What do you remember about the case – nothing official, just looking for background?'

Hamish looked relieved at the words 'nothing official' and sat down at Corstorphine's bidding on the other side of the paper-strewn table.

'It was just an ordinary day, about this time of year. We had an emergency call alerting us to the discovery of a woman's body hanging in the glen, must have been around 1 a.m. as I'd just got back from the beat and was making myself a coffee.'

'Who made the call?'

'Anonymous, sir. Some hiker who didn't want to be identified, probably. He had an Australian accent, I think. Whoever it was had used the public call box on the Inverness road – it's not there now, been taken away.'

'Was the phone dusted for prints?'

The desk sergeant looked surprised, as if this was the first time anyone had suggested checking the public phone for evidence. 'No, sir. I think the DI said it wasn't a worthwhile use of police resources as everyone and their dog would have used that phone some time or other.'

'It's not a phone that would get that much use, stuck in the middle of nowhere.'

Hamish considered for a good while, his eyes staring at a point over Corstorphine's head. 'I suppose not, sir. It was all a bit mad then, with the girl's body and everything.'

'What can you tell me about the girl?'

'Oh, she was a bright thing. Worked as a reporter for the *Courier* – always sticking her nose into everything. The DI used to get quite angry with her, leaking stories he was trying to keep under wraps.' His eyes traversed to today's copy of the paper, front page uppermost on the intervening desk.

'Was she depressed at the time? Did anyone suggest a reason she'd commit suicide?'

'Well, that's the thing, sir. She always looked quite happy, a regular ray of sunshine, but there was a change to her in the weeks before she died. Something wasn't right although she never let on.' Hamish looked defiant for a second. 'Whatever it was that was bothering her, she shouldn't have taken her own life – not with her having a child to look after.'

'What child was this, Hamish?'

The desk sergeant looked faintly surprised that he had to be asked the question, before remembering that Corstorphine was an outsider. 'You'd not know, of course. She had a daughter, she must have been aged around six at the time. She doted on her, a pretty young thing.' He frowned. 'The child was distraught when the social took her from school that day. I had to go along with them, there wasn't a dad, see. Not even sure if June ever married, there certainly wasn't a man on the scene back then.'

His tone held echoes of scandal.

'Where's the girl now?'

He shook his head. 'Nobody knows. She was taken to the old orphanage in City Road, not there any longer of course, turned it into flats. She'd only been there a year or maybe a bit longer when she ran off. She was never found; we organised a few search parties in case she'd taken off into the moors, put her picture in the press.' He bowed his head. 'Terrible for her, I don't think she ever came to terms with her mum's death. God knows what happened to the girl, the DI closed the case after a couple of years – presumed dead.'

Corstorphine listened to the sergeant's words with increasing concern. How had he not heard about this case? If it was reported in the press, then only the local paper had run with the story. Why hadn't the old DI ever mentioned it to him?

'Thanks, Hamish. That's been a great help.'

'Glad to help, sir. There's nothing worse than losing a child, sir.' Seconds ticked by without the sergeant moving from his seat until he shared a sombre look with Corstorphine. 'Nothing.'

The desk sergeant got back to his feet, and slowly made his way back to the front desk. Corstorphine watched as he left the office, wondering whether Hamish was referring to the dead reporter's child or if there was a personal tragedy nearer to home.

How well did anyone know the people they worked with, day in, day out? He knew the old sergeant was married, that they didn't have any children – had they lost a child themselves, in childbirth or to illness? He pursed his lips, aware for the first time since losing his wife that he never really talked to anyone anymore, that his world had collapsed in on itself so much that he inhabited a lonely universe with room only for himself and a ghost. Corstorphine put that unsettling thought to the back of his mind before he opened the bulging file and started reading.

SIXTEEN

The Courier's offices occupied the first floor of a substantial stone-built Victorian building, one of the many built following the construction of the railway in the mid-nineteenth century. The ground floor that used to house giant cast-iron printing presses was now home to a budget supermarket; garish window decorations announcing bargains in primary colours and fun fonts. Frankie sat in her car, watching the steady stream of shoppers as they negotiated automatic doors with reluctant children, buggies and bags. The gamekeeper's comments had rerun in her mind as she drove to the newspaper offices – the sheriff and Oscar being hand in glove for years. True enough, not one complaint for violence had ever stuck, and yet everyone knew Oscar was a vicious bully. What possible reason could the sheriff have for protecting him, and why did he hire Oscar as the estate gamekeeper when he could have had any number of experienced candidates? Frankie looked up towards the first-floor windows with trepidation. She wasn't looking forward to talking to the press, and even less keen to see what they'd construe into print for tomorrow's edition.

The young woman who met her at reception was familiar,

she'd seen her somewhere before. Frankie was good with faces, but it was her clothes that made her stand out – more European casual chic than anything readily available in the high street. She proffered a hand, elegant long fingers clasping Frankie's in a light grip as she welcomed her. 'Hello, I'm Josephine Sables, I have an office where we can talk privately. This way.'

She turned and walked back down the corridor, although Frankie wasn't sure that the verb walk did justice to the balletic glide of the figure she followed, contrasting unfavourably with the stolid gait she herself exhibited. Josephine had pronounced her name in a French style that matched the light trail of perfume she left in her wake. She stopped at a door, holding it open for Frankie to enter. Inside was a table, dominated by a large Apple Mac screen, a filing cabinet adorned with a vase of plastic flowers and two swivel chairs, one of which Josephine immediately occupied. She motioned towards the remaining chair and smiled encouragingly at Frankie as one would to put a child at ease. 'How can I help you, Ms?'

The word hung in the air, a row of z's fading into silence as if a solitary bee had just left the room in search of nectar. 'McKenzie. Detective Constable Frankie McKenzie.'

'Ah. Detective. Is this to do with the murder in the glen?' Her eyes came alive with interest, hazel-brown eyes that held Frankie's in a penetrating gaze.

'You could say that.' Frankie felt uncomfortable under such direct observation and decided to cut to the chase. 'What I'd like to know, Josephine, is where you got any idea that this may have been a murder rather than a suicide. I see you've printed the story in today's *Courier*, what makes you so sure? You'll look pretty stupid if our investigations show it's a suicide.'

Josephine's expression didn't change. 'We have our sources. It's important to us on the *Courier* that we tell the truth to our readers. Are you denying this was a murder? I'd be more than happy to quote you on the record if we have been given incorrect information.'

Frankie cursed inwardly; this wasn't going at all well. 'We are not in a position to either confirm or deny whether this was a murder. All I'm asking is that you refrain from printing allegations which are unsubstantiated, and which could adversely affect our enquiry.'

'What if our stories are substantiated?'

'What do you mean? Only officers concerned with the investigation would be able to confirm any findings, the rest is hearsay.' Frankie paused, aware she'd been given a steer. 'Are you being given information by one of our officers?'

'My sources must remain confidential, you know that, Frankie.'

Frankie's name sounded so much more attractive spoken in a French accent. She shook her head in exasperation. 'Look, all I'm asking is that you let us do our job without making it even more difficult than it already is.' She thought rapidly; identifying the probable source for any leaks shouldn't be that difficult. 'We can help each other here. I'm willing to let you have first knowledge of any real developments we make on this case, but I want something from you in return.'

Josephine sat back in her chair as if in consideration, but Frankie could see she'd taken the bait. 'What can we do for you?'

Frankie took a deep breath. 'There was a reporter on this paper back in 1997. Her name was June Stevens.' She watched Josephine in vain for any flicker of recognition. 'We believe she was working on a story just before she committed suicide. Is there anyone we can talk to who was working with her at the time?'

Josephine shook her head. '*The Courier* has only ever had two reporters on the books at the same time since the turn of the century. I've been here just over six months, I replaced the previous chief reporter who retired last year. The only other reporter is the junior, straight out of high school. He'll last a year at most, then another youngster will take his place.' She smiled conspiratorially at Frankie. 'We take them on as apprentices, a government scheme that allows us to pay them minimum wage. Someone has to write up the hatched, matched and dispatched.' Her smile grew broader. She seemed pleased to have learned a new turn of phrase that sounded almost poetic when spoken in a foreign tongue.

'Would you have her notebook, or a copy of any notes she may have left from that time?'

Josephine made a note on a pad lying open on the desk between them. 'Suicide?' She uttered the word as a question. 'I can have a look in the archives. Why is this important, how does it connect to the murder?'

Frankie let the use of the word murder slip this time. 'We don't know if there is a connection, but we have to investigate the apparent coincidence of them both dying at the same location.' She looked directly into Josephine's eyes so there was no room for any misunderstanding. 'We found a coin under the tree, it hadn't been there for more than a few days. It was minted the same year June Stevens died; that's why we need to look into any connection. You can't use any of this in your reporting, you understand?'

The reporter nodded just once, quick and efficient. 'We are a reputable newspaper, Frankie, and would not want to compromise your investigations in any way.' Frankie relaxed slightly. Maybe this was going better than she'd initially thought. 'Tell me, Frankie, did Oscar come as he died on the tree?'

'What did you say?' She thought she'd misheard the question, or Josephine's grasp of English wasn't as perfect as it had first appeared.

'I wondered if he died with an erection, whether there was

semen on his underwear. I've heard that this can happen when a man dies on the gallows.'

Frankie looked askance at the reporter – there were limits. 'I'm afraid I don't know anything about that – and if I did, I would be the last person to tell you.'

Josephine looked unperturbed at her outburst. 'Well, what can you tell me about the murder of the minister?'

Frankie's moment of self-congratulation at her handling of the press evaporated before it had a chance to attain any sense of permanence. 'What do you mean, murder?' Her words sounded like bluster, even to her own ears.

The reporter's smile reminded Frankie of the look a cat gives a mouse when it has been allowed to escape, only to have a clawed paw impale its tail. Her eyes were both inquisitive but also possessed a calculating edge that hadn't been there before. 'Frankie.' Her name was spoken like a gentle reprimand. 'We've already been told the roof timbers had been sawn through, and I do not think the minister was capable of climbing up the bell tower without assistance.' Josephine adopted a conciliatory tone. 'We have to tell our public what we know; otherwise, we are no better than those national newspapers that sell pictures of fake breasts along with fake news.'

Her hands reached across the table towards Frankie, the act of a supplicant searching for something. 'We can help each other, Frankie. I promise to pass on whatever we discover if you can keep me as up to date with developments as you can. This story will go national, you know that. Soon there will be reporters all over the town, and they won't care who or what they trample over in search of a story. You give me exclusive access and in return we can make the story more sympathetic, show the police in a better light.'

Frankie felt as trapped as the mouse. 'What are you going to print about the minister?'

Josephine nodded, pulling her hands back across the table

to flick over the Mac keyboard, almost-silent keystrokes barely punctuating the silence in the room. 'The next edition will be in the shops tomorrow. If you have a line of questioning that the public may be able to help with, fine – we'll print a request for help.' She stood up, announcing that the interview was over. 'In the meantime, I'll start searching for June Stevens' notebook for you. Do you have contact details?'

Frankie passed over a dog-eared business card with her phone number and took a pristine card from Josephine in return. As they walked back down the corridor, Josephine lifted an A3 sheet from a printer. The headlines screamed *Minister of St Cuthbert's Crushed under Church Bell*. It was folded in half before Frankie could read any further, Josephine passing it to her almost conspiratorially before opening the door that led out to the street. 'Thank you for visiting me, Frankie, I'm sure we can work well together.'

As the door closed, and Frankie stood looking back up at *The Courier* offices, she wondered who'd been interviewing whom. Making her way back to the car, Frankie made a mental shortlist of people who could be feeding the paper information. It wasn't Corstorphine, it sure as hell wasn't her – that left the sergeant and the two uniforms. The only other sources were the fire crew and the building surveyors. Christ, it was a mess! As soon as the print hit the news-stands tomorrow, the proverbial shit would hit the fan. One thing she could agree on with Josephine, two unusual murders happening this close together in the same town would bring the major papers' and broadcast news' reporters in droves. She returned to the station, one part of her mind running through how she was going to tell Corstorphine that the press were all over the story, the other part wondering how a French woman came to be working as a reporter on a provincial Scottish newspaper.

SEVENTEEN

Corstorphine was also deep in thought. The file that the desk sergeant had brought him posed more questions than answers. His predecessor, Inspector Brian Rankin, had retired seven years previously. It was his name on the report into the June Stevens' suicide that Corstorphine had been studying, an errant eyebrow raised higher as he devoured the contents of the document that Hamish had deposited on his desk. The forensics report was light at best, glossing over the woman being found hanging from the lower branches of the old oak in the glen. Cause of death – suicide by hanging. There was no mention of any vehicle. Did the old DI think a young mother would abandon her daughter, carry a heavy rope the length of the glen and then manage to effectively kill herself? The photographs embedded in the file neglected to show any item she could have used as a step to position the noose around her neck before kicking it away. Come to think of it, he had only been able to reach the lower limbs of the tree by using his Land Rover as a makeshift platform, so how the hell had this poor girl managed to climb the tree and tie the rope unaided? Then there was the witness who reported the death, some Australian tourist who had never been identified, calling from a public call box; by rights he should have been a person of interest, but no real attempt had ever been made to trace him. The more he read, the more uncomfortable he felt.

Corstorphine leaned back in his leather seat, cradling the back of his head in his arms. The report contained witness statements which all broadly agreed that June Stevens had been behaving oddly for several months prior to her apparent suicide. None of the witnesses had suggested she was depressed; the words they used had been distracted, worried, frightened.

One report detailed how she had suddenly become overly protective of her daughter, refusing to let her out to play with friends, describing the young child as 'a prisoner, locked in the house'. These were not character statements that he'd associate with a potential suicide, more descriptive of someone suffering from a mental illness. In which case, she might have taken her own life whilst the balance of her mind was disturbed. He glanced up as Frankie's car entered the car park at the rear of the station. The case was long closed, it would be a devil of a job to try and go over the evidence this far on – and there was no way his superiors would sanction anyone digging over ancient history without solid evidence that the original case had been mishandled. Anyway, Corstorphine tried to persuade himself, there probably wasn't anything to connect the girl's suicide to Oscar's murder – just a coin found at the scene which by chance was minted on the date of her death.

He glanced up at the office clock; it was coming up to four. He stood, pulling on his coat as Frankie entered the office. 'How did you get on?' Corstorphine could see from her face that he wouldn't like her answer.

'I met with the reporter, a French woman called Josephine Sables. She knows about the church bell timbers being sawn through. It's going to be in tomorrow's paper.'

Corstorphine took the folded sheet of A3 as if he was

handling something poisonous, opening it out to reveal the story. 'Shit! Who's been feeding her the information?'

'I don't know, sir. Could be one of the team, or it could be the fire crew – or even the building surveyors. Either way, the cat's out of the bag. She's asked for exclusive information in return for finding out what June Stevens was working on.'

'Has she now?' Corstorphine shook his head in frustration, he should have gone to the paper himself. 'What did you tell her?'

'I didn't. Thought I'd run it past you first. She mentioned that the nationals will take note of two murders happening in the same small town this close together.'

Corstorphine sighed heavily, placing the A3 sheet face down on his desk as if he could hide the story for a while longer. 'I guess it was unavoidable, a snared gamekeeper, and a minister killed by his own church bell. We'll have to tighten up our act, Frankie. The assistant chief is going to be all over this as soon as the national press get wind. We've tomorrow at best to make some progress; after that, we'll be tripping over bloody reporters and film crews.'

Frankie stopped at the door, uncharacteristically hesitant. 'One other thing she said, sir.'

Corstorphine paused, wearing what Frankie had termed his impatient face.

'She asked whether Oscar died with an erection, whether he'd ejaculated as he died.'

The detective's right eyebrow responded accordingly. 'What sort of bloody question is that?'

'I don't know, sir, couldn't see why she wanted to know.' Frankie stared at her notebook to avoid looking him in the eye.

'French, you say?'

'Yes, sir, certainly sounded French.'

'Well, that explains that!' He shrugged and grabbed his car keys, thinking furiously. Time was closing in on their investigation, and they still hadn't had the results from the belfry. 'I'm going to pay a visit to Brian Rankin, go over some of the details in the June Stevens' suicide just in case there's a connection. You chase up the forensics report on the church. I hope to God we find something tangible to report, otherwise it's going to get bloody uncomfortable here.'

EIGHTEEN

'Come on in, James. Molly's just put the kettle on. You've time for a tea?'

Corstorphine shook the old DI's hand, stepping into the hallway of an anonymous bungalow on the outskirts of town. The area was full of retired folk, the neat postage-stamp gardens and manicured hedges evidence of those with hours to kill and nothing much to fill those hours.

'Hi, Molly, how are you keeping?' He kissed the woman whose inquisitive face had turned into a welcoming smile as she recognised Corstorphine.

'Och, I'm fine, James, and you're looking more handsome every time I see you!' Her face crumpled into well-worn laughter lines. It was their standing joke that she was on the verge of leaving her husband to run off with the new DI. At least Corstorphine hoped it was a joke.

'I'll bring through a pot, you two must have lots of catching up to do.' She disappeared back into the kitchen, busying herself with cups and saucers, the old mugs being returned to the cupboard in deference to the arrival of a guest.

'How are you keeping, Brian?' He settled into a plush

armchair, noticing the old DI struggling to lower himself into his chair.

'Och me, I'm fine. Overdid the gardening yesterday so my back's giving me gyp. What's the latest on that terrible affair with Oscar? The paper's calling it a murder?'

'That's what I wanted to talk to you about. You remember the reporter who died at the same spot – June Stevens?'

Molly came in with a tray, cups and saucers rattling as she lowered it onto a small table. Her head lifted as she overheard the name. 'That poor lass. Such a terrible thing.' Molly shook her head, as if in disbelief that anything so tragic could have happened in their quiet little town.

'Now, Molly, don't go getting upset. It's all ancient history now – the poor girl is in a better place.' Brian patted her arm. 'You'd better leave us to talk – police business.'

'Police business,' she said disparagingly. 'You've been retired seven years, Brian. I shouldn't think you're going to be of any help to James at all. Don't you go exhausting him, James, he's still recovering from doing all that gardening yesterday.'

They waited until she'd left them alone before Brian spoke. 'Why are you bringing that old case up, James, thought you'd have enough on your plate with Oscar's death?'

'Well, that's why I'm here. I think there may be a link between her death and Oscar's.'

Brian's jaw dropped, the surprise written across his face. 'Linked? How do you mean, was Oscar's death a suicide as well?'

'Not quite. Someone left a coin at the scene; it was minted in 1997, the same year that June Stevens was found hanging from that tree. I'm fairly certain Oscar's death wasn't a suicide, just need to check a few facts with you if that's alright?'

'Aye, happy to help in any way I can.' The old DI indicated the tray to Corstorphine, encouraging him to help himself. He took a cup of tea, adding a splash of milk. 'Have a Tunnocks as well, they'll not keep forever.'

Corstorphine shook his head, wondering if Tunnocks tea cakes did indeed possess some innate quality that made them close to immortal. Certainly, the ones his mother used to keep in a jar were manufactured before use by dates were even invented. 'No, thanks. Got to watch the figure.'

Brian settled back in his chair. 'So, James, how can I help you?'

'I was going over the old case notes on the June Stevens suicide, you were lead detective on that.'

'Aye, that's right. It was a terrible affair, such a young age to want to end it all.'

'That's the thing, Brian, how certain are you that it was a suicide?'

'Och, there wasn't any doubt. She'd been behaving very strangely in the last few months of her life, keeping that daughter of hers locked up in the house. There was no evidence of foul play, nothing that forensics came up with. No, it had all become too much for the lassie. Such a shame, these days she would have had help. It was a different time back then.' He took a sip of tea, followed by a bite of his teacake. 'No, it was as open and shut a case as I'd ever seen.'

Corstorphine carefully sat his teacup back on its saucer and looked steadily at the old inspector. 'There are some things about the case I don't understand.'

'Fire away. It was some twenty years ago, but my memory's still working.'

'How do you suppose she climbed the tree to fix the rope? I had to climb onto the Land Rover roof before I could get up into the lower branches.'

Brian looked askance at Corstorphine. 'She was a good bit younger than you are, James, and fitter.' He looked into some faraway point as if recalling the scene. 'Aye, I think she threw the rope over the branch and tied it that way. Sort of thing kids do all the time when they're making rope swings. I did the same myself as a lad, just need to tie one end to a stone or stick and throw it over the branch.'

Corstorphine nodded. 'Aye, I can see that might be possible. Nothing we can validate now without seeing how the rope was tied.'

'No, that's true enough. Forensics had the rope, of course. I wouldn't imagine that they'd still have it, but it may be worth checking?'

'I'll do that. Another thing, what did she use to climb up into the noose? I couldn't see anything in the photographs taken at the time?'

Brian puzzled for a moment. 'I think there was a boulder or something, she must have dragged it to the tree and stood on it before jumping off. The track's still in use, so it would have been moved to allow vehicles access to the site. Yes, that must have been it.' He nodded to himself before finishing the teacake in a second bite. 'Forensics weren't the power in the land that they are now, whoever was first on the scene would have cleared the track for the emergency vehicles.'

'Who was first on the scene, do you remember?'

'Aye, Hamish. Hamish McKee, he was just a constable back then.'

'OK. Thanks, Brian, that's been a help. Always good to hear first-hand.'

'Glad I've been of assistance. Anything else I can help with, just call, you know where I live.'

Corstorphine finished his tea and rose out of the chair. As he made his way to the front door, he turned back to ask a final question. 'The daughter, what happened to her?'

The old DI shook his head. 'She was taken into care; no other family members came forward.'

'Where was that, Brian, where did she go?'

Brian hesitated as if he was searching his memory. 'The old orphanage in City Road. Closed now, has been for many years.'

'Where did she go after that?'

Brian looked uncomfortable. 'That's something that has been worrying me all these years, James. She ran away after a few months, just vanished into thin air. We put out a nationwide alert for her, but she never showed up. I think her body must be out on the hills somewhere, poor lost lamb.'

'Thanks, Brian. I'll let you know how we get on.' He raised his voice, calling out to Molly who was still clattering around in the back kitchen. 'Bye, Molly, thanks for the tea.'

'Are you not staying, James?' a remote voice called back. 'We'll be having dinner soon, I can easily set another place?' She came into view, wiping her hands on a tea towel.

'That's very kind of you, Molly, but I really have to be going. It's all a bit mad at the moment.'

As Corstorphine drove away from the house, he caught a glimpse in his rear-view mirror of the old DI and his wife standing motionless on the bungalow porch, watching him until they were lost from view. He had a strong suspicion that the old detective was hiding something. His body language had betrayed him when he had asked about the missing daughter, the false searching for lost memories as if he was creating a story that Corstorphine would swallow. As quickly as the thought came to him, he dismissed it. He'd known Brian ever since he'd transferred here, a young detective learning the ropes as the old DI worked the last three years towards retirement. There wasn't even a whisper that he was ever anything other than a straight cop, certainly nothing that Corstorphine had heard. Why that nagging doubt that he was concealing something?

He checked the dashboard clock: 17:44. Nothing he could do without the latest forensics. Corstorphine started to phone Frankie to check up on progress but hung up before completing the call and drove home instead. The day was almost done, and he needed to have a quiet place to think.

Corstorphine lived in a semi-detached Victorian villa in one of the more salubrious parts of town, a house that had been chosen as a good place to bring up a family, three bedrooms for the children that never were. Corstorphine tweaked the heating up a notch to dispel the chill he'd felt on entering the house, the old gas heating creaking into life as radiators filled with hot water, companionable noises that helped maintain the fiction that he wasn't alone. Out of habit, he checked the silent carriage clock on the mantlepiece, the hands frozen at the moment he'd dashed it to the ground after his wife had died – an outlet for the rage that burned his heart. On autopilot, he turned on the TV, tuning into the twenty-four-hour news channel. He found voices filled the empty house more effectively than music, maintaining the fiction that he wasn't alone.

Sinking into his favourite armchair, Corstorphine nursed a large glass of single malt, ice clinking against the glass as he raised the amber fluid to his lips. He kept half an ear on the TV news, just in case the murders had reached the nationals. Nothing – yet. Drinking a toast to whichever saint was the patron saint of journalists, Corstorphine sat and thought through the last few days, searching his mind for clues he might have missed, the common thread that tied the cases together. Before long, the potent mix of whisky, warmth and the comforting sound of the TV combined to lull him into a fitful sleep.

It was night. A full moon hung large and silver in the velvet star-studded sky, lending a silver tint to Glen Mhor as if it had been freshly painted in ethereal colours. Corstorphine glided over the ground, an effortless movement which allowed him the leisure to admire the stars, feel a warm breeze upon his cheeks. Somewhere in the distance a tawny owl called, a familiar twit-twoo echoing down the glen. Corstorphine recognised the

Hanging Tree as soon as it came into view, and his air of contentment metamorphosed into a feeling of unease, growing in intensity as the tree drew ever closer. He tried to turn back and looked down to see that his feet drifted above the ground, caught in some invisible current that had him gripped fast.

The path turned into a fast-flowing burn even as the thought occurred to him, and he struggled to keep his head above the water. On one level, Corstorphine realised he was dreaming, but he still fought the current in a mounting panic as the burn changed into a river in spate, rocks flying past as he was tossed and driven towards the old oak. Suddenly, he was thrown against the tree, fighting to disentangle himself from Oscar's corpse as their limbs entwined like lovers and the water rose higher, threatening to drown him. He struggled free, somehow lifted out of the corpse's cold embrace by rising waters to enter the green canopy above. As the waters quietened, Corstorphine looked in wonder at the gears, moving together in common purpose, the rhythmic tick of the mechanism counting towards the hour until the chimes struck, counting out the hour in sonorous peals.

Corstorphine woke suddenly, the dream leaving him wondering for a brief moment where he was. His doorbell rang again, the sound a distant echo of his dream and he remembered every detail even as he staggered towards the front door, fighting the cramp which threatened to unbalance him at every other step.

'Sorry to bother you, sir, I guessed you'd probably finished for the day, but I thought you'd want to see this.' Frankie stood on the doorstep, holding out a few A4 sheets for his inspection.

'Come on in, Frankie,' he offered, taking the pages and studying them as he headed back to his seat. He held an email from the Inverness forensics department, confirming what he already knew – that the support timbers had been sawn almost completely through. Corstorphine skimmed through the report, taking note of the collection of bone gear fragments which the forensics team had managed to reassemble without any idea as to what they represented. He turned to the last page, a sharp intake of breath the only indication of his surprise as he saw the photograph of another Pope Paul II Vatican coin, the date 1997.

'So, no doubt these murders are linked.'

'No, sir.' Frankie waited as Corstorphine pinched the bridge of his nose, eyes shut tight as he remembered the dream and sought whatever meaning lay behind the images still fresh in his mind.

'Clocks!' Corstorphine almost shouted the word, his eyes now wide open. 'Frankie, who do we know that repairs clocks?'

Frankie stared at him with obvious concern. 'Sorry, sir, I'm not sure I understand.'

'The gears. I think I know why they were used in both murders. I think they're timing mechanisms. We need specialist help, Frankie, we need someone who understands clocks and gears, who can help work out when these were fitted and how long they ran before they completed their tasks.' He shook his head in exasperation. 'These could have been fitted months ago. Until we can recreate the murder scene apparatus, we won't be able to pinpoint when the murderer fitted the devices.'

NINETEEN

Frankie stretched in bed, squinting at the nearby digital clock's green LED display until the numbers swam into focus. Another half hour before she had to leave for the morning shift. She attempted a stronger stretch, culminating the full extension with a fixed idiot grin at the ceiling. She'd watched a TV programme the previous evening where an inspirational Danish woman had insisted that the release of serotonin engendered by such an activity would help keep her happy for the rest of the day. She lay there, waiting patiently for the happiness chemical to work its magic whilst her mind was engaged with the two recent murders.

Corstorphine had proposed that the gears found at each scene were part of a clockwork mechanism, a means of setting the events into motion without the murderer having to be present. Forensics had even come up with a plausible theory for how the bell rope may have been connected via the bits of gear they'd manage to piece together. Frankie had studied the drawing they'd made, the bell rope's up-and-down motion transferred via secondary nylon lines found still attached to the top of the rope and how they could pull the large bone wheel one way, then back the other. The reciprocating action was strong enough to pull the hacksaw back and forth across the oak beam, cutting from underneath so that as the wood weakened, it would naturally open to allow the saw blade deeper access.

Who would want to murder the old minister? How was his death connected to Oscar's? The coincidence of the same coin, the same carved gears being found at both crime scenes, made it clear that the murders were linked.

She swung her legs over the edge of the bed, glancing just for a second at the other empty half and wondering how he was doing. It was like this most mornings, she was still surprised to be alone as she awoke. How many years had it been? Three years since the divorce, three years married. She knew this represented some sort of fulcrum in her life, a point of balance between one chapter and another. She knew other women of a similar age, too old for a casual fling – or at least old enough to find fault with themselves for scratching that itch – and too young to reconcile themselves to living on their own for the rest of their days, all with similar embittered stories to tell of breakup, betrayal, divorce.

Corstorphine had it easy in some ways, death was so much cleaner than a breakup and society allowed you time to grieve. At least she didn't have children, something her ex had been wont to throw in her face during the last tumultuous year of their relationship when love had been replaced by its evil twin. How had it all gone wrong? It was a question she asked herself most days, searching for the faults inherent in herself that had made his love turn to hate. At the back of her mind she knew that the fault wasn't hers alone, but the days had turned into weeks, the weeks into months, the months into years until they each blended into the kaleidoscope of their lives. Seen, but not seen. There, but not there – not really.

Douglas had been the first to realise – a romantic at heart he felt the lack of constant renewal, he needed that mantra of love repeated ad nauseam or he simply stopped believing. Frankie was content with his presence, a comforting occupation of her personal space. Unlike him, she didn't worship at the altar of love, and when the prayers stopped, she didn't even notice. Perhaps that's what made him grow so angry, her simple acceptance of him rather than a constant renewing of her avowed love – she'd driven him away by not loving him in the way he wanted to be loved. Stroked, kissed, held – he needed constant reassurance like a child.

Frankie stood, feeling warm carpet under bare feet. It was for the best. She wanted an equal partner, not a needy manchild. Looking at herself in the bathroom mirror, teeth bared for the electric toothbrush, she decided the Danish woman was speaking crap. This day would be the same as all the others, with a side helping of two murders that needed solving.

The clock repairer's workshop was sandwiched between a Chinese takeaway on the one side and a shop offering cut-price mobiles and unlocking services. The street was home to a ragbag of such businesses: a couple of takeaways, a betting shop, a newsagent's and a funeral parlour complete with purple plastic irises gathering dust in the sombre window. The word dignity was misspelled, leading her to worry how many gravestones in the town might present idiosyncratic messages to the living, cryptic comments about the deceased.

Inside the shop window, a selection of wrist watches shared space with a carriage clock whilst further back in the dim recesses she could just make out a grandfather clock. Every timepiece displayed a different time, none of which agreed with her phone's clock. For some reason, Pink Floyd's track 'Time' started playing in her head and she dismissed it with irritation as she pushed the door open. A bell attached to the door on a coil of brass rang in tuneless urgency to announce a customer, and a humpback figure eventually appeared behind the counter, peering up at her through pebble glasses as if a customer was indeed a rarity.

'I'm DC Frankie McKenzie. I was wondering if you may be able to help me?'

'Have you brought it with you?'

'I'm sorry. Have I brought what with me?'

'What's that? You'll have to speak up. Oh, one moment.' He fumbled with his ears, retrieved two hearing aids and took them over to a large magnifying glass attached to the end of the counter. 'I'll just be a minute,' he advised, turning on a light and concentrating on replacing two small button batteries. Satisfied they were working, he inserted them back into his ears and smiled beatifically up at Frankie.

'Sorry, my dear. What was that again?'

Frankie took a deep breath and started again. 'My name is DC Frankie McKenzie. I'm a detective at the local police station. We're looking for someone to help us with one of our cases, someone who understands clockwork mechanisms.'

He nodded enthusiastically. 'Yes, I'm a horologist. Been working with clocks for nigh on sixty years. What's wrong with the police station clock, is it running slow?'

She wondered if the only clockmaker in the town was going to be of any help. 'It's not the police station clock.' She said each word with emphasis, leaving space between them to avoid misunderstanding. 'We have a crime which we believe involves a clockwork mechanism. Would you be able to look at what we've found and advise us?'

'Clockwork mechanisms?' He said the words as if he doubted her sanity. 'You say the crime involved a clockwork mechanism?'

'That's right.' Frankie began to think up ways of terminating a conversation that had the potential to continue in circles for hours to come. The small shop was restless with sound, manic ticks emanating from the smaller clocks and watches to the statelier measured tick-tocks issuing from the larger timepieces. Somewhere out the back, a clock chimed three o'clock, completely at odds with reality.

'Well, of course I can help!' The shopkeeper peered up at her with indignation shining from each pebble glass. 'There's nobody who knows more about clocks than I do.' He held his chin for a moment. 'Unless you go to Manchester. There's a very good group of horologists in Manchester.'

'We'd rather keep it local if we can,' Frankie answered.

'Well, bring me what you've got, and I'll have a look.'

'Thank you, Mr...?' Frankie realised she was talking to his humped back as he disappeared back into whatever room was behind the counter. No answer came back from her query, quite likely he hadn't heard her. She tugged on the door and the spring-loaded bell accompanied her departure from the shop.

TWENTY

At the station, Corstorphine assembled the team in front of the crazy wall. The minister's and Oscar's pictures both took pride of place, and a new photograph adorned the board in between both mugshots. A young woman, long auburn hair framing an intelligent face. Her name was displayed under the photograph – June Stevens.

'Morning all.' Corstorphine found this opening remark faintly reminiscent of the days of black and white TV, but only Hamish was old enough to have even heard of *Dixon of Dock Green*, and he had a humour deficit. 'Just to update you all, we have found bone gears and a 1997 papal coin at both the scene of Oscar's death and in the rubble at the bottom of the bell tower where the minister of St Cuthbert's died. We need to find whatever connects these two murders. The only working hypothesis I have is from the date on the coins, the year June Stevens was found hanging from the tree in Glen Mhor. I believe her death may be linked to these other two murders, but for the time being, we have no corroborating evidence that can back this up.' He pointed at June's photograph, her face smiling confidently into the camera lens. 'If any of you have any ideas, now would be a good time to share them.'

The only answer was a shuffling of feet as the rest of the team looked at each other. Corstorphine pursed his lips. They had to make progress or risk being sidelined by the Inverness detectives as soon as the story broke.

'OK. Here's what I'm proposing. The killer planned these deaths meticulously. No forensic evidence was found at either scene, so they know enough about police procedures to wear protective clothing. The gears we've found, I believe they were used to create mechanisms that killed both of our victims. Forensics provided this diagram, showing how the bell rope could have transferred energy via the large bone wheel to the hacksaw.' Corstorphine pressed the keyboard space bar, and the sketch of a Heath Robinson device appeared on the screen behind him.

'So, the minister was the cause of his own death – that's sick!' PC Lamb stared with fascination at the screen.

Corstorphine wasn't too sure what the PC meant by 'sick'. That generation tended to turn words on their heads, and he had a feeling that his own interpretation may be at odds with what Lamb meant. He decided to let it pass. 'Yes, Lamb, it takes a certain mindset to create such a scenario. Unfortunately, the mechanism found at the tree was completely destroyed, but we have identified someone who may be able to piece it together.' He looked towards Frankie with hope.

'Yes, sir. I've talked to a local clockmaker. He's offered us his help in trying to discover how the mechanism may have worked. I'll take him what we've found once forensics give us the all-clear on handling the evidence.'

'Thank you, Frankie. There are a number of lines of investigation I want to follow, and small as our team here is, it goes without saying I want all of you to work on these murders to the exclusion of everything else. You'll be aware that *The Courier* has somehow managed to find out nearly as much about these murders as we do. If I find anyone has been speaking to the press, you'll be out of the force and minus a pension before you can draw a breath. Do I make myself clear?'

A muttered yes sir came from the gathering, all finding anywhere to look rather than catch Corstorphine's eye.

'Good. Right now, we have two murder investigations under way, and next to no suspects in the frame. The national newspapers are likely to catch wind of this today, and as sure as night follows day, they will be turning up here tomorrow sniffing around for a story. Unless we want to be made to look totally incompetent, we'd better have something substantial to report by the end of the day. I don't have to say that the top brass will also be taking a special interest in our performance, so it's in all of our interests to crack this fast.'

He pointed to Hamish, standing at the back. 'Hamish, you were first on the scene at the site of June Stevens' death. I want you to dig out your notebook from that day, and you and I will go over the details like it was a fresh investigation. Frankie, I spoke with DI Rankin yesterday, he mentioned June Stevens' daughter was taken to the old orphanage on City Road after her death. She went missing from there after a few months – look into her disappearance and find out what you can about the orphanage.

'Lamb, McAdam, I want you to talk to anyone locally you can find, who worked or stayed at the orphanage. Get me names, dates and anything of note. I also want you to find out if anyone has moved here recently. Don't be too obvious about it, but any new faces, I want to know about them. Any if you find anything, straight to me. If I'm not available, contact Frankie. We'll get together at four-thirty for a debrief and update.' He dismissed them, glad to see the team moving with a fresh sense of purpose.

TWENTY-ONE

Back at her desk, Frankie started looking into the orphanage. A local history site provided her with the name of the organisation responsible for the children's welfare; a Catholic Order known as the Sisters of Holy Mercy. The orphanage closed in 2000 when the local authority took over responsibility for any waifs and strays. It had been put up for sale and over the following ten years the building had deteriorated to such a dangerous state that the council used a compulsory purchase order to have it demolished. The site was finally sold in 2013 to a private developer for a substantial profit and a block of upmarket flats now occupied the site. Frankie puzzled over the name, Sisters of Holy Mercy – it sounded familiar. Her phone rang, interrupting her train of thought. She picked it up, introduced herself and recognised the French accent on the other end of the phone immediately.

'Detective Constable Frankie McKenzie?'

'Speaking.' Her response was brusque, she didn't have time for brushing off the reporter's questions today. 'How can I help you?'

'I was hoping I could help you.'

'What have you got?'

'Margo McDonald paid us a visit yesterday, wanted to tell us her side of the story. Did you know Oscar claimed he was sexually assaulted as a child?'

Frankie frowned at the receiver as if her expression could be detected the other end of the line. 'Margo told you that?'

'Yes, and I believe her. More to the point she told me who it was that abused him.'

Frankie reached for her notebook and pen, trapping the phone between her shoulder and cheek to free up both hands.

'Who?'

'The minister of St Cuthbert's, and members of staff connected with the orphanage that used to be on City Road. The one run by the Sisters—'

'Of Holy Mercy!' Frankie concluded for her.

'I see you are two steps in front of me. This is Margo's story. It's going in tomorrow's paper, together with a background story on the Sisters.'

'What's the story about the Sisters?' Frankie asked urgently before the reporter could hang up.

'The Sisters of Holy Mercy have been associated with child abuse at a number of orphanages throughout the UK and Ireland. There have been successful prosecutions, both against individual nuns as well as visiting clergy and dignitaries who treated the orphanages as their personal paedophile hunting ground. Nothing has ever been reported locally, but if this follows the pattern elsewhere, we might expect anyone who has been abused to come forward after we publish. I thought you should know.'

TWENTY-TWO

Frankie put the phone down and glanced over towards Corstorphine's office. He was bent over some paperwork, taking notes as he read. This couldn't wait.

'Sir?' She stood at the threshold of the office, waiting for his permission to enter.

'What is it, Frankie? I'm expecting Hamish in any minute.'

'I'll be quick, sir. I've just had the reporter from *The Courier* on the phone.' He cast his eyes to the ceiling in exasperation. 'Margo was in with them yesterday, told them Oscar was sexually abused as a kid. They're publishing her story and claiming staff at the orphanage were involved in some paedophile ring. She named the St Cuthbert's minister specifically as one of the abusers.'

Corstorphine's eyes locked with hers as he processed the information. 'Hamish mentioned two days ago that Oscar had accused the minister of abusing him, he was just starting at school at the time. They treated it as a child's fantasy, attention-seeking behaviour from a disturbed child, only Hamish wasn't convinced Oscar was lying even though nothing came of it.'

'Is it the sort of thing a five-year-old child would invent, sir?' Frankie's voice betrayed her outrage.

'Things are different now,' Corstorphine started to explain only to be cut short.

'He'd not have told Margo the same story if he'd made it up. How does that fit with his "big man" image? It's not something he'd mention unless…'

'Unless it was true?' Corstorphine finished the sentence for her. 'Possibly.' He rubbed his fingers across his temple as if attempting to alleviate a headache. 'Hamish made the point, if Oscar was seeking revenge on the minister, who killed Oscar? Added to which it looks very much as if they were both killed by the same person.' He shook his head. 'No, there's more to this, but the link has to be investigated. What do we know about the staff at the orphanage?'

'The group running it were the Sisters of Holy Mercy.'

Corstorphine froze in his seat at the mention of the name.

'Holy fuck! The same bunch that have been convicted of child abuse all over the world? How did this happen under our noses? Someone must have been aware of what was going on? Get a list of everyone working at the orphanage, from the gardener through to the Mother fucking Superior – and find as many regular visitors to the orphanage as you can? Try the social services, they might have taken over the records when the orphanage closed.'

Frankie passed Hamish on the way out. He was carrying an old notebook, the type that bobbies carried on the beat back in the Eighties. She grabbed her coat; the council offices were the only place that might still hold any relevant information about the orphanage.

* * *

'Come in, Hamish, sit down.' Corstorphine ran his fingers through his hair. The day was lining up to be a marathon. 'Take me through June Stevens' case, from the top.'

'Well, sir, we had a call come in at...' The desk sergeant consulted his notebook, a yellow Post-it hanging from the page he opened. '10:27 a.m. The call came from the old public phone box on the main road just opposite the Glen Mhor turn-off. A young male hiker informed us that a woman's body was hanging from the old oak on the Glen Mhor track – he sounded Australian.'

'Why didn't he wait for the attending officer?'

'He was asked to wait until I arrived on the scene, but when I arrived at the call box at...' the notebook was consulted again, '11:02, the caller had gone. I didn't spend time looking for him, thought in all probability it was a hoax. The local lads had a thing about impersonating Australians at the time.' Corstorphine's eyebrow started to rise and Hamish hurriedly continued. 'I drove the squad car down the track, taking it easy because of the suspension, and when I got to the tree, I saw her hanging there. I tried to get her down but could only hold her up by her ankles, so I drove under the tree and climbed up and cut the rope.'

'You drove under the tree. Are you sure?'

Hamish looked worried. 'Yes, sir. I thought there might be a chance she could still be saved, so I had to get her down on the ground to loosen the noose and perform CPR.' He looked down at the floor, speaking quietly. 'I was too late, sir. She was dead.'

'When did the DI get there?'

'Detective Inspector Rankin arrived at 12:20, sir. I called him in on the radio after I'd tried to save her. I had to drive almost completely out of the glen before I was able to get a signal, not that it's any better now.'

'What investigations did he do – whilst you were at the scene?'

Hamish frowned, recalling the dreadful day. 'He spent a while looking at the rope, said he thought she'd probably thrown it over the branch and then secured it. He asked me to look around, see if I spotted anything unusual. I remember he was quite keen to see if her reporter's notebook had fallen out of her pocket, but there wasn't anything that I could find.'

'OK, Hamish. Just one other thing – you didn't have to clear the track of any logs or boulders to get the patrol car under the tree?'

Hamish shook his head. 'No, sir. The track was clear – estate vehicles used it all the time, so it was kept well maintained.'

'Any marks on her body, had her clothes been disturbed – do you think there was any possibility she could have been raped before she died?'

The sergeant looked at Corstorphine, the shock clear in his expression. 'Raped? No, at least I don't think so. That would have been picked up by the autopsy report, by forensics. Her clothes were dishevelled, but then again, you'd expect that after you've struggled on a rope for a few seconds.' His eyes were still wide as he remembered the scene, remembered her face. 'It was her expression, sir. I never want to see another corpse with an expression like that – it was if she'd seen the devil himself.'

'Do you think it was suicide, Hamish?' Corstorphine asked the question quietly, watching him carefully as he formulated his answer.

'I always thought so, sir, until the events of the last few days. I knew the woman, she never seemed the sort to take her own life – and she loved that girl of hers. It doesn't make sense to me. I was just a constable then, sir, and the DI managed the investigation together with the forensics guys when they finally made it from Inverness. If he said her death was a suicide, then that's what it was.'

'Why the doubt now, Hamish? What's changed from twenty-two years ago?'

Hamish's eyes were troubled. 'I've been thinking about the telephone call, about the Australian hiker. Nobody walks along that glen, it doesn't lead anywhere, there's nothing to attract hikers – not even a reasonable hill to climb.' He raised his head to look directly into Corstorphine's face. 'I think now that I recognised the caller's voice. I think Oscar made the emergency call faking an Australian accent, and I think Oscar may have killed her.'

'Why didn't you say at the time? It's a bit bloody late to raise your suspicions now!' Corstorphine's voice rose, showing his frustration.

'I didn't realise it at the time, sir. When I found the body, I believed that the call must have been genuine, and with the DI's report saying it was a suicide, I never had cause to doubt my own version of events. Having to revisit her death now, all these years later – I just see things differently, sir. Things I may have been too green to notice at the time. People were saying she was mad, the balance of her mind was in question, it all made some sort of sense back then. Now I think she was more frightened than mad.'

'OK, sergeant. I'm sorry I raised my voice – this case is starting to get to me. Can you ask around, see if there's anyone still living or working here that used to go to the orphanage? It's time to get some inside knowledge of what went on in that place.'

'Yes, sir. On it now.' The sergeant wheeled smartly around and left Corstorphine to his thoughts. This case was far from being solved by the close of the day; if anything, it was getting murkier by the minute.

Corstorphine stood in front of the crazy wall, trying to process what Frankie and Hamish had told him. Oscar was capable of murder; he had no doubt of it – had the reporter found information about his past and was going to publish? Oscar wouldn't have wanted anyone to know he'd been abused as a child, so he might have killed her just to shut her up. He would have been around twenty then, strong enough to overpower her. What was June Stevens doing in the glen if she wasn't going there to kill herself, something Corstorphine thought less likely by the minute?

Then there were the discrepancies in Hamish's description of the scene and the old DI's remembering. If Hamish was able to drive under the tree, then there couldn't have been the boulder she'd have needed in order to reach the noose – and dead people didn't clear up behind them. He hesitated, just for a brief second, then added DI Brian Rankin's name to the board. There was something that didn't feel right about the investigation into the reporter's apparent suicide. Why the old DI should have wanted to protect Oscar, though, was a question he couldn't even begin to answer.

TWENTY-THREE

Frankie called an old friend on the hands-free as she pulled into the council car park. 'Hi, Susan? Yes, it's me, Frankie. Yes, far too long. I'm here on official business actually, can you meet me at reception? I'm looking for any records you may have on the old orphanage on City Road, lists of the children staying there, staff – that sort of thing. Great. I'm here now, see you in a minute.'

She was shown into one of the rooms down in the basement. The council offices were built in the Sixties, brutalist concrete architecture standing like a soviet slab in the middle of the town. The building was crying out to be demolished, windows rusting and leaking, damp patches adorned walls and ceilings – even the staff had an unhealthy pallor, white skin, listless gait. They reminded her of zombies, creeping around a decaying building waiting for any kind of death to provide release. She shrugged off the depressing image, at least she had managed to find a job that had some sort of purpose. Her friend Susan was once a good-looking young woman, vivacious and fun to be with – at least that's how Frankie preferred to remember her. Now she was old before her time, drained of vitality. She still attempted gaiety as she joked with Frankie, talking about old times, but they both knew those days were never coming back.

'You'll find a list of the children the social services took over when the orphanage closed in this file.' Susan produced a manila folder from a battered filing cabinet with a magician's flourish. 'There's not much on the staff, the Catholic Church dealt with all that.'

'How do you mean, "dealt with that"?'

'They were responsible for running the orphanage before it closed down, so they employed everyone there. We didn't have any responsibility towards the staff, just towards the children – you know, school places, healthcare, that sort of thing.'

'Was there no oversight of the orphanage, health and safety checks?'

'Sure. There would have been annual inspections, and we kept an eye on the children, made sure they were being fed OK, sleeping arrangements were adequate.'

'Were there ever any complaints?'

'How do you mean?'

'Did you ever hear of any of the children alleging improper touching, abuse, were they ever beaten?'

Susan looked shocked. 'Nothing I've ever heard of! No, nothing like that ever went on there. I'm sure of it.' She folded her arms, a self-conscious act of protection against such an allegation.

'Do you mind if I take a copy of this?' Frankie held up the list of children transferred from the orphanage to the council's social services.

Susan looked doubtful. 'You really need a warrant before we allow sensitive information to be taken.'

'Yes, well, I could get a warrant if needs be. I'm just wanting to check a few names against the list – how about I just keep the list for a few days and then shred it. Guide's honour?' Frankie held up her right hand, thumb crossed against her little finger, the others held straight.

Susan smiled, the childish promise they'd both made as young girls fresh in her mind as if it were made yesterday. 'Go on then. Just don't let anyone else know where it came from or my job's mince!'

Frankie left the council building with the newly printed sheet tucked protectively into her body against the strengthening wind. She suspected Susan already thought her job was mince, but her mind was soon attending to the first name she recognised on the list.

TWENTY-FOUR

Corstorphine finally took delivery of the bone gears and associated paraphernalia found in and around the Hanging Tree together with a more detailed forensics report. The bones were thought to be cow skeleton, although they'd sent a sample for DNA testing to confirm. Forensics had suggested Corstorphine check local slaughterhouses to see if their waste disposal systems were up to scratch, then the animal waste companies that plied a living out of abattoir scraps. There were no fingerprints, no foreign material apart from honest Scottish mud and heather and hence no need to quarantine the fragments. If he wanted to try and put the gear fragments back together, he was welcome, as long as he remembered they may well be required as part of the eventual prosecution case.

He examined the collection of clear evidence bags. Each gear must have been painstakingly carved tooth by tooth from an original piece of bone, with the largest wheel constructed from a large bone... Corstorphine wrestled with his memory – the scapula? To design, create and install something like this was a work of genius – genius or insanity. He put the evidence bags to one side, Frankie could take them to her clockmaker, see if he could make sense of the parts.

The crazy wall beckoned, with fresh red lines connecting Oscar to the orphanage. The next step was to see whether the minister had any historical contact with the orphanage. Corstorphine tried to see a pattern, one that might tie Oscar's death to the minister's or connected the orphanage to June Stevens – apart from her missing child which was another line of investigation altogether which apparently implicated DI Brian Rankin. If *The Courier* was going to print Margo's allegations of child abuse at the orphanage, he hoped they had a good legal team to cope with the Catholic Church's response. Surely any abuse of some twenty years ago, if it really had occurred, would have surfaced by now? Those children would now be adults, in their twenties and thirties – some would surely have spoken out.

The Courier would be out by now, with the story of Oscar's abuse at the hands of the minister and the orphanage staff on the front page for sure. Corstorphine grimaced as he recalled Frankie also mentioning that the article would include a line on police brutality, which wasn't going to play well with the assistant chief constable. Four days since Oscar's death, and they still hadn't managed to identify a suspect apart from the Inverness gamekeeper. If Frankie's clockmaker managed to show that Oscar's snare could have been set more than a week ago, then they could have him back in for more questioning. Until then, his alibi held water.

Corstorphine's instinct told him that the orphanage was the key to the whole mystery, but the religious order had long since left and of those that were still alive and traceable – how many would be willing to provide any evidence?

His attention was drawn to the front desk. Hamish's usual slow and world-weary tones had changed into something more upbeat, tinged with a reverential quality as if he was welcoming a head of state.

'*Perhaps the Queen is reporting a missing corgi?*' Corstorphine allowed a rare smile to part his lips, his wife had been a lifelong republican and stood there now, face lit with a cheeky grin. He blinked, and she was gone, but Hamish's voice was approaching complete with, 'Yes, sir. I'll fetch him now, sir.'

The desk sergeant's face appeared around the door, completely blocking Corstorphine's view of the suited character standing impatiently at reception. 'What is it, Hamish?'

'It's Lord Lagan, sir. He's the—'

'Yes, thank you, Hamish. I'm aware who our local member of the House of Lords is. What does he want?'

'He wants to speak to you, sir. Shall I send him through?'

Corstorphine shook his head. 'Not in the middle of a murder investigation, I'll see him in reception.'

Hamish looked askance at the thought of a Lord having to remain in reception but led the way meekly back to his front desk. A tall, expensively dressed man stood on the other side of the glass, his impatience at being kept waiting evident by his restless stance. Corstorphine sighed. The man was an imbecile. He'd met him at a number of civic functions, one time even having to sit next to him at a formal dinner. A more vacuous peacock would be hard to imagine, hair dyed jet black and oiled, a colourful handkerchief tucked into the breast pocket of his fitted suit.

He keyed the door release and stepped through into the reception area, neatly blocking the entrance as the politician confidently strode towards it, as if locked doors never applied to someone as important as him.

'Lord Lagan, sir, what can we do for you?'

He had to step back to avoid Corstorphine, his fluster at being denied entrance to the station leaving him off-balance in a number of ways, as Corstorphine had intended.

'James, pleasure. Call me Reginald. Not as if we haven't met.' His hand shot out in a well-practised manoeuvre, leaving

Corstorphine no alternative but to begin a handshake that was overly strong and seemingly never-ending. He wondered if the short bursts of sentences were an affectation. As a politician he was certainly able to pontificate in long, flowery language whenever in front of a microphone. 'Do you have somewhere we can talk, in private?' His eyes indicated Hamish, who was watching the interchange with great interest.

'I'm sorry, Reginald. The office is off-limits for the time being whilst we investigate these murders. We can talk here, or if you prefer, we could take a walk, get the benefit of rare Scottish sunshine?'

'Good idea. Just need to run some things past you.' He waved in what he must have thought was a matey way to Hamish as they headed out of the police station entrance. 'Good day, Hamish, keep up the good work!'

'Sir,' came the response.

'What can I help you with, Reginald?' Corstorphine repeated the question as they walked along the road.

'Yes.' He looked around him as he walked, checking whether anyone was in earshot. 'Thing is, these murders have caused a bit of an upset.'

Corstorphine nodded sagely, willing him to get to the point. 'Indeed. We're all working flat out to try and resolve the cases as quickly as humanly possible.'

'Good, glad to hear it.' There was a pause as they approached another pedestrian. The MP turned on his 'winning' smile, a strange rictus that lay somewhere between a baboon threat and cheerleader grin. 'Good day. Lovely weather.'

The pedestrian's expression of distaste was sufficient for Corstorphine to surmise he had most probably voted for any party but the one that his companion represented in the House of Lords. It didn't seem to register with Reginald, who waited until they were alone again before continuing. 'Thing is, I was talking with the assistant chief constable at a private meeting yesterday.'

Corstorphine knew that both the politician and the ACC belonged to the same Inverness Lodge, the euphemism for private meeting being one of their ritual-laden Freemason dinners. *Here it comes*, he thought, a private message from the assistant chief delivered on a platform so far untraceable by normal means.

'He's concerned you are wasting your time with the Stevens suicide. Heard through the grapevine. Asked me to point out the priorities in getting this sorted. Save him making it official, didn't want it looking bad on your record.'

Corstorphine absorbed the command, threat and dangling carrot with equanimity.

'That's very kind of you, Reginald, making a special trip.'

'No, no. I was coming over anyway. Have a surgery in a short while. Listen to the people I represent. No, I just offered to pass it on as I was going to be here anyway. My pleasure.'

Corstorphine was sufficiently well-informed to know that the ACC held the post of senior warden or whatever ridiculous title he had, and that he was several levels up on the MP who in all probability owed his job to the murky machinations of the Lodge. So, he'd been told to pass on a message and like a good errand boy had delivered.

'I'll let the assistant chief constable know that our focus is on finding the killer before anyone else is found murdered. Thank you again for passing this on.'

'Not at all. My pleasure.' Reginald made a show of looking at his watch, a self-important man with things to do. 'Look at the time,' he said rather unnecessarily. 'Must dash. Love to the wife.'

Corstorphine watched his progress as he strutted down the road before entering the town hall, where another crowd of flunkies would be anxiously awaiting his arrival with tea and biscuits. He hadn't been particularly bothered about his parting comment – passing his love onto a wife who'd been dead for five years. The man was, as he knew, an imbecile. The message from the ACC, however... now that had been a deliberate attempt to steer the investigation away from June Stevens' death. Why should that be? Corstorphine was never going to be a top-flight detective, he lacked the showman's flair or the shameless appropriation of his team's work as his own – which was why he'd been posted to a quiet backwater where nothing ever happened. Ever used to happen.

The ACC had just made two mistakes. Firstly, Corstorphine's interest in June Stevens' death had been promoted to the top of his agenda. A death that looked like a cover-up at the time, and was now trying to be hushed up again with an untraceable directive from the top. Corstorphine didn't take kindly to being told what to do, or how to do his job – not a character trait that the assistant chief constable would have been familiar with, of course. He also wouldn't know how Corstorphine would never let go of an investigation once he had his metaphorical teeth sunk into it.

The second mistake he'd made was in the choice of messenger. Lord Reginald Lagan might be an idiot, but he knew who to please in order to stay in power. The ACC was a powerful man, there was no doubt of that, but for the Lord to be willing to become his message boy, someone even higher up must be pulling some strings. Someone who had influence over both the police as well as a member of the House of Lords, and that had just lit a fuse under Corstorphine's interest in her death.

He returned to the station and put through a call to the Inverness forensics lab.

'What have you got for us this time, James? We're running a sweepstake on the next murder victim and method of death. There's a tidy sum of money involved.'

'Very droll, but if you don't mind, we have work to do here.

Can you send me the report on a death in May 1997? The victim was a female reporter, June Stevens, found hanging in an oak tree in Glen Mhor.'

He could hear the percussive taps of a keyboard even through the telephone earpiece.

'Here it is, June Stevens. I can't let you have the official report without authorisation.'

'I know that,' Corstorphine replied, exasperated. 'I'm just looking for the basics, cause of death, any forensic evidence that needed further investigation.'

'OK, let's see. Suicide, hanging. That's strange...'

'What. What have you found?'

'Nothing. That's what's strange. The report is pretty much non-existent. This is back in the days when we didn't have to follow set procedure, but even so, I'd have thought to see more on the report than this.'

'So, there's nothing you're able to tell me?'

'Sorry.'

Corstorphine tried another tack. 'Is any of the original evidence in store, her clothing, scene photographs, the rope?'

'No chance. The case was marked solved, and we don't keep anything beyond ten years. Not going to be able to help you, sorry.'

'Yeah OK. Thanks anyway.'

He looked at his phone accusatorily. Why was nothing as easy as they made it seem in detective stories?

TWENTY-FIVE

Frankie parked outside the butcher's shop on the high street, taking advantage of having the patrol car to straddle double yellow lines with impunity. The morning sun had broken through, driving off the last of the morning chill. Shoppers stopped and chatted as they met, a cluster of coffee tables spilled out from the upmarket café down the road, lending a European feel to the town. She wished the sun could dispel the gloom that gathered around her shoulders like a shawl, two deaths in a week tended to have that effect on her.

'Hi, William.' The ginger-haired man turned around in surprise, still holding the marker pen he'd been using to price up meat cuts.

'Frankie McKenzie! Don't often see you in here. How have you been keeping?'

She responded with a genuine smile. They'd been at school together, shared memories and lives that only those brought up in small towns would understand. She'd also stood up for him on more than one occasion when he'd been bullied at school – the ginger hair an open goal for some. William had been a quiet boy, she remembered him as someone on the periphery of things, never really one of the gang even when he was in a gang. He was simply one of life's loners, although he seemed cheerful enough now, standing there with a belly that was just starting to show under his red and white butcher's apron.

'I'm fine, William, just fine. Listen, I want to have a quick word with you if I can?'

He looked faintly surprised, followed by the worried expression that everyone adopts whenever the police want a word. 'It's nothing you've done,' Frankie reassured him, seeing the frown lift as quickly as it had arrived. 'You were an orphan, weren't you?'

She saw the guarded expression fall into place. She wasn't his enemy, she just needed to convince him of that fact.

'Look, I don't want to put you on the spot – and this is just something I'm following up. When you were first put into care, it was the old orphanage you went to, is that right?'

William's expression turned in a moment into one she recognised from school, the bullied boy's acceptance that whatever he did wouldn't stop the attacks, wouldn't prevent the words that often hurt more than the fists. 'What of it?' The words came sullenly, as if someone completely different had taken his place behind the counter.

Frankie hurried on, not wanting anyone else to enter the shop whilst they were alone together. 'I've heard that some abuse may have gone on at the orphanage, did you ever hear or see anything during your time there?'

He looked panicked, it was the only clue she could read. 'No. Nothing. I don't want to talk about it. It was fine, just, just... it was just hard. A hard life for a kid. I'm sorry, I really don't want to discuss those days. With anyone!'

He stared defiantly at her, the friendly welcome replaced with anger. Frankie couldn't understand what she'd done to upset him. 'I'm sorry, William, I didn't mean to cause any upset.

I was genuinely just trying to understand what life was like there, whether there was any truth in what I've heard.'

'Who's been speaking to you?'

'Let's just say I've heard rumours from a few people, William.'

'How many people?'

Frankie wondered where this cross-examination was going. 'I'm not at liberty to tell you. I'm just trying to find out the truth, William – whether anything went on at that orphanage. Can you help me?'

'No. I'm not saying anything.'

A woman came into the shop. 'Morning, madam.' William's voice lost the anger as he greeted the customer with obvious relief. 'If there's nothing else?' He directed this at Frankie, her cue to leave.

'No. That's all. Thank you for your help, William, we'll be in touch.'

She sat back in the patrol car, William's reaction churning in her mind. Something had happened to him at the orphanage, of that she had no doubt. His response had her worried, though; he was fearful of something or someone. What would worry a large man in the prime of his life? Was it a secret he carried inside him or was there a threat hanging over him? Far from putting the orphanage story to bed as she had hoped, he'd just made it become much more real. She consulted the list again. There were a couple of names she recognised. She remembered assemblies where she and the other pupils had stood with heads bowed at the early passing of children not much younger than themselves.

Corstorphine was not going to like this, another line of investigation to add to the existing murders, but what if these children died because of something that had happened to them at the orphanage – what if they were murdered as well?

She made her way back to the police station, still deep in thought as she entered the office.

'How did you get on?' Corstorphine had been standing so motionless in front of the crazy wall that she hadn't realised he was there.

'Oh, fine, sir.' She handed over the sheet with the orphans' names – they'd been countersigned by some of the sisters. 'Managed to talk the council into giving me a list of the kids that were resident at the orphanage at the time social services took them over.'

Corstorphine studied the list with interest. 'Good work, Frankie. Do you know any of them?'

'That's it, sir. Almost the first name on the sheet, William Booth. We were at school together. I've just been to see him; he owns the butcher's in the high street.'

'Booth the Butcher's?'

'Yes, sir.'

'Now that is interesting.'

Frankie couldn't see why the name was of interest to Corstorphine. 'I asked him about his time at the orphanage, sir, he wasn't wanting to talk about it.'

'Go on.'

'Well, sir, he seemed defensive, and I think he was frightened of someone or something. He looked as if he'd seen a ghost when I mentioned it.'

Corstorphine looked down at the list of names again. 'Do any of the others still live here?'

Frankie drew a breath. He wasn't going to appreciate another curveball thrown his way, but what else could she do? 'There are at least three names belonging to children that died whilst I was at school. I never knew them personally, but I remember their names from assembly. It's a big deal when a kid dies, especially if they're a similar age to you. Brings mortality into focus at an early age.'

'And you think there may be something suspicious about these children's deaths, something connected to the orphanage and our murders?'

'Yes, sir.' She felt the relief in getting it out so easily. He'd made the link himself.

'You could be right.' Corstorphine paused and sent her an inquiring glance as if deciding whether to say more. It seemed he decided Frankie could be trusted, as he went on to say, 'I had a visit from our local member of the House of Lords a little while ago.'

'Oh God, not that idiot Lagan?'

'Yes, precisely. He had a message from the ACC. He wants us to stop looking into June Stevens' death, says it's a distraction when we should be concentrating our efforts on the two recent murders.'

'That sounds awfully fluent of him, sir.'

Corstorphine smiled. Sometimes, Frankie reminded him of his wife. 'Why do you think he sent Lagan over to pass on that message?' He examined Frankie keenly from under an upturned eyebrow.

'Probably because he didn't want anything traced back to him if something went pear-shaped, sir.'

'Exactly. More to the point, what does anyone have to fear from us looking at an old case that's been closed for twenty years?'

'I see what you mean, sir. You think there may be someone in authority who may not want us prying too deeply into this?'

'That's precisely what I mean. Unfortunately, that is going to make our job even more difficult than it already is. We've got the next edition of *The Courier* coming out tomorrow, the ACC on our backs and any time now we can expect TV cameras in town.'

'Shall I start working through this list then, sir?'

Corstorphine nodded. 'But before that, I've a broken clockwork mechanism you may want to give your clockmaker to see if it can be patched together somehow. You'd better give him a few snaps of the tree just to help him along – just don't show him anything with Oscar's corpse on it!'

'Sir.' Frankie gathered the plastic evidence bags, a couple of sanitised photographs which she'd cropped with the office scissors and set off for the clockmaker's.

TWENTY-SIX

Corstorphine started to add another layer of complexity to a crazy wall that was soon going to be too small for purpose. The butcher joined the gamekeeper as a potential suspect, characters that reminded him of some children's board game – though neither felt right to him. What if Frankie was right that the butcher William Booth was afraid of something or someone? Who could still exert control over him, prevent him from speaking out about his abuse?

There were plenty of instances when the floodgates opened after one person came out into the open, one person with the strength to face their own fears and name the abuser. There must be so many more instances when the case never comes to court, the evidence too weak, the accused too powerful. If the case didn't get past the Procurator Fiscal, then it was unlikely that former orphans like William would come forward, adding voice upon voice until sheer numbers alone ensured a case had to be prosecuted and brought into the public domain. Given that the ACC was already signalling he wanted this line of investigation closed down, with fairly weighty political support behind him, pursuing an investigation into the orphanage was going to be increasingly problematic.

Corstorphine sat at his desk, entered the Sisters of Holy Mercy into the police database and the reports started flooding in. They had not only run orphanages here in Scotland but had a number of orphanages and unmarried mothers' homes in Ireland – the so-called Magdalene Laundries where pregnant women, some of them just girls, worked in the laundry until ready to give birth. The babies were forcibly taken away, some sold, some just disappeared. This wouldn't be the first institution of theirs where children had been found buried in unmarked graves. The Order itself was subsumed back into the Catholic Church, with many of the nuns living a life of peaceful contemplation in Rome. Corstorphine read that the church refused to pay any damages to the women it had maltreated, hiding behind a wall of sanctimonious silence. Tracking these particular nuns down was going to be an impossible task. He made a start anyway: Sister Mary August 1992, not a lot to go on.

The arrival of the two constables alerted him to the passing hours. It was coming up four-thirty, time for the briefing. The trail for the nuns had gone stone cold. The names provided on the council document – Sister Mary, Sister Angeline and all the others – they weren't even the nuns' real names. It struck him this was as good a way of running a secret criminal operation as any he'd seen, and whenever it looked as if they were about to be exposed, they hid under the sheltering skirts of the papal palace in Rome.

Frankie entered the office, looking over at him and tilting her head at the clock. It had been a long day, they all wanted to get away.

'Right, let's have your reports. Bill, any luck in tracking down anyone who knows anything about the orphanage?'

'Sorry, sir. Nobody I spoke to claimed to have had any

involvement. The local bakery was still miffed that they never used them for bread deliveries, all their food came from some Glasgow warehouse that the Order owned. The children that used to go to the orphanage, none of them stayed in the town – with the exception of William Booth the butcher. No luck in finding where they went either.'

'OK. Thanks, Bill. Lamb, what have you got?'

'Same really, sir. I did get a few people telling me they'd always had their suspicions about the place.'

'In what way?'

'Well, thought there might have been funny goings-on with the children, sir.'

'Yet nobody thought fit to bring this to our attention?'

'No, sir.'

Corstorphine sighed heavily, the rumours would be flying through the town when the latest edition of *The Courier* hit the streets tomorrow.

'What about you, Frankie? Anything we can use?'

'I saw the clockmaker, sir. He's taken the gears and seemed keen to make a start in putting them together. Asked me to come back in a day or two when he should have an idea of what the clockwork mechanism was intended to do.'

'What about the list of children, made any progress there?'

'Drawn a blank so far. It's as if they've gone off-grid, certainly no sign of them on police records.'

'OK, thanks everyone. So this is where we are. The minister is suspected of abusing Oscar as a young child, and he was known to have visited the orphanage on a regular basis. We can assume the same killer, or killers, were involved at each scene.'

He used a laser pointer to indicate names on the board. 'In terms of suspects, we have Oscar's girlfriend Margo McDonald – not a likely suspect in my view; the gamekeeper John Ackerman – no connection as yet to the minister; and William Booth – he had a connection to Oscar and the orphanage but nothing tying him to the minister yet. He also has ready access to animal bones. We haven't had any DNA evidence returned from the two murder sites, so this is going to have to be done by good, steady police work. I know you're all tired, it's been a busy day. Make sure you all get a good rest because tomorrow we have to make some headway in case this lunatic decides to target someone else.'

TWENTY-SEVEN

It was Wednesday morning. Margo scanned the track as her taxi made slow and bouncy progress towards the main road, anxious that the laird's Land Rover would make an appearance. He hadn't come back to the cottage yesterday, so chances were that he'd be wanting to have another search for something – and that something, she was fairly certain, was hidden in the bag on her lap.

'I'm going to have to charge you extra for my bloody suspension.' The driver swerved to avoid another pothole, cursing the state of the track for the umpteenth time.

'You're getting paid cash, take it or leave it,' Margo replied. 'Plenty of other Uber drivers out there.'

He exchanged an unfriendly look with her, then realised that she could mark him down on the app. 'OK, OK, keep... I'll keep to the track.'

It was a clumsy attempt to correct what she knew he was about to say. Being Oscar's girlfriend had its upsides and downsides. The upside was that nobody would dare touch her, not unless they reckoned they could take him on. The downside was now that he was dead, her reputation marked her out as little better than trash.

All the more reason to leave this godforsaken town and start afresh somewhere else, but first she needed more money.

The car dropped her outside the supermarket, leaving her standing on the pavement with a shopping bag as if she was on a weekly shop. She didn't disabuse the taxi driver of this notion, preferring to keep her *Courier* visits as private as possible.

'Hello, Margo, lovely to see you!'

It was the same French woman she'd seen on Monday and come to think of it, there were precious few other people in the *Courier* offices that she'd seen.

'Can I get you a tea or coffee?'

'No, thanks.' Margo cut straight to the chase, 'I've something you may be interested in paying me for.'

Two delicately shaped eyebrows danced upwards in surprise. 'Something we may want to buy? What do you have?' The interest was evident in her voice, and the reporter leaned forward slightly to get a better view of the shopping bag nestling on Margo's lap.

'I'll show you, but I want real money for this – not just a few hundred pounds.'

In the distance, a telephone rang two or three times before an invisible voice answered. So there must be some other people working here, Margo thought. The reporter stood up, closing the door on an empty corridor.

'Show me what you have, and I'll see what it's worth.'

Margo extricated the reporter's notebook from her bag, laying it down on the table so that June Stevens' name was visible on the cover. She could see the hunger in the reporter's eyes as her hands reached forward; Margo placed her own hand down hard on top. 'I want to know what it's worth before you look at it.'

The reporter reappraised Margo, seeing something she had missed on their previous encounter.

'I can't make you an offer on a notebook without seeing what's inside. Let me see the last page she wrote, and we'll see if there's anything worth buying or not.'

Margo hesitated. If she let the reporter read whatever the scribbles meant on the final page, she might get what she needed without paying for it – then again, why should she pay her anything on the basis of a closed notebook? She took the notebook, opening it to the last written page and held it up for the reporter to read. The reporter's eyes flew back and forth across the page without expression. Margo waited until her eyes stopped moving, and snapped the notebook shut.

'Well?'

A smile teased the corners of the reporter's mouth, and Margo knew she'd get something for her trouble.

'I have to talk to my manager. Wait here and we will see what, if anything, the paper is willing to pay.'

Margo sat in the empty office, straining to hear any conversation taking place outside. Apart from the occasional telephone ringing and printer churning out sheets of paper, the offices were quiet. Eventually, the reporter returned, followed by a short rotund man who wheezed as he lowered himself into the only other chair.

'Hello, Margo. I'm Jack Hammond, the editor of this illustrious newspaper and the one who holds the purse strings. Strings to a purse that is very light if you get my meaning.'

Margo knew horse trading when she heard it.

'I can always take it elsewhere. The nationals have deep pockets.' She was completely bluffing, not knowing what the reporter might have gleaned from the scribbles she'd seen.

'We can offer you one thousand pounds, that's all.'

Margo couldn't keep the surprise off her face. All that money for some old notebook? She felt as if she'd struck gold. 'It's worth more than that,' she responded quickly, hoping the surprise on her face implied she'd just been made an insulting offer.

The editor looked at her with pity. 'It's all you're going to be offered. You do realise this notebook is the property of *The Courier*? Instead of offering you money for it, I should by rights be calling the police to let them know you are in possession of stolen property.'

'You're bluffing!'

He stood up, extracting his portly frame out of the seat with some difficulty. 'Good day.'

'No, I'll take it!' Margo almost shouted at him, worried that she'd be left with nothing.

The editor didn't bother turning around. 'Pay her cash and bring me June's notebook.'

Margo left *The Courier*'s offices with more crisp notes filling her purse. Her feet felt as if they were attached to springs as she entered the supermarket, heading for the wine section to celebrate the change in her fortunes. A glance at *The Courier* front page brought her back to earth with a bump – *Child Abuse at the Orphanage* screamed the headlines, and underneath in smaller writing, *alleges Margo McDonald in a* Courier *exclusive*.

She added the newspaper to her shopping bag, folding it so the front cover was obscured from view. 'Shit!' The expletive hissed from between her tightly clenched jaw. When the reporter had listened to her story on Monday, it had felt so good just to have someone to talk to, someone who nodded at the right times, made sympathetic noises. For the first time in her life, Margo had imagined that someone actually gave a damn about her. Now she'd seen the headlines, the truth hit her as hard as one of Oscar's blows – she was just being used and abused again. Worse than that, her story was plastered across the newspaper and would be read by everyone in the town, everyone that knew her now had another window into her miserable life.

Back outside on to the pavement, she was acutely aware of passers-by looking at her, taking turns to point her out. Margo could imagine the conversations taking place around her in hushed tones. 'That's Oscar's whore, that's the woman who's made all those dreadful allegations about poor Reverend Simon McLean, child abuse, lies, bitch, whore.'

She summoned an Uber, relieved to see someone she didn't know in the driving seat and sat in the back, anxious not to have to speak on the journey home. For the moment, Margo just wanted to sit alone with her thoughts. The road turned into rough track and the scenery grew as bleak as her mood. The car pulled into the tight turning circle in front of the cottage – at least the laird's vehicle was still nowhere to be seen.

Margo shut and locked the cottage door behind her in an effort to close out a world that had turned colder and more hateful than it had been when she had first awoken. She sat in the small living room, pouring out a generous glass of wine without any regard to the foetus developing in her womb and drank the liquid in large gulps. It was just as well Oscar was dead; he'd never have wanted that story to come out about his abuse as a child. He'd have killed her rather than let her tell anyone, much less let a newspaper spread the story far and wide. Christ, what if the nationals did take the story up? Margo sat, undecided whether she could face any more news reports, or whether she could make more money from selling her story to the big newspapers.

'Shit!' The word escaped from Margo's mouth as she considered that the reporter's notebook might have been worth more to one of the nationals. Too late now, at least there was a thousand pounds in her purse to add to the money hidden in the pillowcase. Another full glass of wine was in her hands without any memory of her pouring it. She drank it quickly.

What to do now? There were still the photographs. Initially, she had considered them worthless and was on the point of binning them when caution had stayed her hand. If *The Courier* was willing to pay a thousand quid for the old notebook, what might she be offered for the photographs, complete with the skull and crossbones markings?

Margo put down the wineglass, running upstairs to gather the notes stuffed inside her pillowcase and added them to the money she'd received from the reporter. One by one the notes were counted until she had £4600 forming miniature paper skyscrapers on the table next to her wine. She stared at the money, scarcely able to believe how much was there, one hand holding the wineglass and the other cradling her womb. The last of the wine slipped down her throat, and she automatically reached for the bottle, then paused. The wine wouldn't be good for the bairn. An internal struggle occurred, Margo merely an onlooker, the need for drink to deaden the pain of her existence versus the raw emotion of a mother protecting her young. The mother won, and Margo screwed the cap back on a half-empty bottle wondering what had just happened.

The money was a substantial amount, more than enough for her to move and rent somewhere new – but it wouldn't hurt to have some more. *Wait and see what they write in tomorrow's paper*, Margo advised herself. If they mentioned the children, then they'd pay for the photographs – and the graveyard symbols on the back meant something to someone.

She looked out of the cottage window, seeing the empty track winding down the glen with nothing but the shadows of clouds chasing along the flanks of the hills for movement. For the moment, the money and photographs better be hidden away – just in case the laird came back.

TWENTY-EIGHT

Frankie received the first call from a previous resident of the orphanage at 9:41. A hesitant voice close to tears explained how he'd been regularly abused by the minister, that there were other people he could name, but he wanted protection. When she hesitated, the line went dead. The number was unavailable when she tried calling back.

She sat back in her seat, aware of the two constables behind her staring listlessly at their screens. What did they even do all day?

'Have you had any luck with the names on the list?' Frankie had provided copies of the list of children to the two constables in an effort to move the investigation forward. She was juggling so many balls in the air at once she felt she should have joined a circus. The Fiscal was proving a difficult man to reach, and she needed his help to access the reports dating back over twenty years.

'Nothing yet, Frankie.' Lamb at last was starting to take this more seriously. 'Apart from another five of them who are never recorded as having left.'

'Are you sure? The council only had records of three children dying in care.'

'Plain as day. They're all listed in the orphanage records within a six-year period, the last one joined in the same year it closed, but there's no paperwork to say they ever left.'

'That makes eight possible deaths, plus a girl that went missing and there's next to no bloody record of her disappearance.' Frankie shared Corstorphine's frustration. It seemed that every clue they followed turned into a dead end or was so poorly documented they couldn't hope to pursue it any further. She didn't hold out much hope that any postmortem reports they turned up would show anything out of the ordinary. 'Good work, Phil, send their details to me. It could just be shoddy recording. A lot of the paperwork has gone missing.'

'I've got one here,' Bill McAdam interjected. 'Simon Battle. Turned up on the VALCRI search. He's banged up in Barlinnie. GBH.'

'Sure he's one of our boys, Bill?'

'No doubt about it, unless he shares a NI number with another Simon Battle.'

'Good. I'll apply to see him, see if at least we can get one person to tell us what went on in that place.'

Her phone rang again, the calls coming ever more frequently as news started to spread further afield. Frankie recognised the French accent immediately and responded before she could be asked for any leads. 'Good morning, Josephine, no, I don't have any information for you.'

'Actually, Frankie, I called to offer you information.'

'What have you got?' Her voice was resigned, so far the newspaper was leading them by the nose with all the major leads coming straight off the pages of *The Courier*.

'I had another visit from Margo this morning.'

Oh God, Frankie thought. *We need to talk to her before she goes and blethers to the paper again.* She waited for whatever was coming next.

'She handed over June Stevens' notebook.'

'What was she doing with that?'

'I didn't ask. But it's what is written inside in shorthand that I think you'll find of more interest.'

'I'm listening!' Frankie said more brusquely than she should have.

'She was investigating child abuse at the orphanage and somehow knew Oscar was a victim. She'd arranged to meet him in the glen by the tree, why on her own I have no idea. Oscar was, as far as her notebook says, the last person to have seen her alive.'

They both knew what this signified: the last person to have met a murder victim was always the first in the frame.

'There's more. She had a list of names that she believed were involved in the abuse, some of them were nuns who ran the orphanage, but there are a couple of names you may find more interesting?'

'I don't have time for games, who are they?'

'The recently deceased minister, but you have him already. You may like to question the laird, he features prominently in her notes as an abuser, she also listed the retired DI Brian Rankin and another name that I'd rather not mention over the phone.'

'Why are you telling me this?' Frankie's suspicion was growing; these weren't juicy morsels you'd freely hand out if there wasn't a price to pay.

'Quite simply, you need to prove the allegations before we can print them.'

'Hasn't stopped you so far,' Frankie retorted.

'Ah, but Frankie, these have been Margo's allegations, recorded and signed by her. If they were untruthful, we merely suffer a slap on the wrist. Without the evidence our reporter was pursuing, we'd face a massive libel action or even imprisonment if we published allegations of this nature without corroboration. You may also like to wonder whether her investigation was so sensitive that she was killed, and the murder hushed up by your police department.'

Frankie thought rapidly. If the reporter's case was reopened as Corstorphine wanted, then the notebook, and its location for the last twenty years, would become key evidence. 'That item should be handed in to the police, I'll be with you in twenty minutes.'

'Her reporter's notebook and all it contains remain the property of *The Courier*. I'll share some of what she wrote down, but if you want to take the notebook as evidence, you'll have to apply for a warrant – and to do that, you have to officially reopen the investigation into June's death.'

Frankie stared at her screen when the call ended, eyes unfocussed as the enormity of what she'd just been told hit home. Where was bloody Corstorphine when she needed him? 'Anyone know where the DI has gone?'

'He left twenty minutes ago, said he wanted to go over a few things with Brian Rankin,' Bill McAdam advised.

This was so far above her pay grade. She grabbed her car keys and broke out an evidence bag, just in case.

'Off to *The Courier*,' she called to the two bobbies and keyed in Corstorphine's mobile number as she headed out again. 'Come on, pick up!' The phone was ringing on and on before finally switching to voicemail. She terminated the call, stabbing at her phone in frustration. 'Why don't you pick up?'

* * *

Corstorphine had just parked outside the old DI's neat bungalow, reaching into his jacket pocket on the back seat to retrieve his mobile. Missed call from Frankie. 'It can wait,' he muttered to himself. 'First, I need some answers.'

Brian Rankin came out of his garden gate even as Corstorphine opened the car door. 'Brian, can I have a word, in private?'

The old DI's head shot up in surprise. 'James! I didn't see you there, are you trying to give me a heart attack?'

'I hope not,' Corstorphine countered. 'Where are you going, can I give you a lift?'

'I'm just off to the newsagent's, been following the double murder investigation. You can't take the detective out of me that easily!'

Corstorphine felt the implied rebuke that Brian had to buy the paper because his old colleagues no longer involved him in any of their cases. 'I'll run you there, hop in.'

He held the passenger door open for the retired inspector to climb in. 'I wanted to talk to you about this double murder case anyway.'

'Of course, anything I can do to help.'

Corstorphine noticed the guarded look that the old detective sent his way. 'Have you been talking to the ACC, asking him to warn me off looking into the June Stevens hanging case?' He decided that going in straight for the kill would be the optimum approach.

'The assistant chief constable? Why would I have anything to do with someone that senior? I'm retired, James, old and retired and put out to pasture. No, I don't know who may be responsible for interfering in your work, but it's nothing to do with me!'

Corstorphine's eyebrow rose a few millimetres. Brian's voice sounded too outraged. A detective trying to fool another – good luck with that, Corstorphine thought.

'Brian, you're the only person I told about reopening the

Stevens case.' It helped to slip in the occasional white lie, keep them guessing what was fake and what was real.

Brian sat quietly as the car drove along a road of identical houses. Corstorphine tried another prod. 'I've talked to Hamish about the Stevens crime scene, he's adamant that there was nothing she could have used as a step under the tree when he found her. How do you suppose she managed to climb up into the noose, Brian?'

'Are you accusing me of something, James?' The old detective's voice was quiet, controlled.

'I'm just trying to get to the truth. Somehow that case is connected to these two recent murders. I don't think her death was a suicide, Brian, and I want to know why someone like the assistant chief constable wants to stop me looking into the reporter's suicide before I even get started.'

'Let me out here, James.'

Corstorphine pulled into the side of the road, watching his ex-boss intently as he struggled to release the safety belt and open the door. He was attempting to appear calm whilst desperately trying to escape Corstorphine's company. Finally freed of his buckle and out on the pavement, he stood facing him down. 'If you want to talk to me again, James, you'd better do it officially. Don't bother paying any more social calls.'

The door slammed, and the old detective walked towards the shops, back held straight despite the pain he was experiencing just two days ago.

Corstorphine watched him go, trying to work out if Brian was furious, frightened – or a mixture of the two. The short conversation had decided him: June Stevens' death was going to be re-examined in the light of recent evidence from the attending officer. It wasn't going to make him a popular man, especially having been given an unequivocal message from the ACC. It appeared increasingly likely that the reporter had been murdered twenty years ago, and could the same murderer be responsible for the deaths of Oscar and the minister? What motive could connect the three deaths after such a long time? If there was a link to historical child abuse, then the reporter's death didn't fit the narrative.

He drove back to the station, wondering whether his considering the old DI as an accessory to murder was justified, never mind the opprobrium he'd face questioning one of their own. As he saw it, there wasn't much choice – the woman's death twenty years ago had a connection with the two recent murders, the papal coins left at the scene of both crimes was too great a coincidence. It was as if the murderer was deliberately leaving a trail, pointing him towards the events of that day in 1997, opening up the historical child abuse at the orphanage to scrutiny. If that was the case, then the murderer must have suspected that June Stevens' death wasn't a suicide. Whoever it was had to be stopped before taking out their own brand of justice on anyone else; the last thing Corstorphine needed was a vigilante let loose to be judge, jury and executioner. Brian was the only lead he had at the moment; he really had no choice but to bring him in.

TWENTY-NINE

Frankie followed Josephine back into the same sparsely furnished newspaper office that had been the venue of their last meeting, pointedly taking out her notebook to record the conversation.

'Thank you for coming so quickly.' Josephine shot her a quick welcoming smile. 'I've transcribed the most pertinent pages of June's notebook into longhand, but for legal reasons I've been told I cannot pass them on without an official warrant. We have to protect our bottoms I think is the way you say it?'

'Close,' Frankie responded. 'We would say cover your arse.'

'Exactly.' Josephine beamed at her. 'The discovery of June's notebook and Margo's ability to produce it after such a long time is one question that concerns us at *The Courier*. Are you planning to investigate this?'

'Is this off the record?'

'If you want it to be,' Josephine countered.

'Then yes, Margo has apparently had access to a lot more information than she initially led us to believe. So yes, we shall be asking her in for questioning.'

'And will you be reopening the investigation into the death

of our reporter June Stevens? Will this be part of your investigation?'

'I can't answer for the DI who's leading the investigation, apart from saying – strictly off the record – that DI Corstorphine has expressed a desire to look into June Stevens' apparent suicide.'

Josephine nodded slowly; the word apparent was all she needed to know. 'Then you will be able to requisition June's notebook as part of your investigation.'

'That's what you want, isn't it? Us to reopen the case of June Stevens' suicide?'

'This was before my time, well before my time, Frankie, but my editor never believed she committed suicide. He also doesn't believe her daughter ran away from that orphanage.'

Frankie's interest was piqued. 'What does he believe happened?'

A smoker's voice answered from the open doorway. 'I believe she was murdered, and Oscar was the murderer.'

Frankie spun in her seat, startled by the man's voice. A short, bespectacled man who didn't look as if he'd ever seen the inside of a gym stood in the open doorway. He extended a hand which Frankie shook lightly. It was like holding onto a wet sponge.

'I'm Jack Hammond, editor of *The Courier*. Twenty years ago, I was the junior reporter here and worked alongside June. She was not suicidal, I can tell you that. She had a daughter she doted on and a lot to live for.'

'I'm Frankie...'

'I know who you are DC McKenzie. I know all about every member of our local police station, it's my job. Your job is to bring this out into the open so we can report it.'

'I'm sorry, what is it you want brought out?'

The editor wheezed with exasperation. 'The orphanage stayed under the radar all the time it was here, but there are people who knew what went on behind the walls and did nothing about it.' He held June's notebook up in the air, waving it to emphasise his words. 'June was onto them. She'd talked to a few of the children, and they opened up to her, told her things she didn't enjoy hearing. The nuns of Holy Mercy were involved of course, children were regularly given the strap for bed-wetting, locked in cold stone cells without food or warmth for minor transgressions. Then one of the children told June he was being sexually abused, described what was being done to him in such graphic detail that it had to be the truth.'

Frankie felt sick at hearing the editor's words.

'Did she tell you this?' Frankie asked, her notebook and pen completely forgotten. 'Why didn't the nuns report it?'

He grimaced. 'The nuns were complicit in it. Any children reporting such things were beaten so hard they didn't dare mention it again.' He reached into his jacket pocket and pulled out an inhaler, taking a deep breath before replacing it. The rattle in his throat began to abate.

'June suspected children died there, deaths that were never reported. And then of course the building was demolished, sold at a nice profit for the Catholic Church to a developer and any evidence of burial sites lost with it. Did she ever tell me what it was she was investigating? No, she never told me. Thought I was too young and innocent to hear about such depravity in our perfect little town. She gave me clues, though, clues I only realised after her death.' He lowered his head as if in shame. 'I might have been able to help her if she'd only trusted me. Her notebook, though, everything she knew is in here.'

'What is it you had to tell me in person, what is it you found in her notes?'

The editor and Josephine exchanged a knowing look. 'We've already told you that the minister and the laird are listed as paedophiles, two adults the children mentioned by name.'

'Yes, and DI Rankin, you mentioned him as well?' This was

directed towards Josephine, who had remained silent since the editor had entered the room.

'DI Rankin was not mentioned as a predator. He was a regular visitor to the orphanage, but June found nobody who claimed he had abused them in any way – she specifically mentions this in her notes.'

'Why did you give me his name then?' Frankie had to hold back her anger. 'If I'd been able to reach my boss earlier and pass on what you told me over the phone, he would have accused Brian Rankin of being a bloody paedophile!'

Josephine held up a hand to stop her. 'No, what June wrote in her notebook is that he's suspected of covering up the murder of three children that we know died at the orphanage. Three children that were either beaten or starved to death, or never given medical treatment. Then she mentions five children whose deaths were never even officially reported. Your inspector, for whatever reason, prevented what was going on at the orphanage from ever coming out. He's as guilty as those that abused the children, more so!'

Frankie sat quietly, trying to imagine the quiet old inspector as having any involvement in the events Josephine described. 'It doesn't sound like the Brian Rankin I know.' Her voice came quietly, doubtful. 'Why would he even do such a thing? It makes no sense.' She said the last words emphatically, deciding whatever was written in the reporter's notebook wasn't necessarily the truth.

'He did it because not only the laird was involved, but someone else who carried a lot more clout.'

'Who is it?' Frankie asked. 'Who can possibly be so important that you can't even mention his name over the phone?'

The editor looked steadily into Frankie's eyes, as if weighing how much she could be trusted. She passed whatever test he set. 'Lord Lagan,' he said softly.

Frankie stared at him in disbelief. 'Jesus!'

'It may as well be,' the editor replied. 'Imagine if we tried to report that a senior member of the House of Lords was engaged in lewd behaviour at a Catholic orphanage. The last high-profile person to be accused of child abuse only came to light long after he was dead – conveniently. Do you think this was because he was so clever at hiding what he'd been doing that none of his victims ever reported him to the authorities?'

He gesticulated, thrusting the notebook in Frankie's face to emphasise each point. 'He was a famous figure, renowned for his charity work – if the hospitals let on that they knew he was sexually interfering with patients, male, female, young, old... God, he didn't even care if they had a pulse! They'd lose millions of pounds of donations and then have potential damages to pay. Was he protected? Work it out for yourself.' He mopped his brow with a handkerchief. 'If a whisper of these allegations reaches the real power in this land, then you'll find the investigation is closed down before you've even started it. That's why we can't mention these names until you have a firm case against them.'

Frankie shook her head. 'This can't be right; did June Stevens have any evidence to support this allegation? We can't proceed on the basis of an old notebook which we can't even be sure that it did belong to her, much less put people like that in the frame.'

'This is how we should proceed.' The editor spoke quietly. 'First, we need to make copies of this notebook and place them where they can be easily accessed if we are threatened.'

Josephine joined the conversation. 'We would not be the first journalists to suffer an unexpected death because we were about to reveal an inconvenient truth. If killing us will not be able to stop the distribution of June's notebook, then that makes our lives a little bit safer.'

The editor nodded in agreement. 'Secondly, the police have to proceed very carefully. If you give away any hint that you know the full extent of the people involved in the abuse, then you'll be closed down – same as they did with your predecessor, DI Rankin.'

'You think he was leaned on?'

'Leaned on, threatened, told in no uncertain terms from on high to close any investigation down – yes, Frankie, and that is why you will meet resistance from your superiors if they know you're digging. You have to find the evidence, incontrovertible evidence, before your investigation gets closed down and you end up silenced somehow.' He took another puff of his inhaler. 'And I want justice for June – print what those bastards did to the children and put whoever we can behind bars.'

Frankie nodded in mute acceptance. A pair of random murders was developing into something that had the power to change all of their lives, for the worse. 'You're aware that the two recent murders are linked, do you have any idea who may be behind them?'

The editor and Josephine exchanged another of their mute glances. The editor answered. 'At first, we thought Oscar's death was a suicide, until we received information that the mechanism found in the tree was similar to the one found in the church.'

'How did you know about that?' Frankie couldn't help but interject.

Josephine smiled that same ingratiating smile that was beginning to grate on Frankie's nerves. 'We can't identify our sources.'

'Never mind about that!' The editor spoke quickly. 'Oscar and the minister, both killed apparently by the same person. We think that Oscar was hired as paid muscle to close down any potential leaks about the orphanage. It's possible that both of them were seen as witnesses and dealt with by some shadowy government agency.'

'No, I don't think so,' Frankie replied thoughtfully. 'I don't believe any professional assassin would rely on such complicated bone clockwork mechanisms to commit murder. No, this has the feel of someone who has a personal involvement, someone who lives locally and knows the daily routines of these people.' She looked at them both carefully before continuing. 'Someone who is out to avenge the death of June Stevens. Do you have any ideas who, apart from yourselves, may have such a link to June?'

Frankie left *The Courier* offices in a state of near panic. Far from providing another clue that would help them nail whoever was the murderer, the newspaper's staff had dropped a bombshell on the entire investigation. She had to get hold of Corstorphine before he began anything official into June's death. The editor was right in one regard: if the names in June Stevens' notebook were involved in child abuse and the ensuing cover-up, then the full weight of the British establishment would come falling down on them from a great height.

THIRTY

Frankie drove into the police station car park, relieved to see Corstorphine's car parked in its usual spot. She headed straight for his office, knocking smartly on the door. Something in her expression must have alerted him, as he beckoned her in immediately, shutting the door behind her.

'What is it, Frankie? Have we made any progress with identifying the murderer or a motive?'

Frankie calmed herself down, taking a couple of deep breaths as she composed her response. '*The Courier* called me, said Margo had handed in the dead reporter's notebook.'

Corstorphine's surprised expression said it all. 'After all these years. Where has she been hiding it?'

Frankie held up a hand to forestall him. 'There's more, sir. I've not read the notebook, it's in shorthand – but the reporter Josephine Sables has transcribed the contents.'

'We need that notebook as evidence!'

'Yes, sir, but they're only going to release it if we come up with a warrant, which means reopening the investigation into June Stevens' death. The point is, though, June Stevens had identified some of the suspected abusers in her investigation notes. They include Reverend Simon McLean, the minister of St Cuthbert's and the laird – sheriff Anthony McCallum.'

'He's identified as one of the abusers?' Corstorphine asked the question as if unable to believe his own ears.

'That's not all, sir. The editor thinks that Oscar was employed as hired muscle to keep the orphanage abuse under wraps, stop any word of it ever getting out. He thinks that's why Oscar killed June.'

'I think the editor should leave any detective work to people qualified to make such assumptions.'

'There's more, sir. The editor claims that DI Rankin was under orders to keep June's death a suicide, not investigate it fully. The notebook goes on to allege that there were more child deaths than the three that were officially recorded. *The Courier* reckons that five bodies were buried in the grounds and then covered up by the building development works after the orphanage was demolished.'

Corstorphine sat silently as he processed the information. 'We can't have the laird in for questioning, not on the basis of such an unreliable source as a dead reporter's notebook – if that is even her notebook.'

'Sir, I don't think we can do anything officially at the moment.'

'Why on earth not, Frankie?' Corstorphine's irritated voice almost snapped back at her.

'Because, sir, there's one other thing I've not told you.'

'Well, get on with it, we don't have time to play games.'

Corstorphine looked genuinely surprised as Frankie bent her head towards his ear to whisper Lord Lagan's name. His shocked reaction was proof enough that he'd heard her correctly.

'There's no way...'

'I didn't think so either, sir, until I started wondering how such a cover-up could have been made to happen.'

Their eyes met.

'OK, Frankie, this is how we are going to play it. We will need real evidence, not the musings of a long-dead reporter; otherwise, we stand a very good chance of being removed from not only this case but the force altogether. We have to find the children who were at that orphanage, we need them to come clean over what they knew.'

'I've already seen one person, the uncommunicative William Booth.'

'You think someone's got to him?'

'Not sure, sir. If it was Oscar, then he won't be worrying him now.'

'We can have another attempt, maybe I'll speak to him this time. Anyone else?'

'Bill tracked another child down through his NI number, Simon Battle – presently banged up in Barlinnie for GBH.'

'Good. He's not going anywhere, let's have a word with him as well, eh?'

'What about investigating June's death, sir?'

Corstorphine stared out of the window, apparently seeking inspiration in the car park.

Frankie waited patiently for a response.

'We'd better not proceed in any official way, Frankie. I've had my orders and if there's any truth in that notebook, then starting an investigation would be a red rag to a bull. What do you make of the reporters at *The Courier*?'

'I think they're fairly straight, sir, they've helped our investigation along by passing on what Margo told them.'

Corstorphine stroked his chin before responding. 'OK, we may be able to work with them. Let the reporters do some of the dirty work without anyone knowing we're working together.'

He reached for his car keys, suddenly decisive. 'Right. I'm going to pay a social call on the laird, just to sound him out. You arrange for William Booth to come in at his earliest convenience for a chat. If he can be tied to the supply of animal bones, then he may have more than a coincidental connection to the murders – and he'd have a motive for both those deaths. I want you to organise a visit to Barlinnie as well, let's try for first thing tomorrow, eh? See what Mr Battle has to say about his time at the orphanage.'

Frankie asked the constables whether they'd been able to track down any more of the orphans, but no luck so far. Whatever the reason, the children who'd been to that orphanage were proving particularly elusive to find. She looked at the crazy wall. William Booth and John Ackerman shared space with Margo McDonald as 'persons of interest'. How was Corstorphine going to handle the laird, without insinuating that he had been accused of child abuse? It was lunchtime, as good a time as any to see what the old clockmaker had made of the pile of bone fragments she'd dumped on him yesterday.

Frankie pushed open the door to the clockworker's shop, ears tensed against the urgent clanging of the bell, and waited for the owner to make an appearance. In detective work, there were lines of enquiry that had all the makings of a rich lode – a seam of clues and evidence that if mined efficiently provided all you needed to build a substantial case for the prosecution. The converse was also true, some seams might look promising and a disproportionate amount of energy expended before the realisation dawned that you had a heap of fool's gold in front of you. This seam didn't even live up to the expectation of fool's gold.

The old clockmaker appeared, pebble glasses perched on the end of his nose. He reminded Frankie of Pinocchio's cartoon father, Geppetto. She was about to start speaking loudly and clearly when he turned smartly on his heel and disappeared back into the depths of the shop, returning again with an elaborate mechanism suspended in a framework of old meccano metalwork. He wordlessly attached a small weight to a wire and started spinning a metal disc in the middle of the apparatus. The clockwork came alive, bone gears meshing together and moving in an almost silent mechanical ballet.

'There you are, my dear,' the old man announced. 'It really is a quite accomplished work, if I say so myself. I've had to improvise, of course; a lot of the structure wasn't with the parts you provided.'

'What does it do?' Frankie asked, her attention completely absorbed by the industrious apparatus standing on the counter in front of her.

'Well, I don't have all the parts, so I'd have to guess, and if I had to guess, I would say that it is a timing mechanism, designed to operate this lever after a period of approximately one week from setting it.' His heavily wrinkled finger pointed at a piece of bone that jutted out of the mechanism. 'It may have been holding this in the air.' He bent down to retrieve the bone harpoon that they'd first spotted on the track under the tree.

'Why would someone go to so much trouble to make a harpoon fall out of a tree? It doesn't make sense.'

'I read in the paper that the young gamekeeper was killed by a snare?'

'That's right.'

The old man peered at her through his glasses, eyes magnified alarmingly. 'Well then, that bone could have pulled the snare down into place, ready to catch the young chap unawares.'

Frankie looked at him with surprise; even the most unlikely line of enquiry could sometimes produce results. 'Thank you. Thank you,' she repeated. 'A week, you reckon, for this to run its course?'

'I'd say so. Course, I'd really have needed to see the whole thing before it was smashed but judging by the weight of the rabbit, the approximate length of the drop and this drive gear, it's the best I could extrapolate. The rabbit acted as the weight you see, in this case a dead weight.'

The dead rabbit returned in her memory, its furry face twisted in agony. She quickly dismissed the vision so she could concentrate on his explanation.

'The wire would have been wrapped around this drum, which is itself part of the main wheel. Then the teeth here on the main wheel engaged with this centre wheel, which typically drives the hour hand in a clock. These other gears form part of the escapement mechanism, although in this design the horologist has opted for the more modern balance wheel rather than a pendulum – most likely because the pendulum ideally needs to be encased for protection. You didn't find a metal disc anywhere near the tree, did you?'

'We found a coin. Is it important?'

The clockmaker adopted a pleased expression. 'I thought so, something had to act as a balance wheel.'

Frankie felt that she was getting out of her depth. 'What's a balance wheel?'

'It's a gearless disk, usually of metal that oscillates under the applied drive from the clock mechanism. There would have been a small, coiled spring wire attached to the coin – you should see a weld if you look at it under a microscope – that acts to limit the rotational travel in each direction, pulling it clockwise, then anticlockwise in a predictably timed manner. If I'm correct, you'll see a small hole drilled through the middle of the coin, this is where the rest of the mechanism was attached.' The clockmaker was getting into his stride. 'This was the most difficult part to repair, so many small components with some of them still missing. You should have called me in to search the site, I'd know what I was looking for!'

'Well, I'm sorry. If we'd known someone had left a handmade clockwork mechanism attached to the snare, we'd have obviously called you out first.'

The clockmaker didn't understand sarcasm. 'You weren't to know. Shame though, it really is a most accomplished design. Such artistry.'

Frankie decided to get the conversation back on track. 'Do you know anyone who could construct such a device?'

He peered even more closely at the re-assembled mechanism as if it might have been able to show him something previously hidden from sight. 'No. There's nobody I know who could design something like this and carve it out of bone. The trouble is bone splinters so easily, you have to understand what you're dealing with. It becomes even more difficult with older bones; they fracture if you carve without care. No, nobody in this country is capable I'd say.'

'OK. Thanks anyway. Is there some way I can transport this – we may have to use it as evidence.'

'I'll get you a box and some packing material. You'll have to be gentle with it, it's just on a temporary jig.'

He packed the clockwork into a box, filled with bubble wrap and sealed it with tape. 'That should do you for now.'

Frankie was leaving when a thought occurred to her. 'You said nobody in this country could have built it. Is there someone you know about who doesn't live here?'

'France. There used to be a clockmaker in Toulouse called Henri Dupont. He made some unique clockwork mechanisms out of bone. It was something of a speciality for his workshop, although his designs were too macabre for most people's taste.' He paused as Frankie struggled with the box and her notebook, laboriously writing down the name. 'He died five years ago, such a shame to see such an innovative clock artisan go. Still – time and tide.'

THIRTY-ONE

Corstorphine drove the police Land Rover into the glen, turning off at the fork where the metalled road surface led all the way to the laird's big house. The style was Victorian gothic, mock battlements adorned the roof and twin circular towers enhanced the castle-like look of the place. He drove straight in through the open tall wrought-iron gates into the courtyard, parking on loose gravel in front of a substantial double wooden door.

It had been at least a year since he'd last been here, overseeing a security check for the insurers as well as the more nervous types in the judiciary administration. A quick glance upwards reassured him that the security cameras were still in place, nestling improbably beside stone gryphons and lions the original architect had specified as decorative touches. The doorbell consisted of a metal handle, attached to a length of cable that rang the bell in what Corstorphine supposed would originally have been the butler's room. He gave it a pull, and a faint clanging could be heard jangling from the centre of the house.

Whilst he waited for the laird to make an appearance, he wondered why anyone would want to live in such an enormous old house in the middle of a deserted estate. Back in its heyday, there would have been ten, twenty staff employed at the house. The butler, chef, gardeners, serving maids – enough to fill a small village. Now there was just the laird, and the occasional cleaner. Used as Corstorphine was to being on his own, it wasn't something he would ever have actively sought for himself.

He waited a few more minutes without any response, not unduly surprising as there were no other vehicles to be seen. There hadn't been an answer to the landline number either, and the answering machine hadn't worked. Corstorphine decided to take the opportunity to have a look around, he could always claim he was undertaking another security check if the laird reviewed the CCTV footage to find him peering through the windows. There was nothing of any note to be seen at the front, but around the side a small window had been smashed and the frame lay open. Senses suddenly alert, Corstorphine checked his mobile for a signal – unsurprisingly none. He keyed the radio. 'Whisky tango, this is Sierra one-four, are you receiving, over?' A burst of static was his only reply.

'Bloody hills!' One of the disadvantages of living in one of the more scenic and wild areas of Scotland was that radio transmissions were unreliable at best, especially when hemmed in on all sides by mountain-sized chunks of granite. He returned to the car, putting on his latex gloves, hi-vis jacket and belt complete with the tools of his trade – torch, cuffs, pepper spray and truncheon. If whoever had entered the house through the window was still there, then he'd just alerted them by ringing the doorbell. There was nothing else for it but to climb in, a feat more easily visualised than accomplished – especially with all the equipment hanging from his waist. After a short struggle, Corstorphine stood in a cloakroom, the door wide open giving a clear view of the empty hall. He shouted into the empty space. 'Police! There's nowhere to hide, so you may as well come out.'

He listened – nothing but the sound of an empty building. 'Sod it,' Corstorphine advised himself quietly, 'I'll have to search the bloody place.' At the back of his mind was the thought that this gave him the opportunity to have a good poke around into the laird's life, unless whoever had broken into the house was still there. Moving as quietly as he could, Corstorphine explored the rooms on the ground floor, stopping when he noticed drops of blood on the study door handle. Easing the door open without touching the handle, he cautiously peered inside. Nobody there, although there were signs that someone had been rifling through the desk drawers – papers littered the floor. He spotted the landline phone; now he could call in reinforcements.

'Hamish, it's James here.' Corstorphine forestalled the desk sergeant's lugubrious announcement to advise the caller they'd reached the police station. 'Are Frankie and the constables there?'

There was a short pause where Corstorphine could envisage the sergeant walking into the office to perform a headcount. 'DC McKenzie has just arrived, sir, and PC Lamb is at his desk.'

'Tell them to join me at the laird's house in Glen Mhor and bring the forensics kit. There's been a break-in and the laird is nowhere to be seen.' He replaced the receiver without waiting for an acknowledgement, the unwelcome thought that the laird's disappearance was connected to the two recent murders running through his mind.

The boot room beside the kitchen held two large empty dog baskets. The dogs would have put up a fight if someone had broken in, Corstorphine thought, perhaps the laird was out when it happened?

Suddenly, berating himself for being slow on the uptake, he headed for the cupboard which he knew contained the CCTV recorder – thankfully, it was still running. He played it back, looking for signs of an intruder. Nothing for today, the house seemed deserted and the laird's Land Rover didn't make a showing on the drive camera. Operating the rewind control until the cameras showed Tuesday morning, he played it at fast-forward. Again nothing, no cars, no people. With a mounting sense of dread, Corstorphine wound the recorder back to Monday.

At last, there was some normal activity to be seen, the dogs and laird rushing around as the speeded-up review accelerated through the day, until they left in the Land Rover at 07:13 Monday morning. The footage kept running until it finally picked up the intruder at 16:15. Corstorphine hit the pause button. A familiar face was clearly visible in profile – John Ackerman, the gamekeeper they'd interviewed that same day. He sped through the recording until another camera caught him leaving twenty minutes later, something bulky showing under his waxed jacket.

Corstorphine looked through the papers scattered on the study floor whilst he waited for the rest of the team to make it on-site. There was nothing unusual, nothing incriminating. On an impulse, he phoned the Sheriff Court in Inverness, checking when the laird was next expected to be there. Thursday morning, came the disinterested response.

He started to relax, letting the sense of urgency that had overtaken him dissipate. The laird had probably gone off somewhere for a few days, taken his dogs with him. It was likely that John Ackerman took advantage of seeing the house deserted to get his own back, steal some of the family silver. Stupid bugger never even saw the security cameras, Corstorphine thought to himself. Strange the alarm didn't go off. With that thought uppermost in his mind, he checked the alarm system and the worry returned – it hadn't been set. That could only mean that the laird had been expecting to be out for a few hours or had forgotten to set the alarm.

A blue strobe flashing through the downstairs windows attracted his attention and he opened the front door to greet Frankie and PC Lamb. 'There's been a break-in. He got in by breaking the ground-floor window around the side. We need to dust the glass and frame for prints, although the silly bastard shows up on the CCTV.'

'Anyone we know, sir?' Frankie's question was straight to the point as always.

'Our friend John Ackerman looks like he's made off with something that he can readily exchange for cash. We'll pick him up once we're done here. There's also some blood on the study door handle, get a swab for DNA and remember to photograph everything.' He turned his attention to the young PC. 'Lamb, have a look around outside, see if there's any sign of a struggle, anything out of the ordinary.'

PC Lamb turned neatly on his heel. 'Sir! Right away, sir.'

'And Lamb.' Corstorphine called to the departing constable's back. 'See if you can identify another set of tyre tracks outside the wall. Ackerman didn't walk here, but his vehicle doesn't show up on the camera covering the courtyard, looks like he parked outside the wall somewhere.'

'You think there's been some dodgy business with the laird, sir?' Frankie asked as she carefully collected the blood sample off the study door handle.

'I don't think so. Ackerman may be stupid, but he's not going to kidnap a sheriff. No, I expect he's taken himself off for a few days somewhere. He's expected in court tomorrow morning, I think we're best to wait until then before going all out on a missing person search.'

'What about Margo, we should ask her if she's seen him the last couple of days?'

Corstorphine checked his watch: 14:14. Plenty of time to see Margo and then get John Ackerman in for questioning.

'I'll pay a visit to Margo now. When you and PC Lamb are

done here, I want you to bring John Ackerman in. I'd like to see him explain what he was doing in the laird's house after he'd been in to see us on Monday.'

'That's something else I meant to tell you, sir. The clockmaker managed to put together the bits of clockwork we found at the tree, I've left it in the office. He can't be sure without having the original mechanism, but he's of the opinion it would have been set around a week before activating the snare.'

'Leaving Ackerman without an alibi. Good work, Frankie, I'll see you back at the station, can you make it for four o'clock?'

'Yes, sir, this shouldn't take long, and we can do the fingerprint match at the station.'

Corstorphine left them working the scene, heading back along the metalled road to the fork, then following the rougher track down to the gamekeeper's cottage. He noticed the quad bike was still lying on its side in the burn, just before he passed the Hanging Tree still adorned with tattered strips of police tape. Margo came out of the cottage as he approached, closing the door behind her in a clear demonstration that he wasn't likely to be invited in for tea or coffee.

'Hello, Margo, how are you keeping?'

'Fine. What do you want?' The response was brusque, unwelcoming.

'Have you seen the laird recently?'

'That slimeball. No, thank God. He was creeping around here Monday afternoon, haven't seen sight of him since.' Corstorphine could see that she was intrigued rather than attempting to hide anything.

'What time was he here?'

Margo shrugged dismissively. 'No idea, I was in town when he came around. I left the door unlocked for him. Sometime in the afternoon.' She saw Corstorphine's questioning look. 'He's convinced there was some book of grouse numbers that Oscar used to keep. Sounds like a load of rubbish to me, he never kept note of anything. He wanted to look for it.'

'You've been to *The Courier* recently.'

Margo shifted uncomfortably on her feet, looking around her. 'So what?'

'Where did June Stevens' reporter's notebook come from?' Corstorphine asked the question quietly, watching her like a hawk.

Margo's eyes darted about before she answered.

'I found it in the shed.' She nodded in the direction of the locked shed. 'Thought *The Courier* might want it, as it belongs to them really.' She looked pleased with herself for offering a justification.

'Why do you think it was in the shed? A notebook belonging to a young woman who was found dead, hanging in the tree?'

'I don't know,' she responded sulkily. 'Maybe Oscar found it in the heather and stored it in the dry.'

'What else have you found, Margo? You seem to know a lot more about Oscar and events in this town than you told us.'

'I just remembered some things, that's all. None of this is your business. I don't have to tell you anything.' She spat the last words out defiantly, her low regard for the police evident in her expression.

Corstorphine nodded tiredly. 'That's right, Margo, you don't have to tell us anything. However, if you have any interest in helping us find Oscar's murderer before he selects his next victim, I suggest you come to me first.' He shared a meaningful look with her. 'So far, it's people connected to Oscar that have been killed. You don't want to become another body on the list.'

Corstorphine drove back to the station, the image of Margo's shocked awareness that she may be in danger fresh in his mind. *'That really wasn't kind, James.'* His wife's disapproving voice sounded in his ears. He decided to ignore it.

THIRTY-TWO

They sat in the interview room, Frankie and Corstorphine on one side and John Ackerman with his solicitor on the other. Frankie started the voice recorder whilst John Ackerman sat back in his chair, trying hard to look disinterested, but Corstorphine had caught the slight air of panic as he was brought back into the station.

'You know why we're here again, John?' Corstorphine opened the questioning with a leading comment, calculated to ramp up the stress at the start.

'No idea, why don't you tell me?'

'Have you seen Mr Anthony McCallum recently?' Corstorphine countered.

'Have you something to charge my client with, Detective Inspector? Otherwise, we are just going to walk out of here.' The solicitor made a show of closing his file and replacing his pen in a top jacket pocket.

'Run the footage, Frankie.' DC McKenzie pushed play on her laptop, swinging the screen around so both John Ackerman and his solicitor could see footage of him walking around the outside of the laird's house, followed by inside camera views before ending with him leaving the house with his jacket a lot bulkier than it had been. The solicitor rolled his eyes and painstakingly removed his pen once more, opening his file and writing in small, neat script.

'That's not me!' Even the solicitor forgot to keep a poker face, incredulity writ large across his bespectacled features.

'Fingerprints.' Corstorphine said just the one word, as if this alone was sufficient for a conviction.

Frankie passed over a set of prints, clearly photographed on the broken windowpane where his fingers had picked out slivers of glass before entering. She passed over another set of official matching prints, clearly identified as Ackerman's for comparison. 'There are more in the house,' she added before John Ackerman or his solicitor could interject, 'and we fully expect the blood sample we found on an interior door handle to match your DNA.'

John Ackerman's left hand instinctively covered a cut on his right. He looked hopefully at the solicitor sitting beside him, only to receive a slight shaking of the head in response.

Corstorphine almost felt sorry for the gamekeeper, the way he slumped dejectedly into his seat. 'I'd gone there after seeing you. I was still angry that the bastard had his gamekeeper set me up. That was one of his fucking birds and he knew it!'

'Did you have an argument with him?' Frankie questioned.

He looked at her in that same way he had before, wondering why a woman was asking him questions. 'No, there wasn't anyone at home. That's when I decided to break in and try and find some evidence.'

The solicitor was holding up a hand in a futile attempt to stop the flow of conversation. 'I'd advise no comment to any further questions.'

John Ackerman continued as if the solicitor wasn't there. 'I couldn't find anything; the bastard's too clever to leave anything incriminating around. So, I took a shooting trophy, solid silver, thought that would be payback.'

The solicitor sat back with a show of disinterest. If his client wanted to incriminate himself against his advice, there wasn't much he could do.

'Where were you between Friday 9th May and Sunday 11th May, John?'

'You've already asked me all this crap. I told you where I was!'

Frankie opened her notebook, reading the dates she'd written down before responding to his outburst. 'You told us where you were from Monday 12th through to the day Oscar died, Friday 16th. We now believe that whoever was responsible for Oscar's death set the snare sometime over the previous weekend. What were your movements?'

John Ackerman sat up in his seat. 'You're not pinning that on me. I had nothing to do with his death. What is this?' He looked at the solicitor in appeal.

'Are you accusing my client of being an accomplice to murder, officer?'

Corstorphine watched Ackerman shrewdly, he didn't have the composure to hide anything. If he had killed Oscar, it would be as plain as day.

'Not for the moment, but we are charging you with breaking and entering, criminal damage and theft from Mr Anthony McCallum on Monday 19th May. You'd better remember what you were doing that weekend and who you can provide as witnesses, otherwise you could find yourself in deep water.'

'I'd like a word alone with my client, given the nature of these fresh allegations you're making.'

Corstorphine turned off the voice recorder whilst Frankie collected her laptop and paperwork.

'Is ten minutes enough?' Corstorphine directed this to the solicitor, who nodded sharply in his direction. He shut the door on them, walking back to stand in front of the crazy wall with Frankie.

'What do you make of him, sir? Do you think he could have killed Oscar and the minister?'

'It's possible, sometimes it's the most unlikely people who turn into killers. I guess we all have it in us if we're pushed hard enough.' Corstorphine was puzzling over the board. 'I don't think Ackerman's our man, though, Frankie. Being wrongly accused of poisoning raptors and losing your job, that's bad enough, but is that sufficient motivation to risk a long spell in prison? I don't think so. Then there's the minister. There's no obvious link between them. No, our murderer is someone who's capable of cool planning and has an eye for making the punishment fit the crime. Whoever it is, they have planned this for a long time.'

'And they're a dab hand with clockwork mechanisms,' Frankie added. 'The clock repairer mentioned a deceased French clockmaker based in Toulouse as the only person he knew that could make anything like this.' She pointed towards her desk where the boxed mechanism still lay.

'Our reporter's French,' Corstorphine mused out loud.

'Why would there be any connection to France?' Frankie queried.

Reluctantly, Corstorphine added another name to the board – Josephine Sables. 'I don't know, Frankie, there's something we're missing, something we've not been told.'

Without warning, Corstorphine started pulling at the crazy wall, lifting photographs and coloured string off in handfuls. 'We're looking at this all wrong. The orphanage is the common factor, the orphanage and the children who were abused and killed there.' He drew a rough circle in the middle of the board, labelled orphanage. 'These are the children we know about. Oscar, Simon Battle in Barlinnic and our butcher William Booth.' Their names and photographs radiated out from the bottom of the central circle. 'And these are the people who were either in charge, involved or accused of being abusers.' The minister, the laird, Lord Lagan and the old DI were placed at the top of the board. 'The minister has been killed.' He drew a red line obliquely across the minister's name, then did the same with Oscar. 'If it's someone looking for retribution, then we should be concentrating on the orphans that are still alive.'

'Wasn't Oscar one of the victims, though, sir?'

Corstorphine nodded. 'Yes, victim and also muscle for one of the alleged abusers.'

Frankie looked confused. 'How does this relate to the death of June Stevens twenty years ago?'

'You say her notebook contained allegations of who was involved.'

'That's what I was told, sir. Without getting our hands on the book, we have to go by what *The Courier* tell us.'

'OK. Let's assume for the moment they're telling us the truth. Then where are the names of the children, why are we having so much trouble tracking down any of the orphans that were at the orphanage?'

'Maybe Margo has some of that information, sir. She could be drip feeding it to the paper for money?'

'That's entirely possible. I think we're going to have to have another chat with Margo. She wasn't particularly forthcoming when I went to see her.' He checked his watch. 'They've had their ten minutes, at least we can charge John Ackerman for breaking and entering. When the laird reappears, we can find what's missing – add burglary to his charge sheet.' They walked back to the interview room together. 'I'm going to have to open a line of enquiry into June Stevens' suicide, it's the only way I can requisition that notebook.' Corstorphine didn't sound overjoyed at the prospect.

He formally charged the gamekeeper, accepting the solicitor's plea that he be allowed out pending trial. As far as Corstorphine was concerned, John Ackerman was just a distraction. Somewhere out there was a killer who'd already struck twice, and he didn't want any more murders on his patch.

'See if you can track down any more of the orphanage children, they must be out there somewhere.' Another thought finally crystallised in his mind. 'And get in touch with that local company that undertake geological surveys. I want the old orphanage garden scanned with ground penetrating radar in case that's where all of our missing children ended up.'

Corstorphine left Frankie working at her desk, frustrated at the lack of any solid leads in the case. He was also concerned that the ACC would be down on him like a ton of bricks as soon as he heard the reporter's suicide was being reopened. Couldn't be helped, her death was the key to the murderer, he was sure of it. *The Courier* believed that Oscar had murdered her twenty years ago, something Corstorphine thought highly likely – especially as Oscar had possession of her notebook. What made it more likely that Oscar had murdered her, in his view, was the amateur way the scene had been left to make it look like a suicide, a scene that the old DI couldn't possibly have been taken in by. Which left him with the inescapable conclusion that Brian had been 'got at'.

His mobile interrupted his train of thought, the number not one he recognised.

'Corstorphine,' he announced. There was the slightest delay on the other end before a woman's voice replied.

'Hello, James, it's Jenny. I was wondering if you were free for a drink later on tonight?'

A brief moment's panic ensued. Should he, did he have time, did they even have anything in common, what did she want? His wife sat on his office desk, legs crossed, looking down at him in that way of hers. '*For God's sake, James, get out there and enjoy yourself for once!*'

He smiled at her ruefully. '*I don't really want anyone else, it's you I want. It was always you I wanted.'* The conversation was happening in his head, he knew that – it didn't make it any less real.

'Face up to it, James. I'm gone. I'm never coming back. You made me a promise, you said you'd live life for both of us.'

'Oh, hi, Jenny. Yes, that would be good, I could do with a break from work. Where were you thinking?'

'Same place as last time if you like, the food wasn't too bad, and it will save me having to cook for myself. Shall we say eight?'

'Eight is fine. I'll see you then.' He added as an afterthought, 'Looking forward to it.'

'Me too. See you then, bye.'

Corstorphine sat at his desk, aware of his wife's pleased expression looking down from her perch beside him. *'OK, you win. Now let me try and make some sense out of these bloody murders before I lose my job.'* He sat at his desk, computer waiting with infinite machine patience for his input. He'd previously attempted to use the police VALCRI system for a search on bone gears without success, this time he tried Google with Toulouse as a search term. Within seconds, he had found references to the clockmaker Henri Dupont, together with photographs of bizarre clockwork mechanisms fashioned from animal skeleton remains. Not all of them were timepieces, his most celebrated creations were mechatronic animations with a macabre bent. There was a small dog, mostly skeleton apart from the head and two paws clutching an even smaller guitar. The video link beckoned, and the dog became alive – gears whirring in place of a heart, strings plucked and the head inclining towards the camera from where glass eyes observed him with an air of studied boredom.

The site confirmed that the clockmaker had died five years ago, with a note suggesting his creations had soared in value ever since as collectors scrambled to buy them. The guitar-playing dog, entitled Bonzo, was reputedly worth half a million euros. Corstorphine shook his head, partly in reaction to anyone spending that much money on a clockwork dog, partly because the trail was a dead end. On a whim, he searched for any assistants or staff, but he had apparently preferred to work alone. Only one photograph showed the secretive clockmaker at work, bent over the lens of a large, illuminated magnifying glass mounted on his bench. A young girl stood in the background, out of focus and almost lost in the dark background. The caption said Henri Dupont and his daughter, Joie. Corstorphine squinted at the photograph in an attempt to bring the daughter more into focus; she must have been about ten years old. That's another line of enquiry reached a dead end. He stretched, checked the time and logged out – time to go home and grab a shower before his second date with Jenny.

THIRTY-THREE

The room was getting darker. The laird checked his phone – Tuesday 20:14. The dogs had started pawing at the door, looking at him through unfathomable eyes and exchanging whines. 'Lie down!' The dogs responded immediately to his barked command, but how long would they keep obeying him if thirst and starvation overcame their training? He didn't like to dwell on what the next few days might bring, preferring instead to keep the hope alive that he'd be noticed missing before too long. As the building fell into darkness for the second day of his confinement, he slid into an uncomfortable sleep, curled up on the cold flagstone floor with only his tweed jacket to deter the worse of the night's chill. A sound brought him fully awake, eyes straining in the complete blackness, unable to make out anything other than a faint outline of the slit windows where the dark was less oppressive. The dogs were raiding the crisps, he could hear them crunching packets and contents all in one go. Fumbling for his phone, he keyed on the torch, catching two pairs of watchful eyes reflecting the light. 'Leave! Go and lie down!' The dogs left the crisps, taking position back at the door and panting loudly as if they'd been exercising hard. 'Damn them.' The floor was covered in crisps, torn packets and bits of cardboard where they'd chewed through the box. His mouth felt dry, and the image of a cool glass of water appeared in his imagination, accompanied by a desperate thirst. He licked his lips, already starting to crack, and noticed his tongue felt strangely dry and swollen. This wasn't good, they'd only been trapped in the building for a day, and he was already craving water. The dogs didn't look any better, not helped by however much salt they'd just ingested. He stayed sitting watching the dogs for the remainder of the night, until Wednesday's dawn made its presence known by the first birdsong accompanying a sky turning gradually lighter. The third day of his confinement began.

Getting to his feet was a struggle, muscles complaining after the long night spent on cold stone. He hoped the aches and pains he felt were nothing to do with dehydration and was reassured by his bladder insisting on being emptied as soon as possible. With a feeling of distaste, he pissed against the wall in the corner where the dogs had decided would be their toilet. The animals watched him without any reaction as a stream of dark urine splashed against the whitewashed wall.

A stomach cramp hit as he finished, causing him to double in agony for the few seconds it lasted. 'God, not the time to get the runs.' He pressed his face against the window glass, seeing a constricted view of the woods outside. There was no movement, no sign of anyone in the vicinity – why should there be? The track was so far off the beaten track that the only time it ever had any use was when the hunting season started in earnest, when he could charge grossly inflated prices for those that enjoyed shooting the stupid, overfed birds. He shouted anyway, just in case someone was within earshot. His voice sounded weak and croaky, his throat hurting with the effort.

Holding onto the wall for support, for the first time the laird seriously considered that he might actually die in this single-roomed cottage. The thought scared him, causing him to search for words to a God he'd long ago given up believing in. 'I don't know if you exist, but for God's sake help me.' That sounded wrong, he had another attempt. 'I know I've not been a good man, I know I've made mistakes and have sinned, but please God, please find it in your heart to look down on me and save my soul.' That sounded better, he was quite pleased with it.

The moment of self-congratulation evaporated as quickly as it had arrived as one of the dogs stood up, baring sharp incisors and walking towards him on stiff legs. 'Sit down. SIT DOWN!' The animal's eyes narrowed in a most human fashion, assessing how much of a pack leader he was, who was the stronger. The dog sat, its companion watching the interplay and staying motionless, conserving energy. The day stretched out in front of them, followed by another night. The dogs held no moral scruples, this was always going to be about survival. Their owner just hadn't realised it yet. On the floor, the hourglass leaked red sand from the top glass through to the bottom. He estimated there were one or two days of sand still to go, meanwhile he and his dogs were keeping an uneasy truce. The cold store by now was smelling putrid. He'd had to add his own excrement to the dogs' smaller piles. He'd noticed neither dog had passed urine since yesterday, and just now when he'd managed a meagre piss, his own urine was dark, almost brown. His phone had run out of battery just as dawn broke, so he had to guess the time at around midday, give or take a few hours. He'd been suffering with cramps during the night, and even now his body ached in a way he'd never experienced before. His lips had started to crack – he'd tried licking them to provide some respite to the dreadful thirst he was experiencing, but there was no saliva left in his mouth.

He watched the hourglass, red sand still trickling at an almost imperceptible rate from one side to the other. He'd come to associate the timer with whatever time was left to him, and judging by the rate it emptied, there was one day left. Unless he'd lost track of the days, that took him to Thursday when he'd be missed at Inverness Sheriff Court for sure. He just had to survive until then. An inscription he'd not noticed before caught his eye as the sun made a welcome intrusion into the room. Words were carved around the base of the hourglass – *Children Suffer*. He felt as if his heart had been gripped in an ice-cold fist. One hand went to his chest, willing his heart not to give up now, the other turned the base around to reveal more of the inscription – *The Little. The Little Children Suffer*. Was it a message from whoever had trapped him in here?

He rotated the hourglass around, searching for any other inscriptions, any clue as to who might have imprisoned him in this cold stone cell. They were the only words, carved almost invisibly into the side of the smooth black wooden base. *Suffer The Little Children* – he felt a sudden relief as he recognised it was just a biblical inscription. Why leave an overlarge egg timer with a biblical reference to children here with him? A headache started over his left temple, pulses of pain throbbing through his head. His hands left his chest to hold his head, holding it tight as if that might lessen the feeling that his brain was attempting to force its way out of his skull. A groan of pain escaped his dry lips, causing the dogs to pick up their heads from the cold flagstone floor, watching him with an intensity that would have frightened him had his eyes not been screwed tightly shut against the agony.

As the hours wound on, he entered into a delirious sleep where he could no longer tell dream from reality.

He wasn't sure what had woken him. The first hint of dawn cast a faint light into the cold store and he opened his eyes, struggling to unglue them from the crud that threatened to seal them shut, then wider again as the dogs were close. Too close.

'Sit down, DOWN!' The voice, usually so effortlessly commanding, came as a pathetic squeak. The dogs growled, a sound from low in their bodies. Their eyes had become wild; normally submissive, they now stared at him as if he were prey. He lashed out with a foot, only to receive a bite on his calf. The dog increased the pressure, jaws forcing teeth deep into muscle as the laird started a high-pitched scream. The first flow of blood was all the encouragement the other dog required. Jumping onto the prostrate laird's chest, it pushed past his feeble attempts to ward it off with weak arms before biting him in the neck – an ancient programming taking over from the deceptively thin veneer of domestication.

The last words spoken by the laird consisted of a wet bubbling as air mixed with the sudden release of blood. Death did not come quickly, even hastened as it was by the dogs ripping chunks of flesh off his still struggling body. The animals were driven mad by thirst, drinking the salt-laden blood in desperate gulps in an attempt to satisfy that basic need. In the end, it only hastened their demise.

The dogs lay listless, panting in a pool of the laird's blood which already was starting to congeal on their matted fur. Their stomachs were full, for now, but the thirst remained. The laird stared at the blood-spattered white walls, eyes unseeing. His body resembled a badly butchered carcass, white bones protruding from red flesh. Mercifully, the dogs had not eaten his face, but the expression that remained was not one that anyone seeing it would easily forget.

On the floor, the hourglass still counted down the hours. It was at least a day out in its calculation of how long the laird had left to live – but then death by dehydration is not an exact science, especially when you've added two Rhodesian ridgebacks and a box of salted crisps into the equation.

Outside, the sun made leisurely progress behind the trees, sinking towards a horizon turned blood red. The dogs were unable to appreciate the poetic symmetry of colour bestowed on the interior of the cold store as the light turned to a diffuse ochre. As Thursday drew to a close, they lay stiff, cold and lifeless next to their butchered master on the bloodstained floor.

THIRTY-FOUR

Frankie was driving the patrol car to Glasgow, giving Corstorphine the luxury of being a passenger and free to work through his thoughts as they drove to Barlinnie. Last night had been a revelation for him, sharing a meal with Jenny – they had talked completely naturally for three hours without any of the awkwardness that had accompanied their first meeting. She'd made him laugh on more than one occasion, which was akin to a miracle given the stress he was under, and the conversation had flowed as easily as the drink. She'd asked him about the murders, nothing surprising there as the whole town was avidly buying copies of *The Courier* and following the orphanage allegations in as much detail as the paper was allowed to print.

He'd let it slip that they'd found bone gear mechanisms at each scene, the words escaping his mouth before he was able to prevent them leaving. He'd shrugged it off, fairly certain *The Courier* had already printed something about this anyway, but she'd been fascinated. Looking back on it, he had told her too much. Normally, he didn't ever drink more than a small glass of wine with his meal, preferring not to be faced with the wrong end of a breathalyser at the end of an evening, but the drink just appeared as if by magic and he'd ended up booking a taxi for both of them. Memories of a lingering farewell remained at the front of his mind, and he smiled at the recollection like a teenage boy remembering his first kiss.

Jenny had quizzed him about the orphanage, looking for more detail than the salacious comments attributed to Margo. He had to explain that the matter was under investigation and that he was unable to offer any further details. She had been content with that, understanding that he couldn't give details whilst a case was live. She'd said as much – patient confidentiality she called it, in her profession.

The radio came alive with the sergeant's call sign, bringing him back to the present. Corstorphine pulled the microphone free from the cradle and answered. 'Sierra one-four receiving, over.'

'We've had a call from the Inverness Court, sir. The sheriff's not shown up and nobody can reach him. They've asked us to investigate. Over.'

He exchanged a look with Frankie and spun his finger around. She put on the siren and looked for a place to turn around.

'Whisky tango, we're making our way to the laird's house now. Who's on duty this morning, over?'

'PC Lamb, over.'

Corstorphine rolled his eyes. 'Send him out there now, Hamish, we'll join him in about an hour. Over and out.'

A burst of static provided the only response. Frankie had spun the car in a U-turn and was speeding back up the road, flashing blue lights clearing the way ahead. Corstorphine called Barlinnie, advising that they wouldn't be interviewing Simon Battle today. A sick feeling had settled in his stomach. There was something amiss yesterday when they'd been at the laird's house, he knew it. Why hadn't he insisted they undertake a more thorough search of the grounds?

'Do you think he's alright, sir?' Frankie asked, eyes focussed on the road ahead.

'I certainly hope so, Frankie. I certainly hope so.' Corstorphine had an image of the crazy wall in his mind's eye as they sped back along the A-road they'd only just come down. In his imagination a red line was being drawn through the laird's name even as he thought about it.

Lamb was waiting for them on the gravelled drive, standing in his uniform as if on parade.

'Sir!' He attempted a salute as they climbed out of the car, only to be fended off by Corstorphine.

'Never mind that. Have you found anything?'

Lamb looked doubtful, querying his own powers of detection. 'Only this, sir. I saw these tracks yesterday when I was looking for signs of that gamekeeper's vehicle.' He led them out of the courtyard onto the metalled road.

'What are we looking at, Lamb?' Corstorphine asked, casting his eyes around in an attempt to see anything of note at all.

'These tracks here, sir, the ones going down the forest track.' Lamb pointed at a muddy track that entered dense conifers. 'They look like they might belong to the laird's Land Rover. Thing is, sir, they only show a single vehicle. If he'd come back this way, the tracks would cut across each other.'

Frankie crouched down to inspect the tracks more closely. 'I think he's right, sir. Do you think he drove down here and then had an accident?'

Corstorphine had a concern that this was exactly what had happened, although he wouldn't be placing any bets on it being an accident. 'Does anyone know where this track goes?'

They both shook their heads, Lamb pulling out his iPhone to try and load Google Earth only to discover that 3G and 4G didn't exist in the glen.

Frankie inspected the depth of the ruts left by the passage

of a vehicle. 'We'll not get the car down here, sir. If we did manage any distance, we'd probably end up getting stuck.'

Corstorphine had to agree, the patrol car wasn't up to off-roading. 'OK, Lamb – you stay here, see if you can spot anything else that may assist us finding the laird. Frankie, we'll go back to the station and pick up the Land Rover, and some maps if we have them.'

Back at the station, Frankie logged onto her screen and loaded Google Earth, zooming in on the laird's house in an effort to see where the forest track went. She had to give up, the track split several times, making the network of paths that she could make out through the extensive tree plantations more like a maze. The map that Corstorphine had dug out from the office shelves didn't even bother showing anything as ephemeral as a forest track.

'We'll just have to split up once we're in the trees. Ask Hamish for the short-wave walkie-talkies, they should be good for around ten miles, so we can at least keep in touch.' Corstorphine checked the back of the Land Rover for police tape and the first-aid kit. Both were present. Frankie jumped in the front with three walkie-talkies clutched in her hands.

Corstorphine checked the dash clock as he swung out into the high street. 'OK. We've around four hours before the sun starts going down. If we haven't found his Land Rover by then, we'll have to call out the helicopter tomorrow morning, perform an aerial search.'

'We can't call them out now, sir?' Frankie asked.

'No. We're not even into an official missing person enquiry yet, and the ACC has to approve any helicopter use out of the regional budget. There's no way he'd even look at it unless the sheriff has been missing for at least twenty four hours.'

They scooped up Lamb from the big house and entered into the gloom of the forest. Trees were planted so densely together that he needed the lights on full beam to follow the path. The air temperature had dropped by several degrees, the sun's heat unable to penetrate the thick pine foliage. They came to the first fork in the track. Lamb pointed out tyre impressions still evident in the soft earth, so they continued for a mile on a potholed track, the Land Rover pitching and yawing like a drunk at sea. Before long, the track headed up the steeper side of the glen, the trees starting to thin out and let some welcome light back. Another split in the path appeared, and once again Lamb climbed out to check for signs of recent passage.

'It's no good, sir. The ground's too hard and stony to take any imprint. He could have gone either way.'

'You take the left, Lamb, we'll continue on this track. If you find anything, see any recent tracks, call us on the short-wave. Here.' He threw a roll of police tape out of the window. 'You've heard of Hansel and Gretel I take it?'

'Sir?' Lamb voiced a query.

'Just mark which way you've gone with strips of tape on trees, rocks, whatever. So we can find you if we have to,' Frankie impatiently instructed him. They sped on along the higher road, able to make better speed as the visibility was so much better. Crossroads appeared and Corstorphine stopped the car so they could both check the paths ahead.

'This one turns to mud just down here,' Corstorphine advised, 'and there's no sign of any tracks.'

Frankie walked back down from the track she'd investigated. 'He could have gone this way, sir, it's too dry to hold any tracks for long.'

'You take that track, Frankie, I'll cover as much ground as I can this way.' He handed over a roll of police tape, wished her good luck and headed further off into the mountains. The estate covered hundreds of square miles, Corstorphine thought, they could spend days looking for him up here. At least the weather was in their favour, a lot of the time the hills would be covered in mist at this time of year and visibility next to zero. He motored on, jumping out at each fork and looking in vain for any sign that a vehicle had been along this way. After a few more hours, Corstorphine accepted defeat. If the laird had travelled along this road, he'd left no sign of his passing, and it would be getting dark soon. The last thing he wanted was to call out the mountain rescue to find Lamb and Frankie. That would be the final nail in his career's coffin!

THIRTY-FIVE

Frankie meanwhile was back in dense woodland. The track showed evidence that a vehicle had been along it, but whether this was the laird's Land Rover and whether it was a recent track, she couldn't say. Each time she came to a fork, she followed the path displaying the deeper tyre tracks, tying blue and white police tape onto conifer branches as she went. At one point she stopped, imagining she'd heard a vehicle. She listened intently for any sound that could percolate through the dense woodland, realising as she breathed deeply that her breathing was all she could hear. No birds, no animals, not even insects disturbed the perfect quiet. She shivered, not through the cold. Conifer plantations were like graveyards, sucking up all heat and light and leaving nothing for the living, she thought. She checked her watch: 19:08. They'd been searching for hours. There was at best one hour of daylight left. Reluctantly, she turned back on herself and walked as quickly as she could back to the track where Corstorphine had left her. Frankie keyed the short-wave radio. 'This is DC McKenzie. I'm starting to head back to our rendezvous, sir. Nothing found along here. Over.'

Corstorphine responded after a short while. 'OK, Frankie, I'll just have to find somewhere I can back up and turn around. Drawn a blank here too. PC Lamb, anything to report? Over.'

'PC Lamb here. I've found his Land Rover, sir, there's a small building next to it. I'll just take a look. Over,' he added eventually.

'Don't touch anything. Let us know if he's alright. I'll collect Frankie and we'll come to your location. Over.'

* * *

Lamb had shouted out to see if anyone was there. The silence that returned his call was sufficient warning for him to proceed cautiously, checking the trees for snares, the ground for traps. In this overtly cautious manner he approached the window, already suspecting that the spatters covering the glass were blood. He reached into his belt, retrieved his high-powered flashlight and looked in, on a scene of utter carnage.

'Fuck, fuck!' He looked around guiltily in case anyone had heard his involuntary outburst and was relieved to find he was still on his own. Walking around the building until he found a door, he tried the handle with his gloved hands, issuing a silent prayer of thanks when he found it was locked.

'Sir. I've found him. Over.'

Something in his voice must have alerted Corstorphine that this wasn't the good news he was hoping to hear.

'What's his status, Lamb? Over.'

Lamb could hear Corstorphine wrestling with the wheel as he manoeuvred the Land Rover as quickly as he could back down the hill through the dense conifers.

'Bit of a dog's dinner, sir.' Lamb still hadn't lost his knack for an accurate and graphic description of a crime scene. 'Looks like the dogs killed him. There's nothing left alive in there by the looks of it, sir, and the door's locked. I can't gain access. Over.'

'Wait there, Lamb, we'll be with you soon. I can see Frankie ahead. Don't touch anything!'

THIRTY-SIX

The forensics team had arrived from Inverness just before half past eight, meeting with Corstorphine and the local locksmith outside the laird's house. Leading a small convoy of 4x4's the DI led them back up the now pitch-black forest trail to the remote cold store. Dressing in white forensics suits, they watched as the locksmith bent to his work, feeding metal picks into the lock, juggling the internal mechanism in the beam of his head torch. As the minutes went by, he gave up the struggle to open the locked door, complaining to Corstorphine that something was jammed inside the lock.

'Just cut the bloody door open,' Corstorphine's patience had reached the limit. Another long day, another death and still no closer to identifying whoever was responsible for each death. He had no great expectation that the laird's death was some terrible accident, but they needed access to the building before working the scene.

The locksmith fetched an angle grinder out of his toolbox to slice through the deadbolt, sparks flying from the tip of the tool like a firework. As soon as the bolt was cut, the locksmith stood back to allow Corstorphine room to push the door open, releasing a putrid stench of death and faeces. It was immediately apparent nothing was alive in there. The laird had been butchered by his own dogs, throat torn open leaving a raw dark void in his neck from where the dogs had ripped bite-sized lumps of flesh. Muscle and sinew lay exposed like some anatomical examination performed with stone-age tools. The laird's expression had frozen at the moment of death, a nightmarish mask that left no one in any doubt that his death had been excruciatingly painful. One leg lay stripped to the bone, tatters of flesh hanging white against the dark bloodstained tweed. Dogs and man were as stiff as cardboard, rigor mortis leaving them arranged like a grotesque tableau painted in dried blood.

Forensics set up floodlights, propping the door open with one of the lights and the photographer started taking shots, the surgical forensics mask covering her nose insufficient to block out the ripe odours permeating the space. She was in shock, going through the motions like an automaton. Corstorphine pointed out the crisp packets and still functioning hourglass which she duly photographed, leaving the charnel house with relief to take close-ups of the now disassembled door lock in the fresh air.

'What do you make of it, sir, could he have been locked in by accident?' Frankie looked around the blood-spattered room. Like him, she'd be working out how many days the laird had been trapped in there. They both tried to avoid looking at the laird's body – the expression on his face would live with them forever.

Corstorphine merely indicated the hourglass, the papal coin shining in the cold floodlight glare. 'Dust the whole place for prints, especially the door lock, crisp packets and this hourglass contraption. Then bag the lot and look for any DNA. This is the same killer.' He felt an anger building up inside him – three murders and still nothing to go on. It felt as if the murderer was playing a game with him now, deliberately placing clues to identify himself. Even the mode of death: snare for the gamekeeper, church bell for the minister, imprisonment for the sheriff. There was a certain poetic justice in the way each death had been engineered, something almost psychopathic in the attention to detail and cruelty.

'Sir?' PC Lamb called him over to the door lock, spread out on a spare white forensics suit on the forest floor. 'Thought you should see this.'

Inside the door lock new metal parts stood out, shining in the lights and contrasting with the original rust-coloured components. A tightly coiled spring had unwound, engaging to push the deadbolt into the lock position. A single bone jammed against the mechanism, preventing any possibility of unlocking the latch bolt.

'Do you think this could have caused the deadbolt to operate without requiring a key?' Corstorphine directed the question to the locksmith, who was attempting to pack his toolbox whilst casting furtive glances into the building.

'Aye, looks like it. May have been the door slamming shut that set it off. Poor bastard didn't stand a chance of getting out. How long do you think he was in there?'

'Thanks for your help. This is an ongoing investigation, and we can't give out any information. I'd be grateful if you didn't tell anyone about this in case it harms our enquiry.'

'No, of course. Glad to be of service. I'll be on my way. Good night.'

Corstorphine watched him as he drove his 4x4 away through the trees, wondering what it must have been like for the laird locked in the cold store. Monday was the last time he showed up on the CCTV at his house, then Margo said he'd been at her cottage some time Monday afternoon. Could he have been there four days? Frankie stood in the open doorway to the cold store, waiting for him to come back to the scene.

'How long can you live without water, Frankie?'

She thought for a second before replying. 'I think it's something like three days, sir. Probably less if you have nothing to eat except dry salted crisps.'

She'd come to the same conclusion as he had; the crisps had been deliberately left in the building to hasten the onset of death. That wouldn't have been a pleasant way to go, at least Oscar and the minister had died quickly. Could the murderer have deliberately chosen a painful and lingering death for the laird? And the hourglass, the red sand almost completely run through to the bottom glass container. Had the laird made the connection between the hourglass and the time he had left to live? 'There's an inscription on the hourglass, sir.'

'What have we got?' He entered the cold store again, crouching down to read the words carved into the side of the mahogany hourglass base – *Suffer The Little Children*. There was no doubt about the motive now.

'Lamb, can you stay here until forensics have completed their job?'

'Sir,' he acknowledged.

'Good man. Get a lift back to town with them when they're ready to go. We'll arrange for an ambulance to collect the body.' Corstorphine looked doubtfully back at the track. 'May have to ask the mountain rescue team to fetch him. Frankie, you come back with me, we need to talk.' He took another roll of police tape from the back of the Land Rover, making a mental note to order additional supplies. 'Here, seal the place up when you're done.'

Corstorphine turned the police Land Rover around, headlights casting a xenon beam deep into the trees until they found the track, police tape fluorescing silver in the distance and indicating which path to take through the labyrinth forest.

'We might have saved him if we'd only gone looking for him yesterday.' Corstorphine's voice was bitter with self-recrimination. 'Now one of the few people that knew what was going on at the orphanage is dead.'

'It's not your fault, sir. Nobody could have known he was locked in that building. It was a piece of luck that Lamb found him at all.'

'Fuck!' He hit the steering wheel with the flat of his hand, then had to grab the wheel in both hands to keep from driving into the trees. Frankie sat in silence.

'We have to get Brian Rankin in for questioning. He's the last one that we know had a connection with the orphanage who's still alive.'

'Do you think he's in danger, sir?'

'He might be. The notebook claimed he wasn't involved in any abuse, is that right?'

Frankie thought for a while before answering. 'The notebook specifically mentioned that nobody had identified him as an abuser, more as someone who covered up whatever was happening.'

'The laird's death is going to be all over town tomorrow, that locksmith was bursting to get the story out. Two murders are bad enough, three will bring a shitstorm of pain down on our heads.'

'What do you suggest we do now?'

Corstorphine went through his options, such as they were. 'Trouble is, if this orphanage business goes as far up the tree as *The Courier* have suggested, then we are going to have a devil of a job investigating anyone involved. The ACC has already warned me off opening the June Stevens' suicide case, he's not going to take well to my taking a retired DI with an exemplary record into custody, even if it is for his own protection.'

The car pulled smoothly onto the road leading out of the estate, suspension no longer reacting to the ruts and rocks littering the churned-up forest track.

Corstorphine considered what little they knew as he drove

in silence. The murderer knew the movements of each of his victims intimately, he knew Oscar rode his quad bike under that tree every day, standing in the saddle to avoid being bounced by the roots; he knew the minister had to ring the church bell himself, locked in the belfry with no possibility of escape once the timbers had been sufficiently weakened; and he knew the laird would eventually visit the cold store. Routines, habits, learned by patient observation over what, days, weeks, years?

'Whoever the murderer is, sir, he must have been living in this community for quite a while to know each of the victim's movements.' Frankie echoed his thoughts.

'And your point is, Frankie?'

'What if our murderer is one of the abused orphans that we haven't been able to track down?'

'Because they don't appear on the lists, or are going under assumed names?'

'Oscar wasn't listed as an orphan, but he was allegedly abused as a child.'

'Good point. There must be people living here who have concealed any abuse, either too ashamed or embarrassed to bring it into the open.'

'There was that one call I had, sir, following *The Courier*'s article about the orphanage yesterday, from someone who claimed he'd been abused at the orphanage. He rung off before giving a name, and the number was withheld.'

'That's probably the only good that's ever going to come out of that bloody paper. Once these things are out in the open, it encourages people to tell their own stories.'

'Catharsis, sir.'

'Aye. Lancing a big ugly boil that's festered on this town's backside without anyone noticing. Well, they're bloody noticing now.'

They entered the outskirts of the town, yellow sodium lamps surrounded by halos of mist as the evening air chilled.

'Tomorrow's going to be busy,' Corstorphine stated. 'I want that butcher brought in for questioning, first thing. Arrest him if you have to.'

'What charge, sir?' Frankie was genuinely interested.

'Resisting arrest.'

Frankie's laugh broke the tension.

'Hamish can bring in Brian, he can wait in one of the cells until we're ready for him.'

'He won't thank you for that!'

'If he's been covering up for that orphanage, being put in a cell might concentrate his mind,' Corstorphine responded. 'Then we'd better have a chat with *The Courier* – they've been too much in the driving seat throughout this process.'

'Do you think we'll get anything from forensics?'

Corstorphine shook his head. 'Whoever it is, they know enough to keep each scene sterile. I don't hold out much hope. What we do need is some background on our French reporter, just in case she's linked to this clockmaker in Toulouse.'

'What about our man in Barlinnie?'

'We don't have time to see him, the best we can try for is a telephone interview.'

The Land Rover pulled into the station car park.

'Go home, Frankie, there's no point either of us working on this tonight and we need to be fresh for tomorrow.' He climbed into his own car, watching as Frankie drove off. This was either going to end well or end badly. Corstorphine already knew which outcome he'd choose to bet on. His wife looked at him in despair. *'James, have some faith in yourself, man. You're a better detective than all those idiots at HQ and you know it.'*

'Aye.' Corstorphine started his car, heading down roads he knew so well he could drive them with his eyes closed. 'Well, we'll see soon enough.'

His house was the only one in the street without any welcoming lights at the windows. He sat for a while in the drive.

The building stood, in his mind, as a monument to what might have been – and every time he returned home, the absence of warmth, light, laughter only served to turn the knife in his soul.

'I really ought to move, get somewhere smaller.' He spoke the words to himself, but he was letting his wife know that he had to move on. With the words spoken, Corstorphine turned the key in the front door, switched on the lights and TV, dialled up the heat at the thermostat and pulled the first frozen meal his hands encountered from the freezer. Tomorrow, he had three murders to deal with, and still no real suspects in the frame.

THIRTY-SEVEN

'Thank you for coming in, Mr Booth,' Corstorphine addressed the burly ginger-haired man sat facing him in the interview room, 'or would you prefer if I called you William?'

The sullen stare that William wore made it clear that he had better things to do that morning than decide on how he should be addressed by the detective opposite. 'Listen, I've got a business to run. Tell me what I'm here for and let's get this over as quickly as possible. Friday's one of my busiest days!'

'Fine.' Corstorphine nodded towards Frankie, who set the recorder running and informed William that his statement was being recorded. His countenance turned from sullen to worried in a split second.

'Why are you recording me, what do you think I've done?' His skin colour reddened, either rage or guilt, Corstorphine reckoned.

Frankie placed a bone gear onto the tabletop, the largest one that was found intact in the Hanging Tree. The one that had been identified as a cow scapula. It lay in mute reproach, cow accusing butcher.

'What's that?' William's eyes narrowed as he focussed on the bone.

'DC McKenzie has just placed exhibit twelve in front of the witness.' Corstorphine provided the voiceover. 'We were hoping you may be able to tell us.'

'Can I touch it?'

'Go ahead, it's been checked for prints and DNA.' Corstorphine omitted to add that nothing had been found, no point in making any potential suspect feel comfortable.

The butcher picked up the cog, turning it this way and that as he inspected it under the overhead fluorescents. 'Takes some skill to carve a bone like this,' he commented.

'You've carved bones, William?' Frankie asked.

William laughed. 'I'm a butcher, Frankie. The only carving I do is with a meat cleaver, but I know enough about bones splintering to tell you this wouldn't have been easy to carve. Must have used a lathe or something to get teeth that precise.' He placed it back down on the table, looking at them defiantly.

Corstorphine took up the slack. 'Any idea what animal it was?'

'How am I meant to know? The way it's been carved, it could be from anything.'

Corstorphine nodded. 'What do you do with your bones, William, once you've taken the meat and joints off?'

'There's a collection every week. The waste company provides us with wheelie bins for all the waste.'

'Where do you keep the bins?' Frankie focussed in on the specifics.

'Side passage. There's a locked gate to the road; we wheel the bin out for collection on a Thursday.'

'Have you noticed anyone going through your bins, or has the gate been tampered with recently?'

'What's this about?'

'Just answer the question, William.' Corstorphine checked his watch, he had to hurry this along.

'No to both. Anyone destitute enough to rake through bins would check the supermarket waste. There's nae joy to be had in a butcher's bin.' He smiled as if he'd just said something amusing.

'What were your movements two weeks ago, William, have you been anywhere near the laird's estate in Glen Mhor?' Corstorphine fixed him with a laser-sharp stare.

'What, me go anywhere near his estate? You have to be joking! I've kept as far away from that bastard as I can – and Oscar, he's bad news.'

'Did you want him dead, William?' Frankie asked quietly, acting as confessor to the penitent.

He glared at her, angry at the implied accusation. 'I didn't kill him, Frankie, if that's where you're going with this. Oscar...' He sat there in front of them looking like the lost boy he was. 'Oscar was a mad bastard, and he could be cruel – but he was my mate.' His voice dropped to almost a whisper. 'He was one of the few mates I ever had. I'd never kill him.'

'Can you provide any evidence of your movements during the last two weeks, William, anyone that can verify where you were, what you were doing?' Corstorphine pressed on.

'I've been working in my shop every day except Sunday. The shop's open from eight to six every day. I don't take enough to pay for any help, so it's just me. Most evenings when the shop is closed, I'm sorting out the cuts, making the mince, sausages and pies. I go home most days around ten, collapse in front of the TV and then go to bed before starting the same thing all over again. Sunday is the only day I get off, and I've spent every Sunday for the last few months with this girl in Fort William – do you want her number?' William said this more in the way of a challenge, one Corstorphine accepted.

'Yes please, write her details on this sheet and we'll be in touch to verify your statement. What about the minister of St Cuthbert's, have you ever been to the church?'

William laughed as if the idea of him attending church was a great joke. 'Me, go to church?' He started laughing anew. 'Oh man, that's rich.' He calmed down, wiping tears from his eyes. 'When you've been fucked by the minister, you don't go anywhere near his fucking church. Put that in your detective guidebook, Corstorphine. I don't know who killed the bastard, and I'm happy they've got to the minister – but Oscar was my mate. If I had any idea who it was, I'd shop them to you now – but I don't.' He looked them both in the eye without any sign of guile. Corstorphine was inclined to take him at face value.

'Tell me about your time at the orphanage, William. You were there from...' Corstorphine referred to a sheet of paper in his hand. 'Age five to sixteen. Were they good to you there, treat you and the other children well?'

A veil came down across his face, his features at once expressionless. 'I'm not saying anything about that place. I'm the one you should be defending, not treating me as a potential murderer, so either tell me what you're charging me with or I'm out of here!'

Another self-taught bloody criminal lawyer, Corstorphine thought to himself. 'We're just trying to get to the bottom of this, William. You are one of the few people we can identify that went to that orphanage, and we believe there may be a connection between the orphanage and the recent murders. We're just looking for your help, nothing else.'

He snarled in response. 'You lot, you're all in it together. You're the last people I'd ever go to.'

'How do you mean, we're all in it together?' Frankie asked.

'Not you, Frankie, but all the rest of them. We either shut up, or...'

'Or what, William?' Corstorphine's voice came quietly.

'You work that out, big man. There's enough of us died and nothing ever happened, nobody came.'

'We're on your side, William. We are not the enemy. If you don't give us any information, we can't start to put things right for you.'

'Aye right! I don't believe any of you bastards, all you do is protect the rich and famous. People like us – children like us can all be killed and it's as if we never existed.' He folded his arms in determination, lips tightly pressed together to reinforce that he'd said all he was going to say.

'Interview paused at 7:57 a.m.' Corstorphine switched off the recorder and stood up. 'Come with me, William, and keep quiet.'

William stood uncertainly, exchanging a worried glance with Frankie who shrugged in return. They trooped out of the interview room and followed Corstorphine down to the cells. He stopped in front of one of the doors, slid back the peephole and motioned for William to look inside.

William froze when he saw who was locked up and made to speak, until Corstorphine signed a theatrical shush with a finger in front of his mouth. The peephole cover was slid back, and they re-entered the interview room.

'You've banged up the old DI?' William's incredulity showed in his voice.

'Like I said, William, we're on your side, but we need your help – and from others that know what went on – if we are to put those guilty behind bars for a very long time.'

William sat in his seat with a stunned expression on his face. Corstorphine could imagine what the man sat opposite him was going through. William's understanding of a world that ran to an immutable set of rules where those in power took what they wanted with impunity had just been shattered. The implications of what this may mean, what it did mean to him and the others was beginning to sink in. He would have read of other orphanages; other children being abused – it had never occurred to him that the truth could ever be revealed here in a town so tightly controlled by the abusers. Threats were enough to keep him silent, threats and the use of law. Could all of that be about to change? He looked at Corstorphine properly for the first time, tried to see the man underneath. He nodded just once, a quick decisive movement directed at Corstorphine.

'Interview resumed at 8:09 a.m. What can you tell us, William? Are there any other children who were at the orphanage we can contact?' Corstorphine felt the first glimmer of hope since the first murder had occurred, the first encouragement that he might be able to crack this case wide open before the door was bolted shut.

'Speak to Simon, Simon Battle. He's in Barlinnie.'

'Aye, we've already got him on our list, William. Is there anyone else we can talk to?' Frankie pushed harder.

William shook his head. 'Everyone else got the fuck away as quickly as they could. I would if it wasn't for my shop. No, speak to Simon. He was set up by the sheriff to keep him quiet. There's nobody going to risk speaking whilst that bastard's running the courts.'

'The sheriff's dead, William. We found his body yesterday evening. Believe me, you've nothing to fear, but we need to know what you can tell us. Help us to help you.'

William sat with a stunned expression. 'The sheriff? What, murdered?'

Corstorphine and Frankie both nodded in response as he looked from one to the other.

'How? What happened to him?'

'We can't discuss that with you, William, but you've nothing to fear. We're on your side, but we need your help.'

Corstorphine's impassioned plea struck home, coupled with the shock of hearing of the laird's death.

'Simon was set up for the GBH charge. We were all in the same gang with Oscar, the Survivors we called ourselves. Oscar wanted to call us the Ones that Lived – he used to like the Harry Potter books.' He laughed, a short mirthless sound at the thought of Oscar enjoying reading children's books. 'Oscar beat this random guy up one night in town, took a dislike to his posh accent so decked him outside the Ring of Roses one night, then put the boot in proper. We were standing watching, none of us wanted to get involved. Once Oscar started, there was no way of stopping him – unless you wanted to end up in the same state as that poor bastard. We left him in the gutter, guess someone must have seen something 'cos the police siren came as soon as we'd left. Oscar was laughing about it fit to burst, always made him happy, a bit of violence. Anyway, out of nowhere he decks Simon, couple of punches to the face before carrying on up the road as before. Funny thing was, he wiped the guy's blood that was all over his hands and feet onto Simon's clothes. Deliberate like. Turned out Oscar was a witness at Simon's trial, said it was Simon who'd beaten the guy up and he'd heroically tried to stop him. The blood was used to frame Simon, and it was the sheriff who put him away. He knew Simon wouldn't cope with Barlinnie, it was like a fucking death sentence. I don't know how he's surviving in there...'

Corstorphine thought he had an inkling of how Simon might survive inside, especially as someone who'd had a lifetime of abuse.

'Will you sign a statement to this, William? If Simon has suffered a miscarriage of justice, we need supporting witnesses to get him out. We need to know who else was in your gang, in the Survivors.'

William looked trapped for a moment, as if he'd just realised that he'd committed himself to more than he'd intended. 'OK. I'll give you the names. I don't know where most of them are now, just a couple still live here. The rest left long ago, best thing to do. Those that didn't leave, either toed the line like me or ended up on drugs or taken care of – same thing really. An early exit from a shite life,' he said bitterly.

'What names can you give us, William?' Frankie asked gently.

'Margo. Margo McDonald. She was always there hanging onto Oscar like she couldn't bear to leave him. Craig Derbyshire, he works as a sparky for Highlands Power. George Winter, Georgie Porgie we called him. He sleeps behind the cinema most nights, under cardboard. Begs on the streets – you've probably seen him.'

'Is that all?' Corstorphine queried. 'They're the only people that witnessed the attack?'

'They're the only ones left.'

Corstorphine sighed. 'They'll have to do. If you're telling the truth, then we can at least put one wrong right.' He looked William straight in the eyes; this was the part of the interview he really didn't want to hear. 'Tell us about the abuse, William, in your own words. Take your time but try and include as much detail as you can, people, places, dates. I want to know everything you can tell us about what happened to you and the other children.'

William bowed his head, but not before Corstorphine saw the first tears trickle down his face. He spoke in an emotionless monotone, a story too horrific, a childhood betrayed. Corstorphine and Frankie listened in anguish, only stopping to ask him to repeat a word lost in his sobs. At the end of an hour, they let him go, drained of a burden he'd carried for too long. He had provided them with Lord Lagan's name, told them how the lord enjoyed putting all his weight on their small bodies until they could no longer breathe, how some of them were never seen again. The anger in Corstorphine's breast raged white-hot. He would use that anger, focus it where it could do the most good.

'Frankie, take Bill McAdam and track down Margo, Craig

Derbyshire and George Winter. Stick them in the holding cells for the time being, tell them they're witnesses for a major enquiry and it's for their own protection. May not be that far from the truth. I'm going to question Brian. Ask Hamish to bring him into the interview room. He's got some explaining to do.'

THIRTY-EIGHT

Brian Rankin entered the interview room in a rage, pushing the desk sergeant's arm away as he attempted to guide him in. 'What the hell do you think you're doing, Corstorphine? Have you lost your mind?'

Something in Corstorphine's expression took the wind out of his sails, the bluster replaced with doubt. 'Just sit, Brian. Hamish – you stay here with me.'

'Sir.' The sergeant sat beside Corstorphine, giving every impression of wishing to be anywhere else than facing his ex-boss in an interview room.

'Interview commencing Friday 23rd May at 9:07 a.m., present Detective Inspector James Corstorphine, Sergeant Hamish McKee and retired Detective Inspector Brian Rankin.' Corstorphine read out his rights and stared directly at the old DI.

'Look, I don't know what you think you're doing here, James, but it's already gone too far. I want my lawyer present, and I want to make my phone call. You have that on tape.'

Corstorphine nodded, this wasn't unexpected. 'That is your right. Make your call.' He passed over the old detective's mobile.

'Just the one call, Brian, and we'll be keeping hold of your phone, so don't try and be clever.'

Brian gave him a look that would have had Corstorphine backing down previously. Not now.

'Some privacy please and turn the recorder off.'

Corstorphine stood up, motioning the sergeant to accompany him. He stood outside, pulling the door closed. Before it shut completely, he spoke. 'And I wouldn't rush to get out of here, Brian. I don't think it's particularly safe for orphanage visitors at the moment.' He pulled the door shut, taking satisfaction in the old DI's worried expression.

They watched through the glass as the ex-DI made a single call, noticed him glance towards the one-way mirror they stood behind before placing the phone back on the table. 'Pass the phone out to me, Hamish, quickly, before it needs his permission to unlock it again. Sit with him, act the daft laddie, you don't tell him anything – alright?'

'Sir,' Hamish replied uncomfortably. He went back into the room to pass the mobile out to Corstorphine.

A quick check of recent numbers showed Corstorphine that Rankin had spoken to the sheriff on five occasions that week, plus a couple of times to the assistant chief constable dating back to the first time Corstorphine had mentioned the orphanage. That explained the ACC's sudden interest in the suicide investigation. There were a few numbers he didn't recognise – ones that Google returned as local tradesmen – nothing of interest until he saw the local Lord's number. The call was made Monday evening, just after he'd paid the first home visit to the retired detective, and the Right Honourable Reginald Lagan had made an appearance at the police station the very next morning. What would bring a Member of Parliament up from London overnight to put pressure on a small-town police investigation? He thought he had the answer.

The clock ticked towards nine-thirty; where was that

bloody solicitor? As if on cue the front door buzzer sounded. Corstorphine recognised the skull-like features of the town's most eminent and only criminal lawyer through the glass partition. He keyed the door lock to let him enter.

'Morning, Corstorphine. Now what's all this nonsense with Brian in the interview room, has there been some sort of administrative mix-up or something?'

'If only. You'd better come through.' He led the way to the interview room, started the recorder and continued. 'Joined by Mr Wallace Sweeney, solicitor at 9:27 a.m.'

The solicitor made a show of pulling his own recorder out of his briefcase and extracting a folio pad and pen which he arranged carefully in front of him. 'Do you mind?' He indicated his personal recorder.

'Mr Wallace Sweeney has requested that he independently record this conversation with his client, request granted.' An audible click sounded loud in the room as the solicitor turned on his device, then settled back in his chair with watchful eyes on the detective.

'Brian Rankin, can you describe your involvement with the Sisters of Holy Mercy orphanage that used to be situated on City Road?'

Brian and his solicitor exchanged a sharp look before the solicitor nodded imperceptibly.

'I only ever attended the orphanage in my official capacity as a serving member of the local police. There were sadly occasions when a child might pass away through illness, and we had by law to investigate in case there were any grounds for prosecution. None were ever found.'

'There were never any deaths that weren't reported?'

'Of course not. This was a caring, Christian community – not some third-world ghetto.'

'So, there's no way any deaths could have occurred without either yourself or the allocated doctor being made aware?'

'No, of course not!' Brian said with exasperation.

The solicitor placed a restraining hand on his arm. 'Where is this going, detective? My client hasn't been charged with anything and is helping you voluntarily. We are within our rights to leave at any time.'

'Please bear with me, your help is much appreciated.' Corstorphine glanced at his watch, calculating how long it would be before the other witnesses showed up. 'Let me get straight to the point.'

'At last!' the solicitor exclaimed with all the theatricality of someone used to performing in court.

Corstorphine ignored him. 'We've had an allegation, a written and signed statement from one of the orphanage children who was resident at the time you were a regular visitor.' Corstorphine read from the notes he had hastily written during the previous interview. 'He states that you were aware of at least five children who died at the orphanage and whose bodies were buried in the grounds against common law. He says he was present on one occasion when two of the children's bodies were inspected by you, and that he remembers seeing you being physically sick at the sight.'

'This is preposterous,' Brian managed to blurt out, before being cut off by the solicitor.

'My client does not have to sit here and listen to meaningless allegations. If you have no corroborating evidence – which will be the case as you haven't been able to charge my client, then this interview is terminated, and I am advising my client to answer no comment from here on in.'

Corstorphine smiled grimly at the archaic legal language, he'd heard it all before.

'There is also the allegation that the children at the orphanage were to your certain knowledge regularly sexually abused by people that you knew well, and that you took no action against them.'

'No comment.' The solicitor started packing his bag and motioning Brian to stand.

'And it has also been alleged that Mr Simon Battle was framed for grievous bodily harm with your knowledge and connivance to prevent him from telling the truth about the orphanage.'

Hamish looked towards Corstorphine for guidance as Rankin and his solicitor started making their way towards the door. Corstorphine continued unhurriedly. 'Finally, we have evidence that the death of June Stevens in 1997 was not a suicide, and that you wilfully misrepresented her death in order to prevent the prosecution of Oscar Anderson for her murder.'

They were almost running by now, the desk sergeant's panicked expression a response to indecision over what to do. Corstorphine held a hand up to stop him from interfering with their leaving.

'And that the murders of June Stevens, Oscar Anderson, the minister of St Cuthbert's and Sheriff Anthony McCallum are as a direct result of your criminal inaction.'

Brian Rankin's shocked face looked back at him as the news hit home. Corstorphine leisurely made his way to activate the door release, only for them to almost collide with Frankie and Bill McAdam leading three previous members of the Survivors gang into the station. Three additional witnesses who also had the opportunity to put the old DI behind bars.

The desk sergeant stared in confusion as the three of them filed in, each one taking a good hard look at the old DI as they walked past him and understanding in that single glance that they now held the power.

'That went about as well as I could hope,' Corstorphine said conversationally to no one in particular. 'Hamish, put our guests in the cells with the doors unlocked. I'm sorry, we have nowhere else to put you for the moment. You're not under arrest and can walk out at any time.' He held his hands up to stop the clamour that greeted this statement. 'Quiet, listen to me. You of all people know what it's like to have no one to turn to, no one to listen to you. William Booth has freely given a statement about everything, and I mean everything, that went on in that orphanage. If you can spare the time to let us interview each one of you, then we might see some justice in this town, starting with getting your old friend Simon Battle released from wrongful arrest.'

'There's nothing you can do, not whilst the sheriff is still in charge.' Margo's voice cut across the crowded room.

'The sheriff's been murdered, Margo. He was killed yesterday on the estate. This isn't only about righting wrongs, seeing that every child who suffered at the orphanage is given the right to see their abusers punished, it's also about preventing any more murders. One of you either knows or suspects who the murderer is or has information that will enable us to catch him. No matter what happened to you, and I know nothing can ever make that right, nobody can take the law into their own hands. Will you help me?'

'They had it coming.' A dishevelled character in need of personal hygiene spoke up. He had that unhealthy pallor that Corstorphine associated with a lifetime of dissolution, a single-minded dedication to the use of drugs and alcohol to erase a life no longer worth living. It didn't take a detective to work out this must be the homeless guy, George Winter.

'That's as may be, but now's your chance to take whoever was involved to court, see justice be done.' Corstorphine could see he was failing to inspire the three of them, who still stood there viewing him with distrust, in between looking at the exit.

'And there is the matter of compensation you'd be due if we follow this through.' He'd played his trump card, watched the calculating signs appear in their eyes and knew he'd got them.

'Margo, shall we start with you? Hamish, can you make Mr Craig Derbyshire and Mr George Winter as comfortable as possible and we'll have them in as soon as we can? Frankie, in with me please.'

As Hamish led the other two down the stairs, Corstorphine indicated the interview room to Margo. Against her instincts she entered the room, wondering how much she could make out of this – enough to set her up for life?

'I'll have to record this conversation, Margo, and read you your rights. Just tell me the truth. If you lie, then it gives the defence the perfect opportunity to destroy any case we bring. Do you understand?'

She nodded and sat with hands folded protectively across her womb.

Margo ran through everything she'd already told *The Courier*, adding details where Corstorphine pressed for more information. She confirmed that Oscar had beaten up the victim that drunken evening and not Simon Battle.

'Where was the reporter's notebook, Margo? Where exactly did you find it?'

'I found it in the locked equipment store. It was the only place Oscar kept locked up. I wouldn't have even looked for it, but the laird was sniffing about. He knew Oscar had it, at least I think he knew he had something. Oscar always had some kind of hold over him; it wasn't the usual laird/gamekeeper relationship.' She laughed mirthlessly.

'Was there anything else, Margo, anything else that might help us identify who the murderer is?'

Margo reached into her bag and placed the photographs down on the desk in front of her.

'What are these?' Corstorphine queried.

''They were in with the reporter's notebook. I think it's the children who were killed. Someone's drawn a skull and crossbones on the back of eight of them.'

Frankie reached over to take the photographs. They looked like the sort of thing you'd take at a passport photo booth, in the days before colour. She selected one, turned it over to show Corstorphine. There was the roughly inked outline of a skull and crossbones, a child's representation of death.

'Who is this?' Frankie held the photograph face up for Margo to see.

She looked at it momentarily, disinterested. 'Don't know. Friends of Oscar's? Back when he had friends,' she added.

'Who do you think drew the skull symbol on the back?'

'How should I know? I only saw them when I found the tin in the shed.'

'What tin was that, Margo?' Corstorphine's voice was quiet.

'The photos and notebook were kept in a tin, to stop the mice eating them I suppose. It was up in the rafters, I saw it with the flashlight.'

'What else did you find in the tin?'

Margo squirmed uncomfortably. 'There wasn't anything else, just the notebook and photos.'

Corstorphine raised an eyebrow. 'Who could identify these children?'

'I dunno. Ask Craig and Georgie, they stayed at the orphanage. I was just taken there by my parents whenever they volunteered to help. Godly work they called it, working with the Holy Sisters.'

'Did they now? Are they still living here?' Corstorphine sensed another line of enquiry.

'Mum is, my dad died years ago. She's still living at home. I haven't seen her for ten years at least.'

'What's her address?' Frankie took down the address of one of the council houses on the estate.

Corstorphine wrapped up the interview. 'Margo, we'll get a statement of what you've told us which you'll need to sign. Can you stay here for an hour or so until we get that done?'

'I suppose,' came the sulky reply. 'How much do you think we're going to get?'

'That's difficult to say, Margo. How long's a piece of string?' Corstorphine formally concluded the interview, turning off the recorder as Frankie escorted Margo out of the room.

Margo muttered something under her breath as she passed Frankie by. It sounded suspiciously like 'how fucking long is a length of fucking string.'

THIRTY-NINE

'Lamb!' Corstorphine called out from the interview room, and the PC nervously poked his head around the door.

'Yes, sir?'

'Come in. Stop making the place look even more uncomfortable. Here, grab a seat.'

PC Lamb sat uncomfortably beside the DI, wearing an expression that Corstorphine associated with a guilty conscience.

Corstorphine already had a shrewd idea he was the source of the newspaper's inside information; he'd been spotted buying the French reporter drinks in a town bar – nothing stayed secret here for long. Then there were a few idiosyncratic turns of phrase used in the paper which she was unlikely to have learned during the time she'd been here, and the clumsy description of the minister's death incorporating the words dead ringer in an extremely unsubtle way.

'You know the French reporter for *The Courier*, don't you?'

Lamb's crestfallen face was sufficient evidence for Corstorphine, but he had other more pressing concerns. 'Do you know what part of France she's from?'

Lamb's look of relief would have been amusing in any other circumstances. 'Paris, sir. She told me she's from Paris. Came over here a year ago to improve her English and saw the reporter's job advertised.'

'Unusual for a Scottish newspaper to employ a French reporter, isn't it?'

'Well, she worked for *Paris Match* or something, some big newspaper, impressed *The Courier*'s editor so much that he offered her the job there and then.'

Corstorphine frowned as he wrote neat notes in his notebook. 'She's never had any connection with Toulouse?'

'Not that she ever told me, sir. I don't know her that well, sir. Just bumped into her at a few places and had a brief chat.'

'OK. Thanks, you've answered one question.' Lamb's relieved expression faltered as Corstorphine added, 'For the moment. Frankie tells me your father works for Highland Geophysical Research?'

'Yes, sir, he's the CEO.'

'Good. I want you to ask him whether he could do us a massive favour.'

'Yes, sir, certainly. I'm sure he'd be glad to – they're looking for work now the A9 groundworks is winding down.'

Corstorphine passed over a sheet from the ordnance survey, an irregular outline marked in red biro prominent on the page. 'If he can spare the equipment and manpower, I want this area checked with ground penetrating radar this morning or as soon as humanly possible.'

'The site of the old orphanage gardens. What can I tell him you're looking for, sir?'

'Graves. He's looking for shallow unmarked graves that are the size of young children. Keep me informed.'

'Yes, sir. Do you want me to go now, sir?'

Corstorphine bit his tongue. 'Yes, Lamb. Now! And ask your Josephine Sables to pop in urgently. I've something interesting for her. Tell her to bring the notebook, she'll know what I mean.'

Corstorphine rummaged around in his desk, pulling out a small electrical screwdriver and returned to the interview room.

'Hamish, can you bring George Winter to the interview room. Oh, and raise a maintenance report when you get back to the front desk, the recording light seems to have stopped working on the voice recorder.'

By the time the desk sergeant returned, George Winter following in his footsteps like a lost wean, the screwdriver had been returned to Corstorphine's pocket. 'Can you stay in here, sergeant, get Mr Winter comfortable? I just need to get a fresh memory stick for the recorder.'

Corstorphine requisitioned a new USB memory stick and placed the old one on Frankie's desk. 'I know you've already a lot on your plate, but I need a written statement for Margo to sign before she loses patience and leaves. Her interview is on this USB.'

'We're getting calls from the press, sir. They want a TV interview for the evening news and—'

'Stall them. Brian will have called the ACC by now. I reckon we have at best an hour before he marches in here and tries to shut the whole investigation down.'

'He can't do that! We need to find out the truth about those children and we've still to identify the murderer.'

'He can, and he will. It's his prerogative to replace us with a hand-picked team from Inverness if he wants. We just have to make that as difficult as possible for him. Get Margo's words printed out and make sure she signs and dates it, make two copies and countersign them yourself with date and time. I'm going to interview George Winter now, then Craig Derbyshire and hopefully get corroborative statements. Then we'll see how Brian wants to play it once the cards are down.'

Corstorphine returned to the interview room, ran through

the witness briefing and turned on the recorder. 'The time is 10:24 a.m., Friday 23rd May, present DI Corstorphine, Sergeant Hamish McKee and Mr George Winter. The recorder is now running, for the record the voice recorder light has stopped working, we all OK with that?'

They nodded, wondering why he'd made a point of mentioning it.

'OK. George, you were at the orphanage run by the Sisters of Holy Mercy for how long?'

'I don't remember anywhere else, so I must have been there as a baby. I left at sixteen like everyone else did, they didn't want us once we were grown up.'

'Did you ever suffer from any abuse whilst at the orphanage?'

His eyes shot up from contemplation of the table. 'You said the sheriff's been killed, is that right?'

'Yes. His body was found yesterday evening.'

He grinned, eyes suddenly more alive than before. 'Good!'

'Why do you say that, George? Did you have any reason to dislike the sheriff?'

'I hated the bastard, I'm glad someone's got to him.'

'Did you have anything to do with his death, George?' Corstorphine asked gently.

'Me? You have to be joking. I can't even manage to kill meself. Tried enough times.'

'Can you tell us about life at the orphanage, George?' Corstorphine asked again, trying not to look towards the clock ticking each second away one by one.

'It wasn't a place any child should have been sent to. You think you know what hell is, Inspector? Let me tell you. Hell isn't a place where you go when you die, and red devils torment you in fire for all eternity. No, it's a lot worse than that. It's a place where poor defenceless kids are left as playthings for the rich and powerful, where they're used and thrown away like garbage, where they are killed for fun.'

'You saw this yourself?'

'Aye. I saw it. And I saw who did it. Those faces will never leave me, they come out of the dark to torment me even now when I try and sleep. Death will be a fucking relief, but I'm glad they're being taken, one by one.'

Corstorphine leaned forward. 'Who do you remember, George? What are their names?'

He suddenly clammed up. 'I'm not saying anything. You can't do anything about them, they're too powerful.'

'We've already been given names, George. William Booth has given us names, Margo has given us names. The more people give us information, the more we can make sure that we take these abusers down. Will you help us?'

He looked at them both, greasy hair turning grey as it curled over the collar of a coat two sizes too big for him. 'What the fuck. What can anyone do to me now anyway, it's not as if I can sink any lower?'

His eyes cast downwards, unwilling or unable to face the two policemen as he told his tale of lost childhood for the first time in his life. At the end, Corstorphine passed over the photographs of the children. He looked at them as if seeing ghosts.

'Do you recognise any of these children, George? Were they at the orphanage with you?'

'Aye, I know some of them.' He made two small piles, pointing to the pile of eight. 'These are the ones they killed, the people I told you about.' He spelled out their names as he placed each one down, then spread the remaining seven out on the table, pulling out one. 'This is me.' Another three photographs were lifted out of the pile. 'This one's Craig, this one's William Booth, and this one's Oscar.'

'What was Oscar doing at the orphanage?' Corstorphine queried. 'He had parents.'

'Oh, Oscar was the minister's favourite. He brought him along for all the special parties. His parents were in the congregation – they thought the minister was mentoring him, showing him the path to God. Instead...' He let the implications hang in the air.

Corstorphine formally finished the interview at 10:55 a.m., and had the sergeant accompany George back to the unlocked cell. He felt physically and mentally drained, but at least he now had the names of the children in the photographs, and the names of five children whose deaths were never reported. Just one interview to go.

'Bill?' The PC was typing up the sheriff's death on the report sheet. 'Leave that. I want this audio recording typed up as soon as you can, get George Winter to read and sign it, then countersign, date and time. Take two copies.'

He walked over to the front desk to see what the commotion was. Hamish was trying to fend off a growing melee of reporters. 'Clear reception, Hamish, and lock the doors.' In a louder voice, he addressed the throng. 'You'll get a statement in good time. In the meantime, we have a job to do.' He spotted Josephine trying to get in through the crowd of reporters and film crew, motioned her to go around the back to the car park.

'I had a message that you have some information for me?' She seemed totally unfazed by the scrum of reporters out front.

He locked the rear door before anyone else had the bright idea of entering the station that way. 'Come with me.'

His office was an oasis of calm amid a growing storm. 'You've heard the laird has been found dead?'

'Why do you think I'm here? It was all around town by 9 a.m., I've been trying to call you, but the lines are always busy.'

'Yes, well, we didn't design the comms infrastructure with the expectation that we'd be in the centre of a major murder enquiry. Listen, I don't have much time – did you bring the notebook and transcription?'

She dug around in her over-shoulder bag and produced two clear plastic folders. 'My editor said you'd have a warrant before I hand these over?'

'I'll have a warrant for you, eventually. In the meantime, I'm going to give you everything I know.'

She looked at him in surprise. 'Why would you do that? You could jeopardise any prosecution, never mind lose your job!'

Corstorphine offered her a thin smile. 'This is what I want you to do with the information.'

It had gone 11:30 a.m. by the time Josephine had slipped out the back door, shorthand pad full of hastily constructed hieroglyphs. Still no sign of the assistant chief, at least something was going his way today.

'OK, Frankie, how's the statement looking?'

'Finished, sir, and Margo's signed it. She had one look at the front door and decided to stay here a while.'

He grimaced. 'Can't blame her for that. Let's get Craig in for a chat.'

Once again, they sat in the interview room, Frankie accompanying him this time.

'Craig, thanks for your time, I'll try and make this as brief as I can. You were at the orphanage at the same time as George Winter?'

'He was a lot older than me. I was only ten when I went there, same time as that journalist's daughter. George must have been thirteen or fourteen.'

Corstorphine and Frankie exchanged a glance, this was the first time anyone had mentioned the girl. 'What can you tell me about her, what was her name?'

'Abigail Stevens. She must have been five, something like

that. I didn't see much of her; they kept the young ones in a separate part of the building.'

'What happened to her?' Frankie questioned.

'I don't know, as I say, didn't really see much of her. I know she spent a lot of time in the hole.'

'What's that, the hole?' Frankie pressed.

'It was a room, small windows, no heat or anything. Nothing in there but stone walls and floor. If you didn't do what the nuns told you, then you were put in there without anything to eat or drink. Solitary confinement, I think you'd call it now.'

Frankie exchanged a significant look with Corstorphine before asking him to continue.

'I often saw her with that detective who was in here earlier. He was the one who brought her in. I was out playing in the yard when he turned up in the police car with her in the back. I only noticed her because she was screaming, trying to get away.'

'DI Brian Rankin brought her to the orphanage?' Corstorphine asked.

'Aye. He was never interested in the boys, if you get what I mean. We reckoned he had a thing for young girls.'

'Did you ever know that for sure?' Frankie seemed unwilling to believe his claim.

Craig glared at her defiantly. 'Don't you believe anything I've said? You think I'd make stuff like this up?'

Corstorphine held a hand up, a pacifying gesture. 'We believe you, Craig, but we need more than just an idea that Brian Rankin may have been involved in sexual abuse with young girls. Can you state for the record that you saw Brian Rankin involved in any such activity?'

Craig shifted uncomfortably in his seat. 'No. Not for sure. It's just every other visitor that came was there for one thing. He may not have done anything.' He brightened suddenly. 'Oscar reckoned he'd seen the girl in the detective's car in the town the morning she disappeared. Everyone else said she'd run away, probably died on the moors.'

'We'll look into it.' Corstorphine paused, watching Craig closely as he asked the next question. 'What can you tell us of your movements during the last two weeks?'

'You think I was involved in the murders?'

'Were you?'

Craig didn't answer immediately, his eyes fixed on the table between them. 'I've thought about killing the people that did those things to us, yes, of course I have. Any of us will have had the same thoughts.' His eyes raised from contemplation of the table to match Corstorphine's piercing stare. 'I don't have the guts to kill them, I wish I did.'

Corstorphine's eyebrow remained lowered – he was speaking the truth. 'I still need to know where you've been over the last two weeks.'

'I've been replacing power lines north of Inverness over the last month, Monday to Friday. Just call the Inverness office, they'll be able to confirm.'

'And weekends?'

'I spend the weekends with my wife and family.' Craig's expression changed in an instant to pleading. 'I don't want my wife to know about any of this, anything that happened at the orphanage. You can talk to her but don't tell her about the abuse, please. I'm not sure I can take it.'

'We'll not mention anything about the orphanage, Craig, but it's already in the press. I can't guarantee you'll be able to keep your involvement quiet.'

'Then I'm not saying anything.' He made to stand.

'Wait!' Corstorphine held his hand level to the table, indicating that he regain his seat. 'None of us here will release the names of people involved, you have my word on that. The press doesn't know your names, they only have Margo and Oscar – neither of whom were orphans. I'll talk to the reporter at *The*

Courier, make sure she doesn't name any of you even if she somehow manages to get that information. That's the best I can do, Craig. Either way you stand the same risk of being identified. If you don't help us with this investigation, that's your prerogative, but without your help, it will be that more difficult to put these people behind bars. Will you help us, or do you want to live with the possibility you had the one chance to get back at them and bottled it?'

Craig's expression reflected the conflict going on inside his mind, fight or flee.

'I'll give you a statement.' The words came reluctantly, in a quiet monotone.

Corstorphine nodded. 'I'll do everything I can to protect your identity, you and the others. You have my word on it. In the meantime, I want you to remember everyone that you saw at the orphanage, names, dates if you can, what they did.'

As the interview drew to a close, Corstorphine knew he finally had enough detail to make a case, more than enough to prevent the ACC from closing them down.

FORTY

Corstorphine stared at the crazy wall, desperately searching for a clue to stand out and point the way forward. He glanced at the clock, still no sign of the assistant chief – it was only a matter of time. So far, he had the three murders arranged at the top, the minister and sheriff, both of whom each of the former orphans had accused of child abuse, and Oscar who apparently was employed as a hired thug. Circumstantial evidence now placed Oscar at the scene of the reporter's death back in 1997. Oscar would have been about eighteen, certainly old enough and strong enough to have committed the act. If the reporter had been about to go public on what she'd discovered about the orphanage, then there were a number of people who'd have wanted her dead. He added her daughter to the board, Abigail Stevens, and pinned a red string connecting her to Brian Rankin, responsible for bringing her to a place where he must have known she was likely to suffer abuse – yet according to Craig Derbyshire, he may also have been responsible for getting her away some months later. Why?

Corstorphine had photocopied the five small children's photographs and placed them on the board, waiting on word from Lamb and the ground penetrating radar. How five children could just go missing with social services and all the other agencies involved was beyond him. The Sisters of Holy Mercy would have to wait for the moment, there weren't the resources to deal with them until he'd identified and arrested the murderer, although they were as guilty as sin itself. It had to be one of the orphans, they had the motive. He felt this was especially likely given the specific nature of each death, making the punishment fit the individual if not the crime. The way the laird died suggested that the murderer also spent some time in solitary confinement, in the hole as Craig Derbyshire had put it. The similarity to the chosen method of execution couldn't have been mere coincidence.

The suspects then – Margo still remained on the periphery, but he was fairly certain she didn't have the skills or imagination to plan each death so carefully. Craig Derbyshire was a possibility. He'd managed to hold down a job locally and had put his past behind him to a large extent. He had also displayed satisfaction at the mention of each death. His work alibi was likely to stand up to scrutiny, leaving him the weekends to plan and execute each murder – assuming his wife would cover for him. That seemed unlikely if he was desperate to keep his time at the orphanage a secret from her, there was nothing more likely to attract her interest than to involve her in a deception. George Winter was homeless, a drug addict and beggar. He was the unfortunate victim of a life that was loaded against him before he'd even started. Did he have the wherewithal to plan and execute three murders to this level of detail? He was the only one without an alibi, but then again, he would have struggled to remember what year it was, never mind provide a detailed explanation of his movements during the past fortnight. Corstorphine wrote each name down on the wall as he considered them. That left William Booth, the butcher. He lived locally, worked for himself – even so, with limited time he could get away and prime each death trap in readiness for the victim. He was also the only person with ready access to bone to make the devices. Finally, there was the gamekeeper, John Ackerman. The only link he had was with the laird and Oscar, but he had broken into the laird's house. What about the other orphans, those who had been on the council's list, but they had so far been unable to track down?

Corstorphine shook his head. The job was looking impossible – chasing a murderer who left no forensics clues, only bizarre contraptions that must have taken hours to construct. He tried to get inside the murderer's head, to imagine how they would have coped as a child, forgotten and unloved in the cold Victorian orphanage. How did any of them survive?

'Anything I can help with, sir?' Frankie's enquiry brought him back to the present.

'Just trying to identify a likely culprit, Frankie, someone clever enough to plan these murders without leaving any evidence connecting them to the scenes. Somehow, I don't think it's anyone we've put on the board.'

Frankie stepped closer to the crazy wall, her fingers almost touching photographs of the recent victims.

'I think the murderer is trying to tell us something.'

'How do you mean?' Corstorphine watched her intently as her finger traced an imaginary line between photographs and pared-down forensics reports.

'Oscar – he was hanged. Same place as June Stevens. Then the minister, crushed by his own bell. The laird was responsible for locking kids in 'the hole' – it can't be a coincidence that he died locked up, alone in the dark.'

His mind struggled to pierce the fog. The lack of sleep was getting to him.

'The pattern certainly makes these deaths look personal. Someone has been planning these murders for a long time. But Oscar doesn't fit – he was a victim too.'

'Do you think there's going to be another murder, sir, is there someone we should be keeping an eye on?'

Corstorphine rubbed his chin, feeling the stubble rough against his fingers. The relentless string of events was beginning to take its toll, his personal hygiene held hostage to the need for sleep before the next day's fresh horrors. 'The only other person we have identified as an alleged abuser is living in London, and well enough protected from some insane murderer.'

'Insane?'

He turned towards Frankie, eyes red-rimmed where he'd been rubbing them to keep alert. 'Perhaps. Don't they say that it's a fine line between insanity and genius? Whoever our murderer is, they've designed some extremely efficient methods to kill their victims without having to be present at the death.'

'Could be they're squeamish, sir. Don't like the sight of blood.'

'Possibly, Frankie. I'm open to all possibilities at the moment.' He changed tack. 'We need Craig's statement signed before he leaves, and has Bill finished preparing George Winter's statement?'

'I'll check, sir. If not, I'll type Craig's – always knew my touch-typing course would come in useful one day.'

Corstorphine watched her as she spoke to the PC; the resigned look she sent his way told him she'd be typing for the next hour at least. He sat down in his office and looked up the number for Barlinnie. The prison staff weren't keen to arrange an impromptu telephone interview with Simon Battle, making their displeasure felt by taking an eternity to remove him from his cell and into an interview room. Corstorphine waited. He needed an excuse to do nothing, to just sit with the receiver held to his ear whilst the world continued without him. A click announced someone on the other end of the line, followed by a hesitant voice querying who was there.

'This is Detective Inspector James Corstorphine, is that Simon Battle?'

A pause, then a reluctant response to the affirmative. 'What do you want?' His voice betrayed anger, a reluctance to engage. 'Thought you lot were coming here yesterday morning. Did you find something more interesting to do?'

'We had to turn back. Sheriff Anthony McCallum was reported missing. We found his body last night.'

'The laird? No way!' The line lay silent, waiting on confirmation or denial. The silence apparently provided the answer Simon needed. 'Fucking great! You've just made my day! Who got to him?'

'That's one of the reasons I'm talking to you, Simon. I was hoping you may have an idea? I'm investigating alleged child abuse at the City Road orphanage as part of a multiple murder enquiry. I have statements from Margo McDonald, Craig Derbyshire, George Winter and William Booth who have all stated that abuse happened at the orphanage, that you were also a victim – and that Oscar Anderson set you up for the GBH charge you're in for. I can understand you have little to trust the police for, Simon, but I'm determined to get to the truth and won't stand by whilst an innocent man rots in jail.'

The line fell silent again. Corstorphine could picture Simon processing the news, working the angles, trying to trust the enemy.

'Who else has gone, you said multiple murders?'

It was Corstorphine's turn to go silent. No point in holding back, the press would publish the names soon enough. 'Oscar Anderson was killed sometime Friday, the minister Reverend Simon McLean on Sunday and the sheriff yesterday. I think it's one of the orphans taking revenge. Do you have any idea who may be responsible, Simon, before anyone else dies?'

'Those bastards all deserved it, and there are others out there who should be worried. I'm glad they're all dead.'

'Who else should be worried, Simon? Give me some names.'

'You said you knew I was innocent?'

'That's what the four statements I have say, yes.'

'And you're going to get me out of here?' His voice held the first sign of hope, a drowning man clutching a straw tight enough but still having something to hold onto.

'I'm putting the wheels in motion, Simon. I can't promise it will happen anytime soon, but with this new information, I'm confident we can get you released, yes.' Corstorphine held back, feeling the fish nibbling on the line. Strike too soon and he'd lose the catch.

'I don't know who's taking them out, but I'm fucking glad he's out there. You'd better tell that old detective to watch out – he knew fine well what was going on here and did nothing. There's only one other bastard who needs killing. Lord fucking Lagan! Hope he gets to him before you do.'

Corstorphine forgot to breathe for a few seconds, Simon's corroboration of the name Frankie had whispered two days ago made the unthinkable suddenly a real possibility.

'There's nothing else you can give me, no idea who we should be looking for?'

Simon's laugh echoed down the line. 'Man. I've been in here for years – how the fuck am I meant to know who it is?'

Corstorphine let him know they'd be making a return trip to take a written statement and put down the phone.

It was no good, he couldn't put off getting the old DI back in for questioning now that he had sworn statements, unwilling as he was to confront the possibility that his old boss – someone he'd always looked up to – could be implicated in all this. Decision made, he dialled Brian's home number. At least he could provide him with some warning this time, give him the opportunity to explain something to his wife before the squad car collected him.

Brian answered the phone. 'Hello, James, I wondered how long it would take before I heard from you again.'

'We've four signed statements, Brian, implicating you directly in the abuse at the old orphanage. I've no choice but to get you in, officially this time.'

'I never touched any of those kids, James.' His voice held vehement denial. 'So if any of those so-called witnesses have made that claim, then they're lying!'

'You've not been accused of abuse, Brian, but of knowingly hiding it and refusing to investigate any of the children's allegations. Why Brian? Why didn't you help them?' The phone remained mute. 'What about the girl, the reporter's daughter, Abigail Stevens? One of our witnesses claims you brought her to the orphanage after her mother's so-called suicide. Why would you leave a defenceless five-year-old girl in a place like that when you knew fine well what was going on?'

'She was safe there. I made sure of it.' His voice was so quiet Corstorphine had to strain to hear him.

'How could she possibly be safe, man? In the hands of psychopathic nuns and subject to the sexual whims of any number of visitors! Christ, man. I thought I knew you.'

'Nothing ever happened to her. I swear it.'

'Where did you take her, the morning she vanished? Someone saw you with her, Brian, in your car. She didn't just run off and become lost on the moors, did she?'

There was a silence. Corstorphine wondered if the old DI was still on the other end of the line, then he spoke.

'Yes, I took her away from there. I set her up with a new family, somewhere far away where she'd never be found. I knew her mother had been murdered, I was fairly sure it was Oscar who murdered her, left her hanging. I can imagine the sadistic bastard enjoyed telling her how her daughter would end up in the orphanage as she struggled on the rope. It was my poor attempt to make amends, try and make one thing good out of it.'

'Why, Brian? You could have reported it, got the placed closed down, make sure those involved were put away for a long time.'

'What names have you got, James? The laird? The minister?'

'There's more than that, Brian, you'd know better than me. You can add Lord Reginald Lagan to the list.'

Brian laughed, the sound echoing down the line like a lost soul. 'That's why I had no choice, that's why I saw small, bloodied bodies buried in makeshift graves and nobody dared say anything about it. Your investigation will be closed down, you know that, don't you? There's no way the establishment can allow anything this big to get out. What's a few unloved children to the sanctity of the British establishment, James?'

'You can make this right, Brian. Just give us an honest statement naming everyone, and I mean everyone that was involved. I'll take it all the way, I promise. We'll make sure you're protected inside, if it comes to that.'

'I'm sorry, James. I'm so sorry.' A muffled sob was immediately stifled the other end. 'I've got to go now, James. I wasn't a bad cop, there's nothing I could do – not against them.'

'Nobody is above the law, Brian.'

'Yes, they are, James. Some people are untouchable, no matter how bad the crime. Look after Molly for me, will you? She never knew anything about this.'

'Brian! Brian?' The phone was dead. 'Shit!' Corstorphine grabbed the patrol car keys and ran for the door, turning on his heel as he remembered the crowd of reporters out front. 'Frankie! With me, fast!'

Corstorphine spun the tyres on the car park tarmac in his hurry to get out, only to be prevented from exiting the station car park by a large van equipped with a satellite dish. He turned on the siren, gesticulating wildly to the driver to get out of his way. The sound attracted a throng of reporters waving microphones and cameras towards him in an effort to gain a scoop on the town murders, hemming them in even tighter.

By the time he'd cleared the car park exit, they'd already lost five precious minutes.

'You don't think he's going to do anything stupid, do you, sir?' Frankie's worried face stared forward as if willing the car to travel even faster through the town centre.

'I don't know, he sounded… strange. Get out of the fucking way!' A mobility scooter had frozen on the traffic light crossing, the driver staring at the patrol car in shock. Frankie gestured for him to move and they sat impatiently as the rider struggled to engage forward motion. By the time they reached the old DI's house, twenty minutes had elapsed, and Corstorphine's mind was not put at ease by the sight of Molly standing distraught in the road.

'It's Brian. The garage. There was a shot!' Frankie caught Molly as her legs buckled under her, arms waving weakly towards the house. 'Help him, James. Please. Oh God!'

Corstorphine tried the garage door; it was locked. The windows were grubby, covered in dust which he managed to partly clear with his sleeve. What he saw didn't make him feel any better.

'Frankie. Get an ambulance here, fast!' Putting his shoulder to the door, he threw himself against the wood. The whole building shook in response, but the door held. He took a run at the door and it finally burst open, Corstorphine almost falling over the old DI's body as he flew into the garage. Brian Rankin wasn't going to be giving a statement, not with the top of his head missing.

'Fuck! Fuck! Fuck!' Corstorphine spoke the words one at a time, loudly, precisely, clearly. He knelt down and lifted the gun out of the old detective's slack fingers with a pen, dropping it carefully into an evidence bag. 'Where did you get this from?' He didn't expect a reply.

'Brian!' The scream of anguish came from the open door, Frankie holding onto Molly, pulling her back.

'There's nothing we can do, Molly. I'm so sorry.'

Molly cut him short, her words like daggers. 'What did you say to him, James? What have you done to make him do this to himself, to us? WHAT HAVE YOU DONE!' Her voice broke into meaningless sounds, grief piling upon grief as she struggled to make sense of the blood and brains spread over the garage floor and wall. She turned into Frankie, arms wrapped around her as if seeking a safe anchor in a world turned upside down.

Corstorphine's arm went out to comfort her, the gun in his hand still visible in its plastic bag. He withdrew, left her with Frankie. He was the last person she wanted to see.

'I'll secure the scene, sir.' Frankie spoke from over Molly's shaking shoulder.

Corstorphine nodded in gratitude. There was nothing he could do for Molly except to leave.

'Christ, what a mess.' He spoke the words under his breath as he climbed into the police car. 'What a fucking mess.' A feeling of guilt washed over him like an oily tide. Brian would still be alive if he'd only taken him into custody first thing. There had been enough evidence to hold him just with William Booth's statement, never mind the other supporting statements. It had been through a misplaced sense of loyalty that he'd let him go, a gesture towards a friendship that had existed since the day they'd first met. If anyone was guilty of his death, his culpability played a large part. He left the two women wrapped in each other's arms, acutely aware of Molly's accusing eyes following him as he drove away.

FORTY-ONE

Corstorphine met Hamish's questioning expression as he pushed past the huddle of reporters crowding the police station entrance, ignoring the clamour of questions and waiting until the sergeant had locked the door behind him before answering his mute query.

'Brian's dead. I found his body in the garage.'

'Brian? Dead? What happened?' The questions tumbled over each other, words uttered in disbelief. 'God. Poor Molly! What happened, was it an accident?'

'Suicide. He shot himself in the head.'

'Shot himself?' The desk sergeant was reduced to parroting Corstorphine's words back at him, standing frozen in shock. Hamish noticed the evidence bag for the first time as Corstorphine withdrew it from his pocket.

'Can you put this somewhere safe? Frankie's with her, she'll stay until the body's been dealt with. Molly's sister is on her way, she'll be well looked after.'

The desk sergeant carried the package as if it was contagious, the plastic bag gingerly held pinched between finger and thumb. Corstorphine sat down heavily in his office chair, head bowed in exhaustion, held in his hands. Four people had now died in the space of the last seven days, five children were being exhumed from shallow graves – how many more bodies would be found before this was over? He logged in to his computer, searching through the ever-growing list of emails and dismissing each one as he opened them. Nothing new from forensics, nothing on the search for any orphanage children who'd left and to all appearances had disappeared without trace, nothing on June Stevens' missing daughter – Abigail Stevens. 'What was it you knew, Brian? Why kill yourself?' The questions fell on empty air.

Corstorphine crossed over to the incident board, drawing a diagonal red line for Brian Rankin's death on the top row where he shared space with Oscar, the minister and the laird. He replayed the last call he'd had with Brian before the phone went dead. Brian had specifically named Lord Lagan from the House of Lords. Had he made this final confession knowing he was about to kill himself, one last attempt to make amends after hiding the truth for so many years? This was the same name that June Stevens' notebook contained. If someone that senior was involved in child abuse, it would explain the lack of prosecutions, of a blind eye being turned. It would also explain Brian's behaviour in covering up the abuse, even of covering up June's murder if he was leaned on hard enough.

His eye fell on the five children's black and white photographs at the bottom of the board, two of whose bodies Brian Rankin had seen and kept quiet. What if the lord's particular peccadillo caused the death of some of his victims, was that why only two of the survivors named him? Had Lord Lagan purposefully crushed the life out of those small bodies for some sick thrill? Corstorphine felt the anger seething just underneath the surface – they'd need to do more than lean on him to keep him quiet. With a single-minded focus, he concentrated on the crazy wall. Of the alleged abusers only Lord Lagan remained alive, the last of the names provided by William Booth and Simon Battle. At least that was sufficient confirmation that the name in the reporter's notebook was worthy of investigation. Staring at the laird's photograph, Corstorphine was taken back to the conversation he'd had with Frankie just four days ago, although it seemed a lifetime away. She'd mentioned the gamekeeper John Ackerman saying that the sheriff had it coming, that he might be in danger. He'd dismissed it at the time, took Ackerman's warning as bravado – then they'd found the laird's body. The gamekeeper had already been eliminated as Oscar's murderer, his alibi held for the week during which the snare must have been set, although he'd been placed at the laird's house on the day of his disappearance. Did he have the ability to design the laird's trap and put it into place in the weeks before his death? More to the point, Corstorphine had not only failed to protect the laird, but had given Brian sufficient time to arrange his suicide and there was the last potential victim staring haughtily out from his position next to the laird – Lord Lagan. Was he as safe as Corstorphine thought, tucked away in his London home or sitting in the House of Lords? A sudden premonition came to him, and a chill ran down his spine as he searched online for the Inverness Ball, a gathering of the great and good of the Highlands. It was to be held tonight, and Lord Lagan was almost certain to be in attendance. If the killer knew all of their other victims' moves so well, surely they'd be cognisant of the fact that Lord Lagan always had an invite to the ball. He checked his watch: 14:20. The ball was scheduled to begin at seven that evening in a big marquee in the grounds of the Strathcarron Hotel. If his hunch was right, there would likely be an attempt on Lord Lagan's life tonight. He had to be there, if only to see if he could recognise someone who may be the murderer.

First though, the press would have to be dealt with. Corstorphine opened the station door and stood on the step, watching as the reporters and camera crews surged towards him like piranhas in a feeding frenzy. Corstorphine gave them a few seconds to settle, cameras jostling for position and reporters arranging themselves in a self-imposed hierarchy, then he started. 'Thank you for your patience. I'm Detective Inspector James Corstorphine and I'm leading the investigation into the recent murders. I'd like to make a brief statement and then I'll take some questions.' He took a deep breath, looked straight ahead and began.

'We are following a number of lines of enquiry in respect to the unlawful killings of the Reverend Simon McLean, minister of St Cuthbert's; Oscar Anderson, gamekeeper at the Mhor Estate and Sheriff Anthony McCallum, owner of same estate. It is also my sad duty to inform you my predecessor, Detective Inspector Brian Rankin, took his own life this afternoon.' He waited for the hubbub to quieten before continuing.

'I am unable to tell you much about the enquiry for operational reasons, but I can tell you that we are also investigating allegations of historical child abuse at the local orphanage that was run by the Sisters of Holy Mercy prior to 2000. We have been provided with the names of individuals that we will be wanting to interview and are asking for anyone that either stayed or worked at the orphanage to get in touch with us.'

'Is this connected to the murders, Inspector?'

'We have reason to believe that there is a strong connection between the murders and whatever happened at the orphanage, yes.'

'Were any of the victims involved?'

'All murder victims, as well as retired Detective Inspector Brian Rankin, had regular involvement with the orphanage.'

'Had they been accused of abuse, Inspector?'

'I'm unable to answer that question.'

'Do you have a suspect for the murders, Inspector? Are you

not worried that more deaths may occur until you catch the murderer?'

'We are pursuing several lines of enquiry, that's all I can tell you at the moment. Thank you for your time.'

A question cut through the noise, the distinctive French accent making it stand out from the hubbub. 'Inspector! Is it true that June Stevens, the *Courier* reporter found hanging in the very same tree as Oscar Anderson a week ago, was investigating child abuse at the orphanage back in 1997, the same year she died? Can you tell us what happened to her daughter and the other children reported missing from the orphanage, and is this in any way connected to the search for children's bodies in the old orphanage grounds?'

Corstorphine fixed her with a steady look. 'No further comment.' He ignored the increasing clamour of calls requesting more information, closing the station door behind him. Josephine had carried out one task he'd asked of her, putting this information out into the public domain. It was a risky manoeuvre, but once this was broadcast, the story couldn't be kept under wraps any longer. He owed that to the children, a full and fair investigation into the abuse they suffered without any possibility of putting Pandora's toys back into the box.

'Hamish. You'd better radio Lamb, warn him that a load of reporters are heading his way. Tell him to tape off the entrance to the gardens, we're on our way.'

'Sir?' The desk sergeant held his hand over the phone microphone. 'You may want to take this before you go. It's forensics, they've made a mistake with the bones.'

Corstorphine pointed towards his office, grabbing his phone as the call was routed through.

'Corstorphine, what have you got?'

'Afternoon, Inspector, we've had the report back from the DNA lab. Those bones you asked us to test, they weren't cattle as originally thought. They're human.'

He sat in stunned silence for a few seconds as the enormity of the words hit home. 'Human! How can you make such a basic mistake?'

'The bones had been carved. Our first diagnosis is made on bone shape. Any technician here will recognise human skeletal bones, it becomes a lot more complicated when the bones have been worked like this. We shouldn't have let the report go out to you without confirmation from the DNA analysis, one of our junior technicians was overly anxious to give you something as soon as possible.'

Corstorphine swore under his breath, the day was going from bad to worse. 'What can you tell me about the bones, are they from the same individual?'

'They come from five individuals. The finger bone we collected yesterday evening from the laird's cold store lock was the first indication that we were dealing with human remains. That's what made me chase up the DNA results in the first place, get them to fast-track the tests.'

'Jesus, so we have a serial murderer who carves his victims' bones to make traps for new victims?'

'Not necessarily. The bones date to around twenty years ago. Another thing you should know, they're all children's bones. None of the skeletons had reached beyond puberty. I'm getting the report finished, you should receive it in your inbox by close of play today.'

'OK. Thanks.' Corstorphine spoke distractedly, his mind whirling at the ramifications of what had just been said.

'Sorry we let you down on the initial findings.'

Corstorphine muttered an acknowledgement and grabbed his coat. 'Hamish, you hold the fort. Frankie will be back in an hour or so. Bill, you come with me.'

The car park exit had magically cleared following the press statement, just a couple of reporters making a lunge for their cameras as Corstorphine drove out. The site of the old orphanage gardens was just a few minutes away. As the entrance came into sight, they could see it was already blocked by a phalanx of camera crews and reporters struggling to get the best position. PC Lamb stood implacably in the entrance, standing behind a line of white and blue police tape that nobody was willing to risk crossing. Corstorphine instructed PC McAdam to help Lamb man the entrance and dived under the tape to meet the crew of workers wheeling something the size of a small fridge over the ground. An umbilical of wires led to a man sitting on an upturned flight case in the middle of the gardens, laptop perched on his knee.

Corstorphine introduced himself, only recognising PC Lamb's father as he lifted his head up from the display.

'Hello, James. Quite the circus you've got following you around today.'

'It's not by choice, I can assure you. Police work is a damn sight easier without reporters pointing their cameras in your direction. Have you found anything?'

Jonathan Lamb pointed a finger at the screen, where a jumbled mess of lines and colours provided a complicated display. 'This area outlined in red represents where the soil has been recently disturbed. I'd say you have five distinct pits that have been dug within the last year, possibly containing the bodies you're looking for. We're just finishing off the site now.' He stood up, arching his back to stretch. 'Been sitting here for the last three hours,' he offered by way of an explanation. 'Oh, and by the way, the boys found this, thought you'd be interested.'

Corstorphine followed him across the lawn, now criss-crossed with deep tyre treads where the radar had been driven in parallel sweeps. Jonathan pointed to a young oak tree, green leaves freshly budding on the branches. It looked unremarkable, just a sapling complete with stake and protective sleeve. Then Corstorphine noticed the wooden plaque set into the ground, the words written in the same script that he'd seen inscribed on the hourglass.

T*HEY SHALL REMEMBER YOU*

Inset into the wood was a papal coin. He didn't need to check the date to know it was the same as the others, the date 1997. 'Is this where the radar found the graves?'

A single nod confirmed his expectations.

'When do you think the ground was last disturbed?'

'Difficult to say, around a year ago probably. The tree would have been planted at the same time, near as we can tell. Do you think this is where they buried the children?'

Corstorphine nodded slowly, his eyes fixed on the wooden plaque. The children would have been buried twenty years ago, but somebody must have dug them up within the last year – to take the bones or make it easier to find the remains? At least the motive was now unassailable, trouble is how many other people were involved and how in God's name was he meant to track them down before the murderer got to them first? He thanked Lamb's father before excusing himself, returning the call to the forensics department at Inverness.

'Corstorphine here again, I need a team here asap. We have potentially five children's graves to examine in the old orphanage gardens. I'll text you through the location now. You'll have to bring back-up to protect the site; the press are here in force and our team is too thinly stretched as it is.'

He stood looking at the oak sapling and message in silent contemplation. Whoever the murderer was, they were someone who felt no compunction about digging up five children's graves and removing their bones to carve into killing mechanisms. What sort of person was even capable of such an act? Were the bones selected as some twisted tribute, a belated memorial to each dead child? Corstorphine left the two constables looking after the orphanage garden site and returned to the station. Events had moved so fast, he'd hardly had a chance to think, with one thing tripping over the heels of the next.

'Are our guests still in the cells?'

Hamish shook his head before replying in his languorous way. 'No, sir. Once the reporters had cleared off, they decided it was time to go.' He looked momentarily flustered. 'Did you want me to keep them here, sir? I thought they were free to come and go as they pleased?'

'No, it's OK, Hamish. They weren't under arrest.' He couldn't think of anything else to ask them even if they had still been waiting in the cells. A chilling thought had just occurred to him even as he spoke to the sergeant. 'Pass me the evidence locker key, Hamish. I didn't get a good look at the weapon before I bagged it.'

The key was handed over, and he retrieved the gun in its plastic evidence bag, turning it over to reveal an inscription carved into the wooden stock. The writing was in the same flowing script he'd seen written on the hourglass and oak tree plaque. He read it with some difficulty through the plastic cover.

YOU'LL KNOW WHEN IT'S TIME

The gun had been given to the old DI by the murderer, knowing that he'd be implicated eventually as the murders were investigated. Corstorphine experienced the same feeling that he was being played, as he had at the first murder scene. Each death was meticulously and cold-bloodedly planned and executed, each murder following the next like clockwork. Brian would have had the chance of fighting this in court, of proclaiming his innocence or risk being convicted and sent to prison. The old DI must have known he'd be found guilty of abetting in the unlawful burial of the children at the very least, and he'd have known what to expect as a copper behind bars – especially if any connection to child abuse was mentioned. So, Brian had Hobson's choice, no bloody choice at all. The murderer might have just as well held the gun to the old DI's head and pulled the trigger. He called Frankie on the radio, hoping she was still at his house.

'Frankie, Corstorphine here. Can you ask Molly if Brian had delivery of a package recently, one that may have contained the gun? There's an inscription on the stock, looks like it's our same murderer who sent it to him. Over.'

Frankie's response came back, requesting time to talk with Molly. He added the photos he'd taken with his mobile to the crazy wall and included one of the gun stock whilst he waited.

'Molly said he had a shoebox-sized parcel delivered about six months ago. Says she only remembers because he was evasive about what it contained. He'd said it was a pair of shoes, but he hadn't shown them to her until a few days afterwards which she'd found odd. Not as odd as him buying shoes from France, though.'

'Why did she think they came from France?'

'The box had French printing on it.'

'Did she keep the box, or the stamp? Anything that we can use as a lead?'

'No, sir. I asked her that. It went straight into the recycling. Sorry.'

Corstorphine sighed, another possible lead closed down. 'OK, Frankie. How's Molly bearing up?'

'You're not flavour of the moment, sir. She seems to hold you responsible for his suicide, says you pushed him to it. There's family turned up now, sir. I'll just make sure they're all OK, then head back. Over.'

Corstorphine signed off and sat down heavily at his desk. Four people dead within a week, five children's bodies awaiting forensics to exhume them and still no real idea of who the murderer could be. Was it only seven days ago this had all started? It seemed like an eternity, and somewhere out there was a murderer who knew how each of the dominoes was going to fall before the first death had even occurred. He felt seriously out of his depth, a small-town detective facing multiple murders and a serial killer running rings around them all.

With a heavy heart, he opened the file that Josephine had left for him, a transcription of June Stevens' last notebook entries detailing her suspicions and interviews. As he reached the final words, she wrote her concerns about meeting with Oscar in such a remote location. He knew now why her behaviour had changed in the weeks before her death, she knew the extent of the abuse, who was covering it up and how much she was putting herself – and her daughter – at risk by continuing with the investigation.

'You could have helped her, Brian. She didn't need to die, hanging from that bloody tree whilst Oscar taunted her. You could have stopped all this.' His words fell uselessly on the empty air, too little, too late.

FORTY-TWO

Frankie met Hamish as he was leaving at the end of his shift. 'How's Molly coping?' He paused at the police station entrance, one hand holding the door open for her.

'As well as can be expected. It's come as a huge shock to her. Brian was hardly the type you'd expect to have been mixed up in anything like this.'

'Or someone you'd expect to shoot himself.' Hamish shook his head at the futility of a life so easily extinguished. 'I never had a clue he was involved in any of this, Frankie. He'd always been one of the straightest coppers I'd ever met, a real gentleman. I cannae believe it's happening.' He appeared bewildered at the events of the last few days. 'Any of it.'

'Did you know he was the one who took June Stevens' daughter to the orphanage after her mother was found dead?' Frankie still couldn't bring herself to say murdered, as if accepting there had been yet another murder might in some way cause the entire town to unravel. Was the small Highland town really that close to the edge, perched on the edge of an abyss where societal norms collapse and people exact revenge for whatever wrongs had been committed in the past? She struggled to make sense of it, as they all did. One murder would have been bad enough, four deaths in a week felt like they were facing the end of days.

'Aye. I guessed it was Brian who took her there. I didnae know for sure, but he looked out for her. I thought it was out of Christian kindness, but all this has made me question everything.'

'You think he may have been abusing her?' Frankie asked, not really wanting to hear the answer.

The sergeant turned towards her in shock. 'Never! He'd never have hurt a hair on any bairn's head. That's what I cannae understand, why he'd cover up any abuse. It makes nae sense.' He turned to leave, then stopped. 'That's the thing that's been bothering me the most. Brian was always going out at odd times during the day, more often than not he was going to the orphanage. It's almost as if he was keeping an eye on the wee lass, turning up at random times to make sure she was being treated alright. It was like he felt he had an obligation to her, treated her more like a daughter. Does that make sense to you?'

Frankie could see Hamish had been affected by the old DI's suicide. He'd worked alongside him for longer than any of them and the suicide had hit him hard too. 'No, Hamish, nothing makes sense at the moment. Will you be in tomorrow?'

'Aye. The DI wants all hands to the pumps until this mess is cleared up. I'll see you in the morning.'

She watched as he walked slowly down the road until he rounded the corner and was lost to view. Not everything was making sense, it never did in the beginning, not until enough pieces were found to build the jigsaw.

* * *

The DI was sitting at his desk, illuminated by the glow from his computer screen. He looked up as she entered the office.

'Did you manage to get anything more out of Molly?'

'No, sir. She basically went to pieces when her sister and husband arrived. I left them to it, not much else I could do. There was only the one forensics guy turned up, he didn't stay long. The bullet had passed clean through the skull; he found it embedded in the garage wall. Pretty much an open and closed case from his point of view. He asked where the weapon was, told him you'd taken it for safety.'

Corstorphine gestured to the only other chair in his office and waited until she'd sat down.

'I couldn't have left it in place. I'll talk to forensics, explain the scene couldn't be secured. The rest of the forensics team are digging for bodies in the old orphanage gardens. The ground radar detected five likely burial sites all next to each other.' He passed over a photograph of the plaque at the bottom of the young oak. 'This oak tree had been planted on top of the bodies, either using the planting of it as cover for exhuming bones, or as a memorial at the grave site.'

'Exhuming bones, sir?' Frankie's puzzlement reminded him he hadn't updated her properly.

'Sorry, Frankie, there's a lot on my mind. I had the head of Inverness forensics on the phone earlier this afternoon. The bones that they told us were animal bones were human. Children's bones,' he added.

'The missing children?'

'Looks very much like it. It will take weeks to track down any living relatives, if they exist, before we can genetically match the DNA to each name.'

'So, the single bone in the laird's lock?'

'Finger, metacarpal. From a child's second or third finger, they think.'

'That lettering, it's the same as the lettering on the hourglass.' Frankie had spotted what he'd seen on the makeshift graveyard plaque.

'Then there's this. It's on the wooden stock of the gun Brian was sent through the post.' He passed over another photograph, the lettering indistinct through the plastic covering but still clear enough to tell it was the same calligraphy.

'Same killer.'

Corstorphine put his hands to his temples, as if trying to alleviate a headache. 'Yes. It certainly looks that way, they must have known Brian would commit suicide. Whoever we're looking for must be in the town, Frankie; they know too much about each of the victims, their history, their habits. They can even predict how their victims will react. More to the point, they knew what went on at that orphanage and now they're having their revenge.'

The radio interrupted him, it was PC Lamb. 'They've found two bodies so far, sir. Both young children. Over.'

'How long do they need to complete the investigation, Lamb? Over.'

The radio remained silent for a minute until a burst of static announced Lamb's response. 'Going to take all night they reckon, sir. Do you want us to stay put? Over.'

Corstorphine covered the mouthpiece with his hand and swore under his breath.

'They were just children!'

He caught Frankie's eyes on him and took a deep breath before removing his hand.

'Tell them to take as long as they need. Those children have waited all this time to be found – let's do it right. Of course they'd take days over such a dig, every scrap of soil would have to be examined for evidence and the remains dealt with respectfully – or as respectfully as could be managed. I've asked them to arrange for reinforcements from Inverness to man the site. They should be there within the hour. Both of you head back to the shop when they arrive, call me on the radio if I'm not here.'

'Sir.'

Frankie waited until the radio quietened. 'The five children. Do you think the murderer has made five mechanisms, one from each body?'

'There's only three deaths we've seen which involve any bone contraptions. Brian killed himself, so if you're right, there are two more potential victims.' He pulled the photograph of the gun towards him, peering more closely. 'I can't make it out, I'll have to take the gun out of the evidence bag.'

Corstorphine returned seconds later with the clear plastic bag, pulling on latex gloves before laying the gun down on his desk. They both looked at it under the bright office lighting, the light wooden stock revealing itself for the first time under their scrutiny.

'That looks like it may be a bone handle.' Frankie voiced what they both thought.

'In which case, and if you're right, then there's one more target left for this maniac to kill. Get this weapon to the forensics team at the dig, ask them if they can prioritise matching each of the carved bones to the remaining child skeletons.

Frankie left him alone in the station, searching the police database for Lord Lagan's mobile. The phone picked up on the second ring.

'Hello?'

'Lord Lagan? This is Detective Inspector James Corstorphine. Can I ask if you're attending the Inverness Ball tonight?'

'Why do you ask, Inspector?' He managed to make the word inspector sound like something that was beneath his contempt.

'I believe that someone may make an attempt on your life.'

There was a pause. 'What are you talking about?'

Corstorphine wondered at the lack of surprise, almost as if Lord Lagan was subjected to death threats on a regular basis. How many enemies had the man made?

'You'll be familiar with the orphanage run by the Sisters of Holy Mercy?'

'I've heard of it.' His response was guarded.

'You were a regular visitor, Lord Lagan, up until the orphanage closed in 2000. I have written statements from a number of the former children who were resident there. They've made serious allegations against you, sir. I'm going to have to ask you to come in for questioning.'

'That will not be convenient. Do you have any idea how busy I am, Inspector...?'

'DI Corstorphine, sir. I realise you're a busy man, but you will have to come in for questioning, either under your own volition or in the back of a police car. Your decision, sir.'

The phone went silent again, Corstorphine could imagine the lord gauging how open to persuasion he might be. 'What is the nature of these allegations?'

'I'm afraid I'm not able to provide any specifics, sir, but you would be well advised to have legal representation accompany you.'

'I see. Well, there's obviously been some sort of misunderstanding. It's too late for me to find the time today, can we say tomorrow at 10:30 a.m.?'

'Yes, that would be fine, sir. Thank you for your assistance. As you say, I'm sure this is a simple misunderstanding that can easily be cleared up.' Corstorphine smiled as he imagined Lord Lagan listening to his words, unconvinced by the platitudes.

'So, this attempt on my life?'

'Probably nothing, sir, but I have to let you know of any threats. There have been a number of murders recently as you're probably aware – each of the victims had a connection to the orphanage. We're just trying to make sure that anyone who was a regular visitor at the orphanage is given as much protection as we are able to manage until the murderer is caught. I'll ask the Inverness police to provide a discreet presence.'

'Is this really a good use of limited police resources, Inspector? It sounds to me as if this may be an overreaction.'

'That's as may be, sir, but I don't want to risk any more lives until we've managed to catch the killer. I'd rather we were overly cautious at this stage, just in case.'

In case of what? Corstorphine really didn't know. He had no intention of having Lord Lagan in for questioning today, the lord was going to be bait – the Inverness Ball was the trap, and this was the single best plan he could conceive to catch a murderer who left no trace.

Corstorphine was locking his office door, getting ready to leave, when he saw a car sweep into the station car park. Whoever it was had a uniformed officer as a chauffeur and was sufficiently high-ranking that they waited until the driver opened the rear door for them. He was unsurprised to see the assistant chief constable exiting the vehicle, pulling his cap over his head as he caught Corstorphine watching him through the glass. He waved a hand imperiously, indicating that Corstorphine open the rear door for him. Corstorphine sighed heavily; he'd known this was coming.

'What the bloody hell are you playing at, man?' The assistant chief was already well on his way to incandescence. Corstorphine could imagine him watching the news broadcast, his face moving past traffic-light red and into purple heart-attack territory before commandeering a car to talk to him directly.

'Can we talk in here, sir? It will be more private.' Corstorphine pointed towards the interview room, indicating the uniformed driver with a tilt of his head.

The assistant chief marched in without acknowledging him, taking the interviewer's chair. Corstorphine closed the door behind him, leaving them in relative privacy. His eyes flicked towards the voice recorder, left running without any indicator light announcing the fact it was still on record.

The ACC waited for Corstorphine to settle, his eyes narrowed to slits and his face an unhealthy colour.

'I don't know where to begin, Corstorphine.' His hands slammed down on the table for emphasis before clenching and unclenching, mirroring his jaw. 'What do you think you were playing at with that press interview? You know every press interaction is to be routed via head office – we have professionals trained for the job. You've made the whole Scottish police force look like a bunch of inept idiots. God knows, I was already making plans to relieve you of this murder investigation. How many are dead now? Three bodies, and you've driven Brian Rankin to suicide!' He shook his head, almost as if he couldn't believe the words he was saying. 'And now I've had Lord Lagan telling me you're bringing him in for questioning. Under your watch you've allowed some lunatic to kill this gamekeeper, a minister of the church, the bloody sheriff himself and now Brian's dead! What the bloody hell do you think you're playing at?'

'We've had serious allegations...'

'What allegations are those, Corstorphine? The made-up ramblings of a bunch of inadequate homeless people who are looking for a bit of publicity, looking for a payout like all the other cases they've read about?'

'No, sir. These people have only provided signed statements because for the first time in their lives they aren't scared. They aren't scared of the sheriff or the local thug now they're both dead, and they aren't scared of us anymore.'

'Preposterous. What do you mean scared of us?'

'They reported abuse when it started, first to the nuns who accused them of lying before punishing them for their imagined sins. Then they told the only other person who could help, they told Brian Rankin who did nothing. Worse than that, he witnessed five children who died at the orphanage and let them be buried in the grounds so no pathologist's report, no investigation was ever made. That's the link to the murders, sir. Both the laird and the minister have been accused of historical abuse, and it's my belief a former orphan is taking their revenge.'

'Are you quite alright in the head, Corstorphine? The laird and minister abusing children, the DI burying bodies in the orphanage grounds. Do you realise quite how far-fetched this all is?' The assistant chief adopted a conciliatory air. 'Look, I think the stress of the last week with all these murders has been too much for you. I'm relinquishing you of your position with immediate effect, we'll get some psychiatric help arranged for you before we have a proper enquiry into your handling of this case. Quite honestly, Corstorphine, I think this may be the end of the line for you.'

He made to stand up before Corstorphine spoke.

'You may want to reconsider that, sir, bearing in mind that Brian confirmed all this with me before he died.'

The assistant chief stood, one hand in the process of placing his cap back over his receding hairline.

'He gave you this in writing?'

'No, sir.' Corstorphine could almost feel the wave of relief that passed over the assistant chief. 'But he confirmed the name two of our witnesses have in their signed statements as an alleged abuser, and a suspect for the unexplained deaths of five small children whose bodies I believe are buried in the former orphanage grounds – Sir Reginald Lagan.'

The ACC froze, confirming Corstorphine's suspicions that he knew more about the orphanage than he liked to admit.

'I can have you sectioned.' The threat was real – if he couldn't be shut up by the normal chain of command, then a word in the right ear from the assistant chief constable would be enough for Corstorphine to be facing padded cells for the foreseeable future, pumped full of enough drugs to never make a coherent sentence ever again.

'You could, sir. Is that how you threatened Brian?'

The assistant chief made a few unnatural noises, it

appeared speech was temporarily beyond him. Corstorphine wondered whether the defibrillator was fully charged, just in case he'd have to use it.

'You cannot possibly be serious?'

Corstorphine sat in silence, not sure if this was a question requiring an answer. He suspected not.

'Are you suggesting I had in any way prior knowledge of what may have happened at that orphanage?' His eyes had narrowed, searching Corstorphine's face for a clue as to how much information had been uncovered. It hadn't escaped his notice that the assistant chief hadn't denied threatening the old detective. 'And what's the nature of this attempt on Lord Lagan's life tonight, is this another of your mental aberrations?'

'I have good reason to believe that whoever the murderer is, sir, they will take the opportunity of the Inverness Ball to make an attempt on his life. Can I suggest that DC Frankie McKenzie and I attend the event just in case we can spot anyone who may be the suspect? I strongly advise that Lord Lagan does not attend the event and is provided with police protection until we have identified and apprehended the culprit.'

'I don't want you or any of your team anywhere the Inverness Ball! You've gone too far this time, Corstorphine. These are serious allegations, and you've put them into the public domain. The force could be made liable for damages at the very least. You've put me in an impossible situation. You could find yourself facing not just disciplinary action, Corstorphine, you could end up in the High Court.' The assistant chief glowered down on him. 'Where are these statements, man? I want every copy now! And any so-called evidence.' His fingers twitched with impatience.

'I'm sorry, sir. All the statements and evidence are secured in the evidence locker, and Hamish McKee has left for the day. We can get them to you tomorrow?'

Corstorphine tried a winning smile. The expression on the assistant chief's face told him he needed to work on that.

'My men will be here 10 a.m. sharp tomorrow. You and your team are to be here with all keys, passwords and anything else we require to take over this inept investigation and to begin an enquiry into you and this station's activities. I'm going to have to apologise to Lord Lagan tonight. Don't count on receiving a pension, Corstorphine.' He placed his cap firmly upon his head and paused in the doorway. 'You'd better tell your entire team they're all going to be investigated. You're a disgrace to the force!'

'Yes, sir.' Corstorphine was speaking to the door as it slammed shut, leaving him feeling more alone and isolated than the day his wife had died. He stood slowly, feeling the weight of his body as it overcame gravity and inertia, a foretelling of things to come he thought to himself ruefully. Crossing to the other side of the desk, he switched the recorder off and stared at it for what seemed an eternity whilst his thoughts circled and collided against each other, forming dizzying patterns inside his head. He sat down, suddenly faint and sick with it all – sick with the murders and those at the top of the hierarchy who were already trying to save their own skins by sacrificing everyone else.

FORTY-THREE

Lord Lagan adjusted his tuxedo in the full-length mirror, turning to admire his profile with a satisfied expression. A frown crossed his face, carving deep furrows in his high forehead, his eyes creasing into calculating slits. The detective's words repeated in his mind – attempt on his life, serious allegations. Had someone from the orphanage said something? They were all meant to have been silenced. His memories took him into forbidden territory – the rush it had given him as he squeezed the last life out of those children, the ones they had had to secretly dispose of. It would never do if that came to light. When he'd first heard of Oscar's death, it had come as something of a relief – no longer having to worry about what evidence the gamekeeper might have had, on him in particular. With that thug gone perhaps some of the orphans may have felt brave enough to go to the police? And now the sheriff was no longer in play, he had no option but to submit to the indignity of an interview with some junior detective. At least the ACC was fighting his corner, and he had a decent QC lined up to accompany him. He continued frowning at his reflection, pulling in his stomach until the paunch disappeared from sight. This was not very satisfactory, a string of murders making his life difficult. The frown left as quickly as it had arrived. In his experience every problem could be solved if you had enough money and power. He had enough of both to be all but invincible.

The country house hotel where he was staying had been purchased on more of a whim than from any sound business calculation. Lagan had always liked the way the solid stone house owned the landscape, the largest dwelling by far on the single-track back road to Inverness. Set back from the road, the house sat implacably in manicured gardens. Scots pines lent height to the acres of level lawn, sheltering the house from the occasional strong winds that funnelled down the glen. The hotel revenue stream barely made a worthwhile profit, but at least it offered some of the creature comforts he was used to enjoying in London. Where else could he rely on staff to be at his beck and call at all hours? The food was excellent, cooked imaginatively and expertly by one of the finest chefs in Scotland. He glanced out of the leaded glass bedroom window at the driveway and admired a Jaguar XS in Epsom Racing Green. He'd had the car delivered that afternoon, straight from the Inverness showroom. He felt an almost schoolboy excitement at the prospect of driving it to the ball, the smell of new leather, the powerful engine.

A woman crossed the drive from the hotel car park, pausing to look at his car. He watched her as she circled it, studying the sleek lines. He could imagine her wondering who it belonged to, who had such impeccable taste in cars? She looked up at his window, catching him observing her, and she gave a little wave before wandering off to her own car from which she extracted an overnight bag. Another guest – that was almost a full house! He smacked his lips together in satisfaction and headed down to reception, collecting the electronic key which had been left for him. As Lord Lagan operated the car remote, he didn't notice the same woman sitting in her car, nor would he have understood what the device was that she held in her hand.

She watched him drive off, her eyes fixed on his car as it swept down the tree-lined drive until it was lost behind a bank of rhododendrons. With a tight smile, she turned the ignition and leisurely followed the Jaguar into Inverness.

The car lived up to Lord Lagan's expectations. The gentlest touch on the accelerator and he felt the soft leather seat pushing against his back, the headrest resisting his head's inclination to roll back as the car leapt forward. It took less than an hour to reach the Strathcarron Hotel, and he turned into the hotel grounds with a sense of disappointment that this inaugural drive had been so short. Perched high up above the town, the hotel gave the impression of looking down its nose at the rest of Inverness. Built in the Victorian era by an enterprising local, the hotel preceded the railway by only a few months, providing sophisticated accommodation for the sudden influx of fashionable tourists keen to follow in the queen's footsteps. Granite turrets lent a Scottish baronial feel to the place, reminding him of the Highland castle where he'd been raised.

Lord Lagan parked in a bay that had been reserved for him, catching the watchful eye of a uniformed policeman who tipped his head deferentially towards him. At least the ACC had put a few bobbies on-site, not that he seriously expected anyone to try and murder him. The policeman accompanied him as he entered the hotel, keeping a respectful distance until he met the reception committee. The ACC made immediately towards him, discomfort at having to apologise for one of his detective's actions written across his face.

'Reginald, I'm sorry about this business with Detective Inspector Corstorphine. I've had a word, obviously a misunderstanding somewhere along the line. The fellow's not the sharpest tool in the box, I'll be having my men take over the investigation tomorrow.' The assistant chief's words came out in a torrent until Lord Lagan raised a hand in a conciliatory gesture.

'Not your fault. The fellow's just doing his job – I'm sure it will all be cleared up shortly.' He stopped as a waiter proffered glasses of sherry, the tray held in that peculiarly awkward way waiters present such things. He sipped the sherry, a warm alcoholic glow spreading down his throat. The glass was lowered, held delicately between forefinger and thumb and slowly twirled as he studied the contents. 'Although it's a bloody inconvenience. I've had to call in my QC to accompany me – do you have any idea what he charges per hour?'

The ACC's attempt at further mollification was interrupted as a gong announced the ball was about to commence. Lord Lagan led the way down towards the large marquee set up on the hotel lawns, waiting until there was enough privacy to speak to the ACC without anyone else being in earshot. 'You told me this investigation was being closed down. Why is it that the first thing I hear is this detective of yours calling me in for questioning regarding an investigation into historical child abuse?' The words were hissed, completely at odds to the warm, cultured tones he'd been using seconds before.

'I'd told him not to reopen the case into the reporter's death, but Oscar Anderson was found hanging from the same tree and he's made the connection with the orphanage. Now the dead reporter's notebook has turned up, and the press have it.'

'What's in it? Is there any mention of my name?'

The ACC looked decidedly uncomfortable, casting his eyes from side to side like a trapped animal seeking an escape. 'It looks as if Brian Rankin gave Corstorphine your name before he shot himself.'

Lord Lagan was silent for a few seconds as they entered the

marquee, passing another uniformed officer standing stiffly to attention at the entrance. His voice was back to being mellifluous. 'So only the word of a dead man?'

'I couldn't get my hands on the witness statements, there's no knowing what they might contain – or the reporter's notebook.'

Lord Lagan looked at him with distaste. 'You'd better make this all go away, unless you want to be responsible for a defamation case, and I will sue!'

The ACC attempted to pacify him, patting his arm much as one would a small dog only to remove his hand hurriedly at Lord Lagan's distasteful expression. 'I'll personally be taking over the interview tomorrow, Reginald. Don't worry, Corstorphine and his team won't be having any more involvement from now on.'

They took their seats at the top table, greeting other dignitaries that joined them as the marquee filled. The sound of conversation took over until a glass was chimed in the unmistakable call for silence.

'My lords, ladies and gentlemen. Please be upstanding for a toast to His Majesty the King.' Chairs scraped on wooden flooring as the entire audience stood, glasses raised to the canvas roof.

'The King.'

Two hundred voices echoed the words, before the first of many glassfuls tipped down throats. As they retook their seats, the waiters draped white cloths over their arms and carried bowls of soup to the top table, circling the diners and placing the bowls down in one unified movement. It was, Lord Lagan felt, almost like a ballet – each move rehearsed and smooth. Nothing he saw gave him any cause for concern that there might be a murderer waiting nearby.

On the dance floor, six young dancers took position in readiness. Lord Lagan licked his lips as he stared at them, his eyes fixed with an intensity that he attempted to hide. Pre-recorded music started and the girls curtseyed to the top table before starting their routine, skirts whirling and tartan sashes a blur. He surreptitiously checked the other tables; people were engrossed with the food, the dancers or each other – comparing partners, outfits, company – the usual fascinations for those with nothing but time and money to waste. The whole event was making Lord Lagan feel slightly nauseous as if these tempting morsels were put there to tease him, kindling an appetite that he'd managed to keep under control for many years.

Outside, dusk was falling, and the hotel floodlights cast a yellow glow over the car park and immediate environs. A slight breeze ruffled the marquee canvas, the flapping sound lending a soporific quality to the peace of the evening. The uniforms stood outside the marquee entrance, grumbling among themselves of time wasted as the ceilidh band struck up for the first dance. A waitress came outside and beckoned them into the kitchen, a second tent attached to the main marquee where catering staff were starting to clear up after the meal. The policemen disappeared from sight, their mood greatly improved by the offer of refreshments.

Above them in the car park, a figure looked down through binoculars as the men left their positions unattended. Leaving the safety of her car, she carried a small parcel under her arm and made directly for Lord Lagan's new Jaguar. She keyed a remote and the doors unlocked, indicator lights flashing acceptance of the digital radio code she had cloned back at the country house hotel. In the space of a few seconds, she had removed the driver's headrest and fitted an identical fawn coloured leather replacement. The headrest slid neatly into place, twin metal runners engaging with the seat receptacles until it was positioned at exactly the same height. She closed and locked the Jaguar door, making her way back unnoticed to her own car before driving off into the night.

At the stroke of midnight, strains of 'Auld Lang Syne' alerted the uniforms that the evening was drawing to an uneventful close. Lord Lagan made his way back to the Jaguar, swaying slightly on his feet as he fumbled for the key and sat in the driver's seat. With a slight gesture of acknowledgement to the policeman tasked with accompanying him back to his car, he drove carefully out of the car park. The uniform watched him go, a feeling of resentment fading as he realised there were some people it was better not to breathalyse. At least he didn't have to be the one acting as an unofficial taxi service for the ACC.

Once out on the open road, Lord Lagan pushed his foot down to the floor, feeling the exhilarating surge of power as he was pressed back into his seat. Inside the headrest, an accelerometer detected the forward motion and triggered a small clockwork mechanism into life. It was comprised of readily available electronic components which worked silently, taking power from a couple of 9-volt batteries. The car and its driver hurtled along the main road, slowing down to take the smaller road which briefly ran alongside Loch Ness before heading onwards towards Loch Mhor and Lagan's hotel. The clockwork mechanism bided its time, counting down towards a pre-set assignment as the car sped along the narrow road past isolated whitewashed cottages. Then, without warning the electronic timepiece triggered a small but powerful solenoid, forcefully pushing a syringe through the headrest into the back of Lord Lagan's neck. Simultaneously, a syringe pump whirred quietly as it administered a small quantity of liquid through the needle into his flesh.

The car swerved, Lord Lagan swearing as he fought to regain control of the careering vehicle with one hand as the other encountered the needle poking out of his headrest. 'What the bloody hell?' His hand came away with a speck of blood showing darkly in the light from the dashboard. He slowed down, looking for somewhere to pull over so he could investigate further. He was cursing the bloody idiot that had left their sewing needle in the leather when he experienced the first effects of paralysis. With a sense of increasing dread, he realised that the hands clasping the steering wheel were no longer his to control. It was as if his hands, and now the arms attached to them, belonged to someone else – some godlike puppeteer had replaced his own arms with unresponsive dead weights. His mobile lay within reach, but his hands refused to obey his increasingly frantic demands to call for help.

The brake pedal was under a foot that no longer obeyed his command to push downwards. When his lips became numb, his mouth feeling as if a dentist had just injected novocaine into the gums. A cold sweat beaded his forehead and a chill travelled down his spine as his heart began to physically stutter in his chest. He could feel it frantically beating as if determined to escape the confines of his ribcage. A desperate need for air took precedence as the first warning signs of suffocation entered his primal brain, the autonomous action of breathing in, breathing out no longer responding to messages from medulla to diaphragm. It was at this point that he realised he was going to die, his body frozen into inaction with a mind that remained as sharp as ever. The car continued to creep along the road towards a hedge as his brain screamed a warning that he needed to breathe. With surreal awareness, he sat in the warm leather seat, a disembodied passenger in a car slowly forcing its way off the road and into the undergrowth. The engine finally gave up the fight against the obstinate foliage as a wheel sank into a ditch, coughing one last protest before stalling to a halt. Lagan's heart gave a few massive leaps, a last attempt to keep pumping blood around his body, but it was too late. Saliva speckled his lips, already turning blue as the oxygen was starved from his system. One last breath escaped his mouth, denying him a final opportunity to cry out as pain spread along every nerve in his body. The headlights illuminated pastureland, glinting off the still black waters of Loch Mhor. It was, in its own way, a beautiful scene but of no consolation as he continued to suffocate, drowning slowly on dry land.

FORTY-FOUR

Corstorphine woke from a troubled sleep, scrabbling around beside his bed for the mobile that had finally managed to intrude on his consciousness. He squinted at the number before admitting defeat, eyes too old to focus that soon after wakening and keyed the green accept button.

'Corstorphine,' he announced, blearily checking the alarm clock again for confirmation that it really was just after 6 a.m.

'Inverness CID here, DCI Ashfield.'

Corstorphine struggled to match a face to the name, his memory eventually returning a tall, gaunt fellow that he remembered thinking didn't seem to like him very much. 'DCI Ashfield, sorry, sir, I've just woken up.'

'Well, you'd better finish waking up and get yourself down to the station sharp because I need you to run through some CCTV footage I've just sent you.'

'Can I ask what this is about, sir?' He climbed out of bed, reaching for fresh underwear with one hand whilst keeping the mobile held against his ear.

'The assistant chief tells me you warned Lord Reginald Lagan an attempt might be made on his life last night?'

The silence told Corstorphine he was expected to respond. 'That's right. I advised him not to go to the Inverness Ball. When he made it clear that he wasn't minded to take my advice, I asked the ACC to put a few uniforms on the ground, just as a precaution.'

He could almost hear the DCI on the other end of the line processing his comments, the silence extending to a few seconds before a response came back down the line.

'Shame he didn't listen to you. His body was found this morning by a farmer at four o'clock. Driven his Jag into a hedge and died with the car stuck in a ditch. It looked like a heart attack at first sight, then we spotted a needle stuck in the back of his neck. Forensics are on it now, but they mentioned your name.'

'Why? What have forensics found?' Corstorphine had a sinking feeling that he knew what was coming next.

'It's a strange one. Looks like the headrest has been tampered with, some sort of timing mechanism has been put in there that jabbed a needle into Lagan's neck after he'd been driving for a while. Forensics can explain it to you in more detail, but we need you to look at the camera footage. The CCTV picked up a woman breaking into his car whilst it was parked at the Strathcarron Hotel. Quality isn't great at that distance, but you may recognise her as someone you've been looking at in connection with all this?'

'Certainly, sir. I'll check the footage at the station.'

'Get back to me as soon as you've seen it – the chief constable is going ballistic.'

Corstorphine threw on some clothes and drove to the station, his mind freewheeling over the dramatic events of the last week. Whilst obviously trying to keep open minds, they had been convinced they were looking for a man, someone strong and agile enough to spy on the gamekeeper and laird, climb the Hanging Tree and bell tower, someone who possessed the cold analytical fury to plan each death down to the last detail. If it was a woman behind the murders, then she must have had a connection to the orphanage – and Margo McDonald was the only suspect he had that fitted the bill.

The station was dark when Corstorphine arrived, thankfully free of any reporters blocking the entrance. He entered his password into the computer and downloaded the video sent from the Inverness police. The image showed a floodlit car parking area adjacent to the hotel, the timestamp in the upper right corner of the frame telling him the footage was from yesterday at 21:14. The picture had that peculiar grainy effect that night vision footage always displayed, reducing the level of detail to well below anything of any practical use. A figure appeared in the frame walking towards what he took to be Lord Lagan's car. She was carrying a package under her arm, too far away to make out the face but she looked feminine – something in her build, her walk; if only he could see her face more clearly. She lifted her head, almost as if she knew she was being observed and gave a little wave towards the camera. She must have at that point operated a car remote as the car's indicators flashed in response, overloading the night vision camera and wiping out her image. By the time the image stabilised she was in the car, doing something around the driving seat. Whatever she was doing took under thirty seconds, then she left the car with what looked like the same package under her arm. Corstorphine could only see her back as she disappeared out of the frame.

'Shit!' The expletive was heartfelt. There was nothing he could use from the footage, they'd need a better picture from somewhere. Whoever this was, it certainly wasn't Margo; this woman had a slimmer build and appeared a good head taller. He checked his mobile for the last call, dialling the DCI's number.

'DI Corstorphine here, sir,' he answered in response to the

DCI's brusque acknowledgement. 'There's nothing I can get from the footage, sorry.'

'I'm not surprised. Talk to the forensics team, they're prioritising this case – you may be able to provide some assistance.' The phone went dead, leaving Corstorphine with the distinct impression that the DCI's opinion of him had just dropped even lower from the subterranean point it had started from. At least forensics answered their phone with a cheerful tone, becoming even happier when they realised Corstorphine was on the other end of the line.

'Your murderer has been busy, taking out a lord this time!'

His murderer? Corstorphine hesitated, searching for the right words to let forensics know that the murderer was not someone he particularly wanted to claim as his own. The forensics guy filled the space for him.

'Gary won the sweepstake. His entry was Lord Reginald Lagan. Killed by the parliamentary mace. You have to admit that's close.'

Corstorphine wondered at the psychology of finding enjoyment in predicting another's death, especially before 7 a.m. Perhaps that's what happened to you if you worked in forensics, a way of coping with the daily toil of death and injury. 'What have you got on the murder method?'

'Ah, that's why we thought of you. Whoever it was installed a syringe in the car headrest, activated by an electronic timer. Similar to your murders but what really gave it away as your murderer was the bone case the electronics had been packed into. Quite a work of art, looks like it was milled in a machine shop. We're running the DNA now, what's the betting it comes back as one of your child skeletons?'

'What was in the syringe?' Corstorphine pressed for more information, anything that might give him the clue – any clue – to the murderer.

'Something pretty evil. Must be a neurotoxin of some kind

to affect him that quickly, although getting a dose injected straight into his neck wouldn't have helped him any. It looks as if he managed to give himself a second dose when his hand went behind his neck, probably to check what had just stung him. It may take a while before we get any feedback on what's left in the syringe, to be honest we were all a bit wary of handling it.'

Corstorphine ran through the video footage in his mind. 'I think the murderer swapped headrests, I saw her carry a small package to his car and fiddle about around the driving seat. She had thirty seconds at most.'

'She?'

'Yes, she. It looks like we're dealing with a woman as far as the only video we have of the suspect shows. What about the poison, the neurotoxin – any ideas where that could have come from?'

'Difficult to say without knowing what it is. It's not the sort of thing you can buy over the counter at the chemist's.'

Corstorphine felt a chill run down his spine, settling in his stomach like a lead weight. He needed to look at that video again. 'Can you get back to me with anything you find?'

The voice on the other end of the line paused. 'We've been told you're off the case, Corstorphine. The ACC was quite specific about that yesterday.'

'I've not been told anything official, so as far as I'm concerned, I'm still working the case. Just send me what you find and if I'm no longer involved, then I won't bother looking at it.'

'OK.' The response was dubious. 'Soon as we hear anything, I'll be in touch. I'll pass on your comments about swapping the headrest to the Inverness detectives, they're handling Lord Lagan's murder.'

As soon as the line went dead, Corstorphine ran the CCTV footage again. Just as she raised her hand towards the camera, he could see the woman's fingers waving one after the other before the picture was flooded with light. He was glad he was alone, sitting at his desk – he was fairly certain he knew now who the murderer was. Opening his desk drawer, he pulled out the print Frankie had given him, a newspaper article about the innovative French clockmaker Henri Dupont. The photograph of the Toulouse clockmaker showed him standing behind some animatronic construction made from bone but there, to the side, was a girl standing almost lost in the shadows. He'd never checked the date, after all, Henri Dupont had died five years ago – it felt irrelevant. With a sinking feeling, Corstorphine searched online, pulling up the same photograph and reading the date, 2002. Abigail Stevens would have been about eleven years old – around the same age as the girl in the photograph. On a whim, he searched for the meaning of her name. Abigail – *my father's joy*. Like clockwork, Corstorphine's memory returned the French for joy – joie. Joie Dupont, it couldn't be coincidence! June Stevens had never provided the name of her daughter's father, yet Brian had told him he'd taken her far away where she'd be safe. Had the old detective managed to track down the girl's father, taken her to France to start a new life? Could it be that she and her father had plotted revenge on her mother's murderers or was he taking this too far? Either way, he had no real evidence, just the coincidence of a characteristic wave and a feeling from deep in his gut.

His phone rang, and he recognised the same ebullient forensics officer from earlier.

'Hi, Corstorphine. The lab results have come back on the toxin. Luckily, it's a quiet time in the lab before the day starts so they fast-tracked it. Tetrodotoxin – found in pufferfish, blue-ringed octopuses, poison dart frogs – you get the idea. It's a particularly nasty one, over a thousand times more toxic than cyanide. The poor bastard didn't stand a chance, he'd have been dead within minutes. The thing is, this toxin causes total body paralysis whilst the mind is unaffected. He'd have been fully aware that he was dying, and most likely felt everything as he suffocated. She must have had it in for this one!'

Corstorphine thanked him for the information and sat quietly whilst he thought what to do next. Women were not typical suspects, but Abigail Stevens had the motive. Her mother murdered by Oscar Anderson – he'd have enjoyed telling the young girl the gruesome details of what he did to her mother before he hanged her in the tree. The minister – had she told him the truth, looking for someone to believe her and help her escape from the orphanage? What had the minister done, did he abuse her when she came to him for help? The laird, she'd taken a lot of trouble to make his a slow death. Was he responsible for having her locked in the hole, that cold stone cell that Craig Derbyshire had said she'd often been confined in, maybe because she wouldn't stop talking about her mother's murder? Then Lord Lagan, this was personal. She had wanted him to suffer, needed him to feel the pain and panic as he fought unsuccessfully for breath. What had he done to her as a young child to keep that anger alive after so many years? And Brian, the old DI. Had she given him the gun out of mercy, payment for him taking her out of the orphanage and providing her with a new life? She'd demanded interest from him for not pursuing her mother's killer, for letting the children suffer and die. That payment could only be his death.

The station door opened, alerting Corstorphine to the time. It was 7:30 a.m. and the team would all be arriving in the next half hour to put in another day's hunt for the murderer. Hamish put his head around the door, the frown lifting off his face as he saw the DI sat at his desk.

'Morning, sir. You been here all night?'

Corstorphine shook his head. 'No, sergeant, just the last hour.'

The exhaustion he was feeling must have been written

across his face, as the sergeant offered to make him a coffee. Corstorphine watched him as he made ponderous progress towards the corner of the shared office that served as a kitchen, before looking again at the young girl's picture in the photograph. Could that really be June Stevens' daughter, spirited away from the orphanage to Toulouse – and was Jenny Peck the same person, just some twenty years older? What if he was wrong? He massaged his temple, attempting to allay the fog of indecision. The only evidence he could bring to bear was the woman in the CCTV waving at the camera the same way Jenny had waved to him the first time they'd met, beckoning him over to her table in the restaurant. Corstorphine reran the recording, squinting at the screen as if that would bring the grainy image into some kind of focus. If he could only prove the girl in the photograph was the love child of June Stevens and Henri Dupont. She would have had the motive – God knows what she experienced after her mother's death. She'd also had the opportunity to learn how to make mechanisms out of bone. Could Abigail Stevens really be Jenny Peck?

It was a long shot at best, and if his gut feeling was right, then he was about to question a woman whose life had already been destroyed, who'd already paid more than enough for the harm that had been done to her. Had she been so wrong to take the law into her own hands? Corstorphine knew the orphanage abuse would never have come to light if it wasn't for her actions. He started searching online for a more recent photograph of Joie Dupont, eventually finding her pictured beside one of her own artworks which had sold for thousands of dollars just two years previously. He stared at the picture in shock – there was no room for doubt now.

One by one the team arrived at the station, and Corstorphine told them to be ready for a briefing at eight o'clock. When they were assembled and waiting patiently, he took a deep breath and left his office, standing against the crazy wall.

'Morning all.' The humour had been sucked out of the phrase. He looked each one of them in the eye – they were a loyal bunch, worried about what he had to tell them, bewildered by the deaths.

'Lord Lagan died last night as he drove back from the Inverness Ball. It very much looks like the same killer was responsible, this time using a timing mechanism to inject a lethal toxin into his neck.'

'How did they get to his neck?' The desk sergeant spoke for all of them.

'The syringe and delivery system were concealed in his car headrest. It very much looks as if she swapped headrests over whilst his car was parked up at the Strathcarron Hotel.'

'She, sir?' Frankie was first off the starting line, as usual.

'I've seen video footage from the hotel's CCTV, although the quality is too poor to make an identification, it's pretty clear that it was a woman.' Corstorphine took a deep breath. The next words were going to come at a personal cost. He was the only person who'd seen Jenny in the flesh, had kissed her. He realised he was at risk of becoming a complete laughing stock. The woman had deceived him completely, he'd taken her at face value, who wouldn't? He couldn't even be sure what she really looked like, whether her hair or eyes were the colours he remembered. All he had was her approximate height and build, and how her lips felt. He shook his head as he stood in front of the small group, in frustration and anger they all rightly presumed – not knowing these emotions were directed purely at himself.

'This is a piece of art sold in a New York gallery two years ago.' The painting displayed on the screen showed a young woman standing next to a surrealist painting almost as tall as she was. A female figure hung from an old oak tree – the noose connected to clockwork gears visible in the leaves. Two twisted branches forked outwards looking for all the world like the hands of a clock, twisted into grotesque shapes. The piece was entitled *Whirligig*. 'The woman in the picture is Joie Dupont, her father was the clockmaker Henri Dupont who was famous for creating animatronic sculptures out of bone. I know her as Jenny Peck, she's a staff nurse at the hospital and I believe she is June Stevens' missing daughter. Frankie, I want you to accompany me to the hospital. McAdam, Lamb – follow us in the patrol car and cover the back of the hospital in case she makes a run for it. Don't use the siren, I don't want her to know we're coming for her.' Corstorphine couldn't help but see Lamb's exaggerated mouthing the words 'uniform dating' out of the corner of his eye. He chose to ignore it, there would be worse to come.

Moments later, Frankie climbed in beside him and they drove off, Lamb and McAdam following closely behind as they headed towards the hospital. 'How did you make the connection, sir?'

Corstorphine's mind was in a turmoil, doubts chasing around his head in a kaleidoscope of activity. 'I may be wrong, Frankie. Christ knows I may be wrong.' He drove in silence, attempting to collect his thoughts into some kind of logical order. 'I viewed video footage from the hotel car park first thing this morning, the Inverness CDI called me just after six to see if I recognised anyone. The picture wasn't clear, but I could see it was a woman, and she waved at the camera.'

'Sir?'

A reluctant smile escaped Corstorphine's tight lips. He could see how this sounded. 'The woman had a distinctive way of waving, fingers bending down towards the palm like a Mexican wave. My date the other night, Jenny Peck, waved to me in exactly the same way.'

'Jesus. She was your date?'

Corstorphine nodded, keeping his eyes fixed on the road. He could imagine Frankie's expression without having to see it.

They pulled into the hospital car park and waited for the two constables to make their way around the back before entering the building.

'Can I help you?' The receptionist looked surprised as they entered. Corstorphine held up his badge, seeing the worry leave her face.

'DI Corstorphine and DC McKenzie. I don't suppose one of your staff nurses is in just now, Staff Sister Jenny Peck?'

'Jenny, yes, she's just started the day shift, ward two. Can I ask what this is about?'

Corstorphine knew his luck wasn't that good. 'How long has she been on duty?'

She checked a screen, tapping an enquiry onto the keyboard. 'Since 7 a.m., she'll be on the ward, still doing the handover I expect.'

'Can you call her down to reception?'

The receptionist looked doubtful. 'I can ask her to pop down if she's free?'

'Thanks. Make some excuse for needing her at reception but do not mention the police.' They took a seat, watching the lift doors as the receptionist relayed his request for Jenny to visit reception. He sat in quiet contemplation, wondering how he was going to deal with the next few minutes. A chime announced the lift's arrival, and a stout middle-aged woman in a nurse's uniform caught his eye as the doors slid apart. Corstorphine rose to his feet, an apology already on his lips. He'd never seen this woman before.

Corstorphine sat in the car outside the hospital, trying to make sense of the last hour. Whoever it was that he'd shared dinner with, shared a long kiss with – she was not Jenny Peck the staff nurse. She must have known who he was from the beginning, beckoning him over without any introduction. Of course, she would have researched who she'd be up against and came up with a washed-up detective and his small-town police crew. Had she been laughing at him the whole time, or did that kiss mean anything at all? It had felt to him as if she'd meant it at the time. Christ, what a fool he was.

'At least you've identified the murderer, sir.' Frankie attempted to make the best of it for him.

'It's all circumstantial, Frankie. The Procurator won't move without solid forensic evidence or a confession.' Corstorphine led the small convoy back to the station, unsure which of the many emotions he felt at that moment would come out on top. On the one hand, he felt relief that the murderer had been identified, in his mind at least. Relief and the satisfaction that his team would come out of this with reputations intact despite what would be said about his dalliance with the murderer. Fighting that was the disappointment at being unable to bring 'Jenny' in for questioning, and the embarrassment at being taken in so easily. Overriding all these was the hope that she'd escape, never to be brought to justice. Free, probably for the first time in her life.

Back at the station he assembled the team once again, grateful that Lamb hadn't seen fit to make one of his humorous comments. 'The woman we are looking for has been masquerading as Jenny Peck, a staff nurse. We believe her real name is Abigail Stevens, June Stevens' daughter. She also goes by the name Joie Dupont. It's possible she's still in the town, but her behaviour in the CCTV footage from the Strathcarron Hotel leads me to believe she's left the area. I want you all to make finding any trace of her a priority, any flats suddenly left empty, missing hotel guests – you know the drill. If we're lucky, she may have left something behind that will help us catch her.' Corstorphine said the words without any real hope behind them. She'd been meticulous in covering up her tracks. 'Frankie, see what you can get on Joie Dupont. See if the French police have anything on her, any recent photographs.'

The phone rang and PC Lamb took the call, holding the receiver out towards Corstorphine.

'This is DCI Ashfield. The ACC has asked me to formally advise you that this investigation into the murders is to be handled by the Glasgow Major Investigation Team. They'll be with you in an hour or so. Make sure all relevant information is made available to them when they arrive. In the meantime, under no circumstances are you or any of your team to talk to the press. Is that understood?'

'Yes, sir. Understood.' Corstorphine ended the call, handing the receiver back to Lamb.

'Do you think we'll ever find her, sir, this woman?' PC Lamb looked hopeful.

'Possibly, Lamb. But whether there's enough evidence to mount a successful prosecution...'

'Do you think that's the end of it, sir? The end of the murders?' Bill McAdam's question mirrored the same thought that Corstorphine had been toying with.

'I hope so, Bill. That's everyone now dead who the witnesses told us was involved. Each one has been accounted for.' He struggled unsuccessfully to find the right words to tell them they'd all been taken off the case, some way of making it less of a kick in the teeth. 'We've been taken off the murders, Glasgow MIT are on their way now and I need you all to offer them your full support.'

'So, what do we do now?' The sergeant voiced the question they all wanted to know the answer to.

Corstorphine looked at each of them in turn, the tiredness and stress of the week apparent on each face.

'We wait for the MIT to arrive, pass over our files and take some well-earned leave. You've all been through a lot, and I know everyone here has put in a lot of unpaid overtime. I'll see you back here on Monday, assuming I've still got a job.'

'Are we not going after this woman then, sir, or the nuns?'

'No, Lamb. This case now belongs to the MIT, they'll be working hand in glove with Interpol to try and find her and they'll question the nuns. Our part in this is over, just the paperwork to do.'

The groans that followed his comment were a sign that they'd all get back to normal, back to policing a town where nothing much happens. No doubt the press would make a feast of the events of the last week, and some scars would never heal, but he knew that was the end of the murders. As he waited for the Glasgow team to arrive, Corstorphine realised he'd have to let the MIT know that he'd met the killer. Tell them he'd sat down and had dinner with her and shared the first kiss he'd had since his wife had died. That admission could be the end of his career – a backwater detective like him would be lucky to survive dating a murderer during a killing spree. Corstorphine leaned back in his seat, the office door shut against the animated voices of his team as they railed against being sidelined by some Glasgow detectives. Why had she waved at the camera? Did she know he'd recognise her from that gesture? If she hadn't come back to avenge her mother's death, to deal her own brand of justice to those involved in abusing her and the other children – what then? He knew the answer. Nothing would have happened, the orphanage abuse would have remained concealed, the guilty would have never faced justice.

As Saturday drew to a close, Corstorphine left the station under the charge of a group of Glaswegian detectives. Opening his front door, he wondered why the house felt different. Was it because his wife no longer waited in the hall to welcome him as often as she used to? Was it because he struggled sometimes now to see her face when before it had been as clear as day? He put on the kettle, as much to fill the silent house with some sort of noise as to make a cup of tea.

There it was, the reason the house felt different. Corstorphine walked quietly into the living room, listening for the sound that had alerted him. The house was no longer as silent as it used to be. The steady tick of the carriage clock he had broken when he returned from seeing his wife die in hospital, the clock he'd thrown to the ground in impotent rage but kept because it reminded him of her – its rhythmic heartbeat once more told him that he was alive. His hands trembled as he removed the clock from the shelf, turning it around to reveal the back. There, in a flowing script that he knew only too well was the one word:

Merci

A LETTER FROM THE AUTHOR

Thanks so much for reading *The Bone Clock*. If you want to join other readers in hearing all about my new releases, you can sign up for my newsletter here.

www.stormpublishing.co/andrew-james-greig

Please consider leaving a review. This can help new readers discover a book you've enjoyed and gives us all a big boost!

I very much look forward to sharing my next book with you. You can peer under this author's bonnet at:

andrewjgreig.wordpress.com

- facebook.com/andrewjamesgreig
- x.com/AndrewJamesGre3
- instagram.com/andrew_james_greig
- tiktok.com/@andrewjamesgreig
- bsky.app/profile/andrewjgreig.bsky.social